W9-AZB-651

# 1<sup>st</sup> to Die

Also by James Patterson:

*The Thomas Berryman Number*
*Season of the Machete*
*See How They Run*
*The Midnight Club*
*Along Came a Spider*
*Kiss the Girls*
*Hide & Seek*
*Jack & Jill*
*Miracle on the 17th Green*
          (with Peter de Jonge)
*Cat & Mouse*
*When the Wind Blows*
*Pop Goes the Weasel*
*Black Friday*
*Cradle and All*
*Roses Are Red*

# 1st
# to Die

A NOVEL BY

# JAMES
# PATTERSON

BOOKSPAN LARGE PRINT EDITION

LITTLE, BROWN AND COMPANY

BOSTON    NEW YORK    LONDON

This Large Print Edition, prepared especially for Bookspan, contains the complete, unabridged text of the original Publisher's Edition.

Copyright © 2001 by James Patterson

All rights reserved. No part of this book may be reproduced in any form or by any electronic or mechanical means, including information storage and retrieval systems, without permission in writing from the publisher, except by a reviewer who may quote brief passages in a review.

The characters and events in this book are fictitious. Any similarity to real persons, living or dead, is coincidental and not intended by the author.

ISBN 0-7394-1654-5

Printed in the United States of America

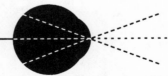

This Large Print Book carries the
Seal of Approval of N.A.V.H.

# Acknowledgments

My thanks to the following people, whose hard work and expertise helped in the writing of this book.

Dr. Greg Zorman, Chief of Neurosurgery, Lakeland Hospital, Fort Lauderdale, Florida, who I'd like on my side in a crisis.

The lovely and talented Fern Galperin, Mary Jordan, Barbara Groszewski, and Irene Markocki.

## Prologue

# INSPECTOR
# LINDSAY BOXER

It is an unusually warm night in July, but I'm shivering badly as I stand on the substantial gray stone terrace outside my apartment. I'm looking out over glorious San Francisco and I have my service revolver pressed against the side of my temple.

*"Goddamn you, God!"* I whisper. Quite a sentiment, but appropriate and just, I think.

I hear Sweet Martha whimpering. I turn and see she is watching me through the glass doors that lead to the terrace. She knows that something is wrong. "It's okay," I call to her through the door. "I'm okay. Go lie down, girl."

Martha won't leave, though, won't look away. She's a good, loyal friend who's been nuzzling me good-night every single night for the past six years.

As I stare into the Border collie's eyes, I think that maybe I should go inside and call the girls. Claire, Cindy, and Jill would be here almost before I hung up the phone. They would hold me, hug me, say all the right things. *You're special, Lindsay. Everybody loves you, Lindsay.*

Only I'm pretty sure that I'd be back out here tomorrow night, or the night after. I just don't see a way out of this mess. I have thought it all through a hundred times. I can be as logical as hell, but I am also highly emotional, obviously. That was my strength as an inspector with the San Francisco Police Department. It is a rare combination, and I think it is why I was more successful than any of the males in Homicide. Of course, none of them are up here getting ready to blow their brains out with their own guns.

I lightly brush the barrel of the revolver down my cheek and then up to my temple again. Oh God, oh God, oh God. I am reminded of *soft hands,* of Chris, and that starts me crying.

Lots of images are coming way too fast for me to handle.

The terrible, indelible honeymoon murders that terrified our city, mixed with close-ups of my mom and even a few flashes of my father. My best girls — Claire, Cindy, and Jill — our crazy club. I can even see myself, the way I used to be, anyway. Nobody ever, *ever* thought that I looked like an inspector, the only woman homicide inspector in the entire SFPD. My friends always said I was more like Helen Hunt married to Paul Reiser in *Mad About You*. I was married once. I was no Helen Hunt; he sure was no Paul Reiser.

This is so hard, so bad, so wrong. It's so unlike me. I keep seeing David and Melanie Brandt, the first couple who were killed, in the Mandarin Suite of the Grand Hyatt. I see that horrifying hotel room, where they died senselessly and needlessly.

*That was the beginning.*

## Book One

# DAVID AND MELANIE

# Chapter 1

Beautiful long-stemmed red roses filled the hotel suite — the perfect gifts, really. *Everything* was perfect.

There might be a luckier man somewhere on the planet, David Brandt thought as he wrapped his arms around Melanie, his new bride. Somewhere in Yemen, maybe — some Allah-praising farmer with a second goat. But certainly not in all of San Francisco.

The couple looked out from the living room of the Grand Hyatt's Mandarin Suite. They could see the lights of Berkeley off in the distance, Alcatraz, the graceful outline of the lit-up Golden Gate Bridge.

"It's incredible." Melanie beamed. "I wouldn't change a single thing about today."

"Me either," he whispered. "Well, maybe I wouldn't have invited my parents." They both laughed.

Only moments before, they had bid farewell to the last of the three hundred guests in the hotel's ballroom. The wedding was finally over. The toasts, the dancing, the schmoozing, the photographed kisses over the cake. Now it was just the two of them. They were twenty-nine years old and had the rest of their lives ahead of them.

David reached for a pair of filled champagne glasses he had set on a lacquered table. "A toast," he declared, "to the second-luckiest man alive."

"The second?" she said, and smiled in pretended shock. "Who's the first?"

They looped arms and took a long, luxurious sip from the crystal glasses. "This farmer with two goats. I'll tell you later.

"I have something for you," David suddenly remembered. He had already given her the perfect five-carat diamond on her finger, which he knew she wore only to please his folks. He went to his tuxedo jacket, which was draped over a high-backed chair, and returned with a jewelry box from Bulgari.

"No, David," Melanie protested. "You're my gift."

"Open it anyway," he said to her. "This you'll like."

She lifted the top. Inside a suede pouch was a set of earrings, large silver rings around a pair of whimsical moons made from diamonds.

"They're how I think of you," he said.

Melanie held the moons against the lobes of her ears. They were perfect, and so was she.

"It's you who pulls my tides," David murmured.

They kissed, and he unfastened the zipper of her dress, letting the neckline fall just below her shoulders. He kissed her neck. Then the tops of her breasts.

There was a knock on the door of the suite.

"Champagne," called a voice from outside.

For a moment, David thought of just yelling, "Leave it there!" All evening, he had longed to peel away the dress from his wife's soft white shoulders.

"Oh, go get it," Melanie whispered, dangling the earrings in front of his eyes. "I'll put these on."

She wiggled out of his grasp, backing toward the Mandarin's master bathroom, a smile in her liquid brown eyes. *God, he loved those eyes.*

As he went to the door, David was thinking he wouldn't trade places with anybody in the world.

Not even for a second goat.

# Chapter 2

Phillip Campbell had imagined this moment, this exquisite scene, so many times. He knew it would be the groom who opened the door. He stepped into the room.

"Congratulations," Campbell muttered, handing over the champagne. He stared at the man in the open tuxedo shirt with a black tie dangling around his neck.

David Brandt barely looked at him as he inspected the brightly ribboned box. Krug. Clos du Mesnil, 1989.

"What is the worst thing anyone has ever done?" Campbell murmured to himself.

"Am I capable of doing it? Do I have what it takes?"

"Any card?" the groom said, fumbling in his pants pocket for a tip.

"Only this, sir."

Campbell stepped forward and plunged a knife deep into the groom's chest, between the third and fourth ribs, the closest route to the heart.

"For the man who has everything," Campbell said. He pushed his way into the room and slammed the door shut with a swift kick. He spun David Brandt around, shoved his back against the door, and powered the blade in deeper.

The groom stiffened in a spasm of shock and pain. Guttural sounds escaped from his chest — tiny, gurgling, choking breaths. His eyes bulged in disbelief.

This is amazing, Campbell thought. He could actually feel the groom's strength leaking away. The man had just experienced one of the great moments of his life and now, minutes later, he was dying.

Campbell stepped back, and the groom's body crumpled to the floor. The room began to tilt like a listing boat. Then everything began to speed up and run together. He felt as if he were watching a flickering newsreel. Amazing. Nothing like he had expected.

Campbell heard the wife's voice and had the presence of mind to pull the blade out of David Brandt's chest.

He rushed to intercept her as she came from the bedroom, still in her long, lacy gown.

"David?" she said with an expectant smile that turned to shock at the sight of Campbell. "Where's David? Who are you?"

Her eyes traveled over him, terror ridden, fixing on his face, the knife blade, then her husband's body on the floor.

*"Oh, my God! David!"* she screamed. *"Oh, David, David!"*

Campbell wanted to remember her like this. The frozen, wide-eyed look. The promise and hope that just moments ago had shined so brightly were now shattered.

The words poured from his mouth. "You want to know why? Well *so do I.*"

"What have you done?" Melanie screamed again. She struggled to understand. Her terrified eyes darted back and forth, sweeping the room for a way out.

She made a sudden dash for the living

room door. Campbell grabbed her wrist and brought the bloody knife up to her throat.

"Please," she whimpered, her eyes frozen. "Please don't kill me."

"The truth is, Melanie, I'm here to save you," he said as he smiled into her quivering face.

Campbell lowered the blade and sliced into her. The slender body jolted up with a sudden cry. Her eyes flickered like a weak electric bulb. A deathly rattle shot through her. Why? her begging eyes pleaded. Why?

It took a full minute for him to regain his breath. The smell of Melanie Brandt's blood was deep in his nostrils. He almost couldn't believe what he had done.

He carried the bride's body back into the bedroom and placed her on the bed.

She was beautiful. Delicate features. And so young. He remembered when he had first seen her and how he had been taken with her then. She had thought the whole world was in front of her.

He rubbed his hand against the smooth surface of her cheek and cupped one of her earrings — a smiling moon.

What is the worst thing anyone has ever

done? Phillip Campbell asked himself again, heart pounding in his chest.

Was this it? Had he just done it?

Not yet, a voice inside answered. Not quite yet.

Slowly, he lifted the bride's beautiful white wedding dress.

# Chapter 3

It was a little before eight-thirty on a Monday morning in June, one of those chilly, gray summer mornings San Francisco is famous for. I was starting the week off badly, flipping through old copies of *The New Yorker* while waiting for my G.P., Dr. Roy Orenthaler, to free up.

I'd been seeing Dr. Roy, as I still sometimes called him, ever since I was a sociology major at San Francisco State University, and I obligingly came in once a year for my checkup. That was last Tuesday. To my surprise, he had called at the end of the week and asked me to stop in today before work.

I had a busy day ahead of me: two open cases and a deposition to deliver at district court. I was hoping I could be at my desk by nine.

"Ms. Boxer," the receptionist finally called to me, "the doctor will see you now."

I followed her into the doctor's office.

Generally, Orenthaler greeted me with some well-intended stab at police humor, such as, "So if you're here, who's out on the street after *them?*" I was now thirty-four, and for the past two years had been lead inspector on the homicide detail out of the Hall of Justice.

But today he rose stiffly and uttered a solemn "Lindsay." He motioned me to the chair across from his desk. Uh-oh.

Up until then, my philosophy on doctors had been simple: When one of them gave you that deep, concerned look and told you to take a seat, three things could happen. Only one of them was bad. They were asking you out, getting ready to lay on some bad news, or they'd just spent a fortune re-upholstering the furniture.

"I want to show you something," Orenthaler began. He held a slide up against a light.

He pointed to splotches of tiny ghostlike spheres in a current of smaller pellets. "This is a blowup of the blood smear we took from you. The larger globules are erythrocytes. Red blood cells."

"They seem happy," I joked nervously.

"They are, Lindsay," the doctor said without a trace of a smile. "Problem is, you don't have many."

I fixed on his eyes, hoping they would relax and that we'd move on to something trivial like, You better start cutting down those long hours, Lindsay.

"There's a condition, Lindsay," Orenthaler went on. "Negli's aplastic anemia. It's rare. Basically, the body no longer manufactures red blood cells." He held up a photo. "This is what a normal blood workup looks like."

On this one, the dark background looked like the intersection of Market and Powell at 5:00 P.M., a virtual traffic jam of compressed, energetic spheres. Speedy messengers, all carrying oxygen to parts of someone else's body.

In contrast, mine looked about as densely

packed as a political headquarters two hours after the candidate has conceded.

"This is treatable, right?" I asked him. More like I was telling him.

"It's treatable, Lindsay," Orenthaler said, after a pause. "But it's serious."

A week ago, I had come in simply because my eyes were runny and blotchy and I'd discovered some blood in my panties and every day by three I was suddenly feeling like some iron-deficient gnome was inside me siphoning off my energy. Me, of the regular double shifts and fourteen-hour days. Six weeks' accrued vacation.

"How serious are we talking about?" I asked, my voice catching.

"Red blood cells are vital to the body's process of oxygenation," Orenthaler began to explain. "Hemopoiesis, the formation of blood cells in the bone marrow."

"Dr. Roy, this isn't a medical conference. How serious are we talking about?"

"What is it you want to hear, Lindsay? Diagnosis or possibility?"

"I want to hear the truth."

Orenthaler nodded. He got up and came around the desk and took my hand. "Then here's the truth, Lindsay. What you have is life threatening."

"Life threatening?" My heart stopped. My throat was as dry as parchment.

"Fatal, Lindsay."

# Chapter 4

The cold, blunt sound of the word hit me like a hollow-point shell between the eyes.

*Fatal, Lindsay.*

I waited for Dr. Roy to tell me this was all some kind of sick joke. That he had my tests mixed up with someone else's.

"I want to send you to a hematologist, Lindsay," Orenthaler went on. "Like a lot of diseases, there are stages. Stage one is when there's a mild depletion of cells. It can be treated with monthly transfusions. Stage two is when there's a systemic shortage of red cells.

"Stage three would require hospitalization. A bone marrow transplant. Potentially, the removal of your spleen."

"So where am *I*?" I asked, sucking in a cramped lungful of air.

"Your erythrocytic count is barely two hundred per cc of raw blood. That puts you on the cusp."

"The cusp?"

"The cusp," the doctor said, "between stages two and three."

There comes a point in everybody's life when you realize the stakes have suddenly changed. The carefree ride of your life slams into a stone wall; all those years of merely bouncing along, life taking you where you want to go, abruptly end. In my job, I see this moment forced on people all the time.

Welcome to mine.

"So what does this mean?" I asked weakly. The room was spinning a little now.

"What it means, Lindsay, is that you're going to have to undergo a prolonged regimen of intensive treatment."

I shook my head. "What does it mean for my job?"

I'd been in Homicide for six years now, the past two as lead homicide inspector.

With any luck, when my lieutenant was up for promotion, I'd be in line for his job. The department needed strong women. They could go far. Until that moment, I had thought that I would go far.

"Right now," the doctor said, "I don't think it means anything. As long as you feel strong while you're undergoing treatment, you can continue to work. In fact, it might even be good therapy."

Suddenly, I felt as if the walls of the room were closing in on me and I was suffocating.

"I'll give you the name of the hematologist," Orenthaler said.

He went on about the doctor's credentials, but I found myself no longer hearing him. I was thinking, Who am I going to tell? Mom had died ten years before, from breast cancer. Dad had been out of the picture since I was thirteen. I had a sister, Cat, but she was living a nice, neat life down in Newport Beach, and for her, just making a right turn on red brought on a moment of crisis.

The doctor pushed the referral toward me. "I know you, Lindsay. You'll pretend this is something you can fix by working harder.

But you can't. This is deadly serious. I want you to call him *today.*"

Suddenly my beeper sounded. I fumbled for it in my bag and looked at the number. It was the office — Jacobi.

"I need a phone," I said.

Orenthaler shot me a reproving look, one that read, *I told you, Lindsay.*

"Like you said," — I forced a nervous smile — "therapy."

He nodded to the phone on his desk and left the room. I went through the motions of dialing my partner.

"Fun's over, Boxer," Jacobi's gruff voice came on the line. "We got a double one-eight-oh. The Grand Hyatt."

My head was spinning with what the doctor had told me. In a fog, I must not have responded.

"You hear me, Boxer? Work time. You on the way?"

"Yeah," I finally said.

"And wear something nice," my partner grunted. "Like you would to a wedding."

# Chapter 5

How I got from Dr. Orenthaler's office, out in Noe Valley, all the way to the Hyatt in Union Square, I don't remember.

I kept hearing the doctor's words sounding over and over in my head. In severe cases, Negli's can be fatal.

All I know is that barely twelve minutes after Jacobi's call, my ten-year-old Bronco screeched to a halt in front of the hotel's atrium entrance.

The street was ablaze with police activity. Jesus, what the hell had happened?

The entire block between Sutter and Union Square had been cordoned off by a barricade of blue-and-whites. In the hotel entrance, a cluster of uniforms crowded about, checking people going in and out, waving the crowd of onlookers away.

I badged my way into the lobby. Two uniformed cops whom I recognized were standing in front: Murray, a potbellied cop in the last year of his hitch, and his younger partner, Vasquez. I asked Murray to bring me up to speed.

"What I been told is that there's two VIPs murdered on the thirtieth floor. All the brainpower's up there now."

"Who's presiding?" I asked, feeling my energies returning.

"Right now, I guess you are, Inspector."

"In that case, I want all exits to the hotel immediately shut down. And get a list from the manager of all guests and staff. No one goes in or out unless they're on that list."

Seconds later, I was riding up to the thirtieth floor.

The trail of cops and official personnel led me down the hall to a set of open double doors marked "Mandarin Suite." I ran into Charlie Clapper, the Crime Scene Unit crew chief, lugging in his heavy cases with two techs. Clapper's being here himself meant this was big.

Through the open double doors, I saw roses first — they were everywhere. Then I spotted Jacobi.

"Watch your heels, Inspector," he called loudly across the room.

My partner was forty-seven, but he looked ten years older. His hair was white, and he was beginning to bald. His face always seemed on the verge of a smirk over some tasteless wisecrack. He and I had worked together for two and a half years. I was senior, inspector-sergeant, though he had seven years on me in the department. He reported to me.

Stepping into the suite, I almost tripped across the legs of body number one, the groom. He was lying just inside the front door, crumpled in a heap, in an open tuxedo shirt and pants. Blood matted the hair on his chest. I took a deep breath.

"May I present Mr. David Brandt," Jacobi intoned with a crooked smile. "Mrs. David Brandt's in there." He gestured toward the bedroom. "Guess things went downhill for them quicker than most."

I knelt down and took a long, hard look at

the dead groom. He was handsome, with short, dark, tousled hair and a soft jaw; but the wide, apoplectic eyes locked open and the rivulet of dried blood on his chin marred the features. Behind him, his tuxedo jacket lay on the floor.

"Who found them?" I asked, checking his pocket for a wallet.

"Assistant manager. They were supposed to fly to Bali this morning. The island, not the casino, Boxer. For these two, assistant managers do wake-up calls."

I opened the wallet: a New York driver's license with the groom's smiling face. Platinum cards, several hundred-dollar bills.

I got up and looked around the suite. It opened up into a stylish museum of Oriental art: celadon dragons, chairs and couches decorated with imperial court scenes. The roses, of course. I was more the cozy bed-and-breakfast type, but if you were into making a statement, this was about as substantial a statement as you could make.

"Let's meet the bride," Jacobi said.

I followed through a set of open double doors into the master bedroom and stopped. The bride lay on her back on a large canopy bed.

I'd been to a hundred homicides and could radar in on the body as quick as anyone, but this I wasn't prepared for. It sent a wave of compassion racing down my spine.

The bride was still in her wedding dress.

# Chapter 6

You never see so many murder victims that it stops making you hurt, but this one was especially hard to look at.

She was so young and beautiful: calm, tranquil, and undisturbed except for the three crimson flowers of blood spread on her white chest. She looked as if she were a sleeping princess awaiting her prince, but her prince was in the other room, his guts spilled all over the floor.

"Whaddaya want for thirty-five hundred bucks a night?" Jacobi shrugged. "The whole fairy tale?"

It was taking everything I had just to keep

my grip on what I had to do. I glared, as if a single, venomous look could shut Jacobi down.

"Jeez, Boxer, what's goin' on?" His face sagged. "It was just a joke."

Whatever it was, his childlike, remorseful expression brought me back. The bride was wearing a large diamond on her right hand and fancy earrings. Whatever the killer's motive, it wasn't robbery.

A tech from the medical examiner's office was about to begin his initial examination. "Looks like three stab wounds," he said. "She must've showed a lot of heart. He got the groom with one."

What flashed through my mind was that fully 90 percent of all homicides were about money or sex. This one didn't seem to be about money.

"When's the last time anyone saw them?" I asked.

"A little after ten last night. That's when the humongous reception ended down-stairs."

"And not after that?"

"I know this isn't exactly your terrain, Boxer," Jacobi said. He broke into a grin.

"But generally people don't see the bride and groom for a while after the party."

I smiled thinly, stood up, looked back across the large, lavish suite. "So surprise me, Jacobi. Who springs for a room like this?"

"The groom's father is some Wall Street big shot from back east. He and his wife are down in a room on the twelfth floor. I was told it was quite a shindig downstairs. Up here, too. Look at all these goddamn roses."

I went back over to the groom and spotted what looked like a gift box of champagne on a marble console near the door. There was a spray of blood all over it.

"Assistant manager noticed it," Jacobi said. "My guess is, whoever did this brought it in with him."

"They see anyone around?"

"Yeah, a lot of people in tuxes. It was a wedding, right?"

I read the champagne bottle label. "Krug. Clos du Mesnil, 1989."

"That tell you something?" Jacobi asked.

"Only that the killer has good taste."

I looked at the blood-smeared tuxedo jacket. There was a single slash mark on the side where the fatal knife wound had gone through.

"I figure the killer must've stripped it off after he stabbed him." Jacobi shrugged.

"Why the hell would he do that?" I muttered out loud.

"Dunno. We'll have to ask him."

Charlie Clapper was eyeing me from the hallway to see if it was okay to get started. I nodded him in. Then I went back to the bride.

I had a bad, bad feeling about this one. If it's not about money . . . then . . . sex.

I lifted the fancy tulle lining of her skirt. The coldest, bitterest confirmation sliced through me.

The bride's panties had been pulled down and were dangling off one foot.

A fierce anger rose in my chest. I looked into the bride's eyes. Everything had been ahead of her, every hope and dream. Now she was a slaughtered corpse, defiled, possibly raped on her wedding night.

As I stood there, blinking as I stared down at her face, I suddenly realized that I was crying.

"Warren," I said to Jacobi, "I want you to speak with the groom's parents," I said, sucking in a breath. "I want everyone who was on this floor last night interviewed. If they've checked out, I want them traced. And a list of all hotel staff on duty last night."

I knew if I didn't get out now, I couldn't hold back the tide any longer. "Now, Warren. Please . . . now."

I avoided his eyes as I skirted past him out of the suite.

"What the hell's wrong with Boxer?" Charlie Clapper asked.

"You know women," I heard Jacobi reply. "They always cry at weddings."

# Chapter 7

Phillip Campbell was walking along Powell Street toward Union Square and the Hyatt. The police had actually blockaded the street, and the crowd outside the hotel was growing quickly. The howling screams of police and emergency vehicles filled the air. This was so unlike civilized and respectable San Francisco. He loved it!

Campbell almost couldn't believe he was headed back to the crime scene. He just couldn't help himself. Being here again helped him to relive the night before. As he walked closer and closer on Powell, his adrenaline surged, his heart pounded, almost out of control.

He edged through the mob that populated the final block outside the Hyatt. He heard the rumors swirling through the crowd, mostly well-dressed businesspeople, their faces creased with anguish and pain. There were rumors of a fire at the hotel, a jumper, a homicide, a suicide, but nothing came close to the horror of the actual event.

Finally, he got close enough so that he could watch the San Francisco police at work. A couple of them were surveying the crowd, *looking for him.* He wasn't worried about being discovered, not at all. It just wasn't going to happen. He was too unlikely, probably in the bottom 5 percent of the people the police might suspect. That comforted him, thrilled him, actually.

God, he had done it — caused all of this to happen, and he was only just beginning. He had never experienced anything like this feeling, and neither had the city of San Francisco.

A businessman was coming out of the Hyatt, and reporters and other people were asking him questions as if he were a major celebrity. The man was in his early thirties and he smirked knowingly. He had what they all wanted and he knew it. He was lording it over everyone, enjoying his pitiful moment of fame.

"It was a couple — murdered in the penthouse." He could overhear the man. "They were on their honeymoon. Sad, huh?"

The crowd around Phillip Campbell gasped, and his heart soared.

# Chapter 8

What a scene! Cindy Thomas pushed her way through the murmuring crowd, the looky-loos surrounding the Grand Hyatt. Then she groaned at the sight of the line of cops blocking the way.

There must've been a hundred onlookers tightly pressed around the entrance: tourists carrying cameras, businesspeople on their way to work; others were flashing press credentials and shouting, trying to talk their way in. Across the street, a television news van was already setting up with the backdrop of the hotel's facade.

After two years spent covering local interest on the Metro desk of the *Chronicle,* Cindy could feel a story that might jump-start her career. This one made the hairs on her neck stand up.

"Homicide down at the Grand Hyatt," her city editor, Sid Glass, had informed her after a staffer picked up the police transmission. Suzie Fitzpatrick and Tom Stone, the *Chronicle*'s usual crime reporters, were both on assignment. "Get right down there," her boss barked, to her amazement. He didn't have to say it twice.

But now, outside the Hyatt, Cindy felt her brief run of luck had come to an end.

The street was barricaded. More news crews were pulling up by the second. If she didn't come up with something now, Fitz-patrick or Stone would soon be handed the story. What she needed was inside. And here she was, out on the curb.

She spotted a line of limos and went up to the first one — a big beige stretch. She rapped on the window.

The driver looked up over his paper, the *Chronicle,* of course, and lowered the window as she caught his eye.

"You waiting for Steadman?" Cindy asked.

"Uh-uh," the driver replied. "Eddleson."

"Sorry, sorry." She waved. But inside she was beaming. *This was her way in.*

She lingered in the crowd a few seconds longer, then elbowed her way to the front. A young patrolman blocked her path. "Excuse me," said Cindy, looking harried. "I've got a meeting in the hotel."

"Name?"

"Eddleson. He's expecting me."

The entrance cop paged through a computer printout fastened to a clipboard. "You have a room number?"

Cindy shook her head. "He said to meet him in the Grill Room at eleven." The Grill Room at the Hyatt was the scene of some of San Francisco's best power breakfasts.

The entrance cop gave her a careful once-over. In her black leather jacket, jeans, sandals from Earthsake, Cindy figured she didn't look the part of someone arriving for a power brunch.

"My meeting," said Cindy, tapping her watch. "Eddleson."

Distractedly, the cop waved her through.

*She was inside.* The high glass atrium lobby, gold columns rising to the third floor.

It gave her a giggle, all that high-priced talent and all those recognizable faces still outside on the street.

And Cindy Thomas was first in. Now she only had to figure out what to do.

The place was definitely buzzing: cops, businesspeople checking out, tour groups, crimson-suited hotel staff. The chief had said it was a homicide. A daring one, given the hotel's prominent reputation.

She didn't know *which* floor. Or *when* it had taken place. She didn't even know if it involved a guest.

She may be inside, but she didn't know shit.

Cindy spotted a cluster of suitcases unattended on the far side of the lobby. They looked as if they were part of some large tour. A bellhop was dragging them outside.

She wandered over and knelt by one of the bags, as if she were taking something out.

A second bellhop passed by. "Need a taxi?"

Cindy shook her head no. "Someone's picking me up." Then, sweeping a view of the chaos, she rolled her eyes. "I just woke up. What did I miss?"

"You haven't heard? You must be the only one. We had some fireworks in the hotel last night."

Cindy widened her eyes.

"Two murders. On thirty." He lowered his voice as if he were letting her in on the secret of her life. "You happen to run into that big wedding last night? It was the bride and groom. Someone broke in on them in the Mandarin Suite."

"Jesus!" Cindy pulled back.

"Sure you don't need these brought out to the front?" the bellhop asked.

Cindy forced a smile. "Thanks. I'll wait in here."

On the far side of the lobby, she noticed an elevator opening. A bellhop came out, wheeling a cart of luggage. It must be a service elevator. From what she could see, the cops hadn't blocked it off.

She wound through the lobby traffic toward the elevator. She punched the button, and the shiny gold door opened. Thank God, it was empty.

Cindy jumped in and the door closed.

She couldn't believe it. She couldn't believe what she was doing. She pressed 30.

The Mandarin Suite.

A double homicide.

*Her story.*

# Chapter 9

As the elevator came to a stop, Cindy held her breath. Her heart was pumping like a turbine.

She was on 30. She was in. She was really doing this.

The doors had opened to a remote corner of the floor. She thanked God there wasn't a cop waiting in front of them.

She heard a buzz of activity coming from the other end of the hall. All she had to do was follow the noise.

As she hurried down the hallway, the voices grew louder. Two men in yellow jackets bearing "CSU" in large black letters walked past her. At the end of a hall, a group of cops and investigators stood in front of an open double doorway marked "Mandarin Suite."

She wasn't only inside; she was right in the fucking middle of it.

Cindy made her way toward the double doors. The cops weren't even looking in her direction; they were letting in police staff who had come from the main elevators.

She had made it all the way. The Mandarin Suite. She could see inside. It was huge, opulent, with lavish decor. Roses were everywhere.

Then her heart almost stopped. She thought she might be sick.

*The groom, in a bloodstained tuxedo shirt, lay there on the floor.*

Cindy's legs buckled. She had never seen a murder victim before. She wanted to lean forward, to let her eyes memorize every detail, but her body wouldn't move.

*"Who the hell are you?"* a brusque voice suddenly demanded. A large, angry cop was staring directly at her face.

All of a sudden, she was grabbed and pushed hard against the wall. It *hurt.* In a panic, Cindy pointed to her bag and her wallet, in which a photo press credential was displayed.

The angry cop began leafing through her IDs and credit cards as if they were junk mail.

"Jesus." The thick-necked patrolman scowled with a face like a slobbering Doberman. "She's a reporter."

"How in hell did you get up here?" his partner came over and demanded.

"Get her the hell out," Doberman barked to him. "And keep the ID. She won't get within a mile of a police briefing for the next year."

His partner dragged her by the arm to the main elevator bank. Over her shoulder, Cindy got a final glimpse of the dead man's legs splayed near the door. It was awful, terrifying, and sad. She was shaking.

"Show this *reporter* the front door," he instructed a third cop manning the elevator. He flicked her press ID as if it were a playing card. "Hope losing this was worth the ride up."

As the doors closed, a voice yelled, *"Hold it."*

A tall woman in a powder blue T-shirt and

brocade vest with a badge fastened to her waist stepped in. The cop was nice looking, with sandy blond hair, but she was clearly upset. She let out a deep sigh as the doors closed.

"Rough in there, Inspector?" the cop accompanying Cindy inquired.

"Yeah," the woman said, not even turning her head.

The word *inspector* went off like a flash in Cindy's mind.

Cindy couldn't believe it. The scene must be beyond awful for an inspector to be that upset. As the elevator descended, she rode the entire thirty floors just blinking her eyes and looking straight ahead.

When the doors opened to the lobby, the inspector rushed off.

"You see the front door," the cop said to Cindy. "Go through it. Don't come back."

As soon as the elevator doors had closed, she spun around and scanned the vast lobby for a sight of the detective. She caught a flash of her going into the ladies' room.

Cindy hurriedly followed her in. Just the two of them in there.

The detective stood in front of a mirror.

She looked close to six feet tall, slender and impressive. To Cindy's amazement, it was clear she had been crying.

Jesus, Jesus. She was back on the inside again. What had the inspector seen to get her so upset?

"You okay?" Cindy finally inquired in a soft voice.

The detective tensed up when she realized she wasn't alone. But she had this look on her face, as if she were on the verge of letting it all out. "You're that reporter, aren't you? You're the one who got upstairs."

Cindy nodded.

"So how did you make it all the way up there?"

"I don't know. Luck, maybe."

The detective pulled out a tissue and dabbed at her eyes. "Well, I'm afraid your luck's over, if you're looking for something from me."

"I didn't mean that," Cindy said. "You sure you're all right?"

The cop turned around. Her eyes shouted, *I've got nothing to say to you,* but they lied. It was as if she needed to do exactly that, talk to someone, more than anything in the world.

It was one of those strange moments when Cindy knew there was something under the surface. If the roles just shifted, and she had the chance, the two of them might even become friends.

Cindy reached into her pocket, pulled out a card, and placed it on the sink counter in front of the detective. "If you ever want to talk . . ."

The color came back into the inspector's pretty face. She hesitated, then gave Cindy the slimmest, faintest edge of a smile.

Cindy smiled in return. "As long as I'm here . . ." She went up to the sink and took out her makeup kit, catching the policewoman's eye in the mirror.

"Nice vest," she said.

# Chapter 10

I work out of the Hall of Justice. The Hall, as we referred to the gray, ten-story granite slab that housed the city's Department of Justice, was located just west of the freeway, on Sixth and Bryant. If the building itself, with its faded, antiseptic halls, didn't communicate that law enforcement lacked a sense of style, the surrounding neighborhood surely did. Hand-painted bail bondsman shacks, auto parts stores, parking lots, and dingy cafés.

Whatever ailed you, you could find it at the Hall: Auto Theft, Sex Crimes, Robbery. The district attorney was on eight, with cu-

bicles filled with bright young prosecutors.
A floor of holding cells on ten. One-stop
shopping, arrest to arraignment. Next door,
we even had the morgue.

After a hasty, bare-bones news conference, Jacobi and I agreed to meet upstairs
and go over what we had so far.

The twelve of us who covered homicide
for the entire city shared a twenty-by-thirty
squad room lit by harsh fluorescent lights.
My desk was choice — by the window,
"cheerily" overlooking the entrance ramp to
the freeway. It was always covered with
folders, stacks of photos, department releases. The one really personal item on it
was a Plexiglas cube my first partner had
given me. It was inscribed with the words
*You can't tell which way the train went by
looking at the tracks.*

I made myself a cup of tea and met Jacobi in Interrogation Room 1. I drew two
columns on a freestanding chalkboard: one
for what we knew, one for what we had to
check out.

Jacobi's initial talk with the groom's parents had produced nothing. The father was
a big-time Wall Street guy who ran a firm
that handled international buyouts. He said

that he and his wife had stayed until the last guest had left, and "walked the kids upstairs." They didn't have an enemy in the world. No debts, addictions, threats. Nothing to provoke such a horrible, unthinkable act.

A canvass of guests on the thirtieth floor had been slightly more successful. A couple from Chicago had noticed a man lingering in the hallway near the Mandarin Suite last night around 10:30 P.M. They described him as medium build, with short, dark hair, and said he wore a dark suit or maybe a tuxedo. He was carrying what may have been a box of liquor in his hands.

Later, two used tea bags and two empty push-throughs of Pepcid tablets on the table were the clearest signs that we'd been bouncing these questions back and forth for several hours. It was quarter past seven. Our shift had ended at five.

"No date tonight, Lindsay?" Jacobi finally asked.

"I get all the dates I want, Warren."

"Right, like I said — no date tonight."

Without knocking, our lieutenant, Sam Roth, whom we called Cheery, stuck his head into the room. He tossed a copy of the afternoon *Chronicle* across the table. "You see this?"

The boldface headline read, "WEDDING NIGHT MASSACRE AT HYATT." I read aloud from the front page. "Under a stunning view of the bay, in a world only the rich would know, the body of the twenty-nine-year-old groom lay curled up near the door." He knotted his brow. "What, did we invite this reporter in for a house tour of the crime scene? She knows the names, maps out the scene."

The byline read Cindy Thomas.

I thought of the card in my purse, letting out a long sigh. *Cindy goddamn Thomas.*

"Maybe I should call her up and ask her if we got any leads," Roth went on.

"You want to come on in?" I asked. "Look at the board. We could use the help."

Roth just stood there, chewing on his puffy lower lip. He was about to close the door behind him, but he turned back. "Lindsay, be in my office at a quarter of nine tomorrow. We need to lay this thing out carefully. For now, it's yours." Then he shut the door.

I sat down on the table. A heavy weight seemed to be pressing on me. The whole

day had passed. I hadn't found a single moment to deal with my own news.

"You okay?" Jacobi asked.

I looked at him, on the verge of letting it
all out, or maybe crying again.

"That was a tough crime scene," he said
at the door. "You should go home, take a
bath or something."

I smiled at him, grateful for a sudden, out-
of-character sensitivity.

After he left, I faced the mostly blank
columns of the board. I felt so weak and
empty I could barely push myself up.
Slowly, the events of the day, my visit to
Orenthaler's, wove their way back into my
mind. My head spun with his warning: *Fatal,
Lindsay.*

Then I was hit with the crushing realization. It was going on eight o'clock.

I had never called Orenthaler's specialist.

# Chapter 11

That night when I got home, I did sort of take Jacobi's advice.

First, I walked my dog, Sweet Martha. Two of my neighbors take care of Martha during the day, but she's always ready for our nightly romp. After the walk, I kicked off my Aerosole pumps, tossed my gun and clothes on the bed, and took a long, hot shower, bringing in a Killian's with me.

The image of David and Melanie Brandt washed away for the night; they could sleep.

But there was still Orenthaler, and Negli's.

And the call to the specialist I had dreaded the whole day and never made.

No matter how many times I lifted my face into the hot spray, I could not rinse the long day away. My life had changed. I was no longer just fighting murderers on the street. I was fighting for my life.

When I got out, I ran a brush through my hair and looked at myself for a long time in the mirror. A thought came into my mind that rarely occurred to me: I was pretty. Not a beauty, but cute. Tall, almost five-ten; decent shape for somebody who occasionally binges on beer and butterscotch-praline ice cream. I had these animated, bright brown eyes. I didn't back down.

How could it be that I was going to die?

Tonight, my eyes were different, though. Scared. Everything seemed different. Surf the waves, I heard a voice inside me say. Stand tall. You always stand tall.

As much as I tried to press it back, the question formed: Why me?

I threw on a pair of sweats, tied up my hair in a short ponytail, and went into the kitchen to boil water for pasta and heat up a sauce I had put in the fridge a couple of nights before.

While it simmered, I put on a CD, Sarah McLachlan, and sat at the kitchen counter with a glass of day-old Bianco red. I petted Sweet Martha as the music played.

Ever since my divorce had become final two years ago, I had lived alone. *I hate living alone.* I love people, friends. I used to love my husband, Tom, more than life itself — until he left me, saying, "Lindsay, I can't explain it. I love you, but I have to leave. I need to find somebody else. There's nothing else to say."

I guess he was being truthful, but it was the dumbest, saddest thing I'd ever heard. Broke my heart into a million pieces. It's still broken. So even though I hate living alone — except for Sweet Martha, of course — I'm afraid to be with somebody again. What if he suddenly stopped loving me? I couldn't take it. So I turn down, or shoot down, just about every man who comes anywhere near me.

*But God, I hate being alone.*

*Especially this night.*

My mother had died from breast cancer when I was just out of college. I had transferred to the city school from Berkeley to assist her and help take care of my younger sister, Cat. Like most things in her life, even Dad's walking out, Mom dealt with her illness only when it was too late to do anything about it.

I had seen my father only twice since I was thirteen. He wore a uniform for twenty years in Central. Was known as a pretty good cop. He used to go down to this bar, the Alibi, and stay for the Giants game after his shift. Sometimes he took me, "his little mascot," for the boys to admire.

When the sauce was ready I poured it over fusilli and dragged the plate and a salad out to my terrace. Martha tagged along. She'd been my shadow since I adopted her from the Border Collie Rescue Society. I lived on Potrero Hill, in a renovated blue Michaelian town house with a view of the bay. Not the fancy view like the one from the Mandarin Suite.

I sat down, propped my feet up on a neighboring chair, and balanced the plate on my lap. Across the bay, the lights of Oakland glimmered like a thousand unsympathetic eyes.

I looked out at the galaxy of flashing

lights, felt my eyes well up, and for the second time that day I realized that I was crying. Martha nuzzled me gently, then she finished the fusilli for me.

# Chapter 12

Quarter to nine the next morning, I was rapping at the fogged window of Lieutenant Roth's office at the Hall. Roth likes me — *like another daughter,* he says. He has no idea how condescending he can be. I'm tempted to tell Roth that I like him — *like a grandfather.*

I was expecting a crowd — at least a couple of suits from Internal Affairs, or maybe Captain Welting, who oversaw the Bureau of Inspectors — but, as he motioned me in, I saw that there was only one other person in the room.

A nice-looking type dressed in a chambray shirt and striped tie, with short, dark hair and strong shoulders. He had a handsome, intelligent face that seemed to come to life as I walked in, but it only meant one thing to me:

Polished brass. Someone from the department's press corps, or City Hall.

I had the blunt, uneasy feeling they'd been talking about me.

On the way over, I had rehearsed a convincing rebuttal about the breach in press security — how I'd arrived late on the scene myself, and the real issue was the crime. But Roth surprised me. "'Wedding Bell Blues,' they're calling it," he said tossing the morning's *Chronicle* in my face.

"I saw it," I replied, relieved to focus back on the case.

He looked at Mr. City Hall. "We'll be reading about this one every step of the way. Both kids were rich, Ivy League, popular. Sort of like young Kennedy and that blond wife of his — their tragedy."

"Who they were doesn't matter to me," I answered. "Listen, Sam, about yesterday . . ."

He stopped me with his hand. "Forget about yesterday. Chief Mercer's already been on the line with me. This case has his full attention."

He glanced at the smartly dressed political type in the corner. "Anyway, he wants there to be close reins on this case. What happened on other high-profile investigations can't happen here." Then he said to me, "We're changing the rules on this one."

Suddenly, the air in the room got thick with the uneasy feel of a setup.

Then Mr. City Hall stepped forward. I noticed his eyes bore the experienced lines of someone who had put in his time. "The mayor and Chief Mercer thought we might handle this investigation as an interdepartmental alliance. That is, if you were up for working with someone new," he said.

"New?" My eyes bounced back and forth between the two, ultimately settling on Roth.

"Meet your new partner," Roth announced.

I'm getting royally screwed, a voice inside me declared. They wouldn't do this to a man.

"Chris Raleigh," Mr. City Hall Hotshot said, extending his hand.

I didn't reach out to take it.

"For the past few years," Roth went on, "Captain Raleigh has worked as a Community Action liaison with the mayor's office. He specializes in managing potentially sensitive cases."

"Managing?"

Raleigh rolled his eyes at me. He was trying to be self-effacing. "Containing . . . controlling the damage . . . healing any wounds in the community afterwards."

"Oh," I shot back, "you're a marketing man."

He smiled. Every part of him oozed a practiced, confident air I associated with the kind of men who sat around large tables at City Hall.

"Before that," Roth went on, "Chris was a district captain over in Northern."

"That's Embassy Row." I sniffed. Everybody joked about the blue-blooded Northern district, which ranged from Nob Hill to Pacific Heights. Hot crimes there were society women who heard noises outside their town houses and late-arriving tourists locked out of their bed-and-breakfasts.

"We also handled traffic around the Presidio," Raleigh countered with another smile.

I ignored him. I turned to Roth. "What about Warren?" He and I had shared every case for the past two years.

"Jacobi'll be reassigned. I've got a plum job for him and his big mouth."

I didn't like leaving my partner behind, dumb-ass wisecracks and all. But Jacobi was his own worst enemy.

To my surprise, Raleigh asked, "You okay with this, Inspector?"

I didn't really have a choice. I nodded yes. "If you don't get in the way. Besides, you wear nicer ties than Jacobi."

"Father's Day present." He beamed. I couldn't believe I felt a tremor of disappointment shooting through me. Jesus, Lindsay. I didn't see a ring. *Lindsay!*

"I'm taking you off all other assignments," Roth announced. "No conflicting obligations. Jacobi can handle the back end, if he wants to stay on the case."

"So who's in charge?" I asked Cheery. I was senior partner to Jacobi; I was used to running my own cases.

Roth chortled. "He works with the mayor. He's an ex–district captain. Who do you think's in charge?"

"How about, in the field you lead?"

Raleigh suggested. "What we do with what we find is mine."

I hesitated, giving him an evaluating stare. God, he was so smooth.

Roth looked at me. "You want me to ask Jacobi if he's got similar reservations?"

Raleigh met my eyes. "Look, I'll let you know when we can't work it out."

It was as good a negotiation as I was going to get. The deal had changed. But at least I kept my case. "So what do I call you? Captain?"

With a casual ease, Raleigh tossed a light brown sport coat over his shoulder and reached for the door. "Try my name. I've been a civilian now for five years."

"Okay, Raleigh," I said with a faint smile. "You ever get to see a dead body while you were in Northern?"

# Chapter 13

The joke in Homicide about the morgue was that in spite of the lousy climate, the place was good for business. There's nothing like the sharp smell of formaldehyde or the depressing sheen of hospital-tiled halls to make the drudgery of chasing down dead leads seem like inspired work.

*But as they say, that's where the bodies are.*

That, and I got to see my buddy Claire.

There wasn't much to say about Claire Washburn, except that she was brilliant, totally accomplished, and absolutely my best friend in the world. For six years, she had been the city's chief medical examiner, which everyone in Homicide knew was as underdeserving a title as there was, since she virtually ran the office for Anthony Righetti. Righetti is her overbearing, power-thumping, credit-stealing boss, but Claire rarely complains.

In our book, Claire is the Office of the Coroner. But maybe the idea of a female M.E. still didn't cut it, even in San Francisco.

Female, and black.

When Raleigh and I arrived, we were ushered into Claire's office. She was wearing her white doctor's coat with the nickname "Butterfly" embroidered on the upper-left pocket.

The first thing you noticed about Claire was that she was carrying fifty pounds she didn't need. "I'm in shape," she always joked. "Round's a shape."

The second was her bright, confident demeanor. You knew she couldn't give a damn. She had the body of a Brahman, the mind of a hawk, *and* the gentle soul of a butterfly.

As we walked in, she gave me a weary but satisfied smile, as if she'd been up working most of the night. I introduced Raleigh, and Claire flashed me an impressed wag of the eyes.

Whatever I had accumulated over the years in street smarts, she threw off in natural wisdom. How she balanced the demands of her job, and placating her credit-seeking boss, with raising two teenage kids was a marvel. And her marriage to Edmund, who played bass drum for the San Francisco Symphony Orchestra, gave me faith that there was still some hope for the institution.

"I've been expecting you," she said as we hugged. "I called you last night from here. Didn't you get the message?"

With her comforting arms around me, a flood of emotion welled up. I wanted to tell her everything. If it weren't for Raleigh, I think I would've spilled it all — Orenthaler, Negli's — right there.

"I was beat," I answered. "And beat up. Long, tough day."

"Don't tell me." Raleigh chuckled. "You guys have met."

"Standard autopsy preparation." Claire

grinned as we pulled apart. "Don't they teach you that stuff down at City Hall?"

He playfully spread his arms.

"Uh-uh," said Claire, squeezing my shoulder. "This you gotta earn. Anyway," she regained a tone of seriousness, "I finished the preliminaries just this morning. You want to see the bodies?"

I nodded yes.

"Just be prepared: these two don't make much of an advertisement for *Modern Bride.*"

She led us through a series of closed compression doors toward the Vault, the large, refrigerated room where the bodies were stored.

I walked ahead with Claire, who pulled me close and whispered, "Let me guess. You gave Jacobi a kiss on the nose, and all of a sudden there was *this charming prince.*"

"He works for the mayor, Claire." I smiled back. "They sent him here to make sure I don't faint at the first sign of blood."

"In that case," she replied, pushing the heavy door to the Vault open, "you better hold on to that man tight."

# Chapter 14

I had been having very close encounters with dead bodies for six years now. But what I saw sent a shiver of revulsion racing through me.

The mutilated bodies of the bride and groom were lying side by side. They were on gurneys, their faces frozen in the horrifying moment of their deaths.

*David and Melanie Brandt.*

In their stark, ghostly expressions was the strongest statement I have ever seen that life may not be governed by anything fair or clement. I locked on the face of Melanie.

Yesterday, in her wedding dress, she had seemed somehow tragic and tranquil.

Today, in her slashed, naked starkness, her body was snarled in a freeze-frame of grotesque horror. Everything I had buried deep yesterday rushed to the surface again.

Six years in Homicide, and I had never turned away. But I turned away now.

I felt Claire's hand bolstering my arm, and leaned into her.

To my surprise, it turned out to be Raleigh. I righted myself with a mixture of anger and embarrassment. "Thanks." I exhaled. "I'm okay."

"I've been doing this job eight years," Claire said, "and this one, I wanted to turn away myself."

She picked up a folder from an examining table across from David Brandt. She pointed to the raw, gaping knife wound on the left side of his chest. "He was stabbed once in the right ventricle. You can see here the blade pierced the juncture between the fourth rib and the sternum on the way in. Ruptured the AV node, which provides the heart's electrical powering. Technically, he arrested."

"He died of a heart attack?" Raleigh asked.

She pulled a pair of tight surgical gloves over her hands and red-lacquered nails. "Electromechanical dissociation. Just a fancy way of describing what happens when you get stabbed in the heart."

"What about the weapon?" I spoke up.

"At this point, all I know is that it was a standard, straight-edged blade. No distinguishing marks or entry pattern. One thing I can tell you is that the killer was medium height, anywhere from five-seven to five-ten, and right-handed, based on the angle of impact. You can see here the path of the incision is angled slightly upward. Here," she said, poking around the wound. "The groom was six feet. On his wife, who was five-five, the angle of the first incision was slanted in a downward path."

I checked the groom's hands and arms for abrasions. "Any signs of a struggle?"

"Couldn't. The poor man was scared right out of his mind."

I nodded as my eyes fell on the groom's face.

Claire shook her head. "That's not exactly what I meant. Charlie Clapper's boys scraped up samples of a fluid from the groom's shoes and the hardwood floor in the foyer where he was found." She held up a small vial containing droplets of a cloudy liquid.

Raleigh and I stared at it, uncomprehending.

*"Urine,"* explained Claire. "The poor man apparently went in his pants. Must have been a gusher."

She pulled a white sheet over David Brandt's face and shook her head. "I figure that's one secret we can keep to ourselves.

"Unfortunately," she said with a sigh, "things didn't happen nearly as swiftly for the bride." She led us over to the bride's gurney. "Maybe she surprised him. There are marks on her hands and wrists that indicate a struggle. Here," she pointed to a reddened abrasion on her neck. "I tried to lift some tissue from under her nails, but we'll see what comes back. Anyway, the first wound was in the upper abdomen and tore through the lungs. With time, given the loss of blood, she might have died from that."

She pointed to a second and third ugly incision under the left breast in a similar location to the groom's. "Her pericardium was filled with so much blood you could've wrung it out like a wet dishrag."

"You're getting technical again," I said.

"The tissuelike membrane around the heart. Blood collects in this space and compresses the muscle so that the heart can no longer fill with blood from the main return. Ultimately, it ends up strangling itself."

The image of the bride's heart choking on her own blood chilled me. "It's almost as if he wanted to duplicate the wounds," I said, studying the knife-entry points.

"I thought of that," said Claire. "Straight line to the heart."

Raleigh furrowed his brow. "So the killer could be professional?"

Claire shrugged. "By the technical pattern of the wounds, perhaps. But I don't think so."

There was a hesitancy in her voice. I looked up and fixed on her grim eyes. "So what I need to know is, was she sexually molested?"

She swallowed. "There are clear signs of some sort of postmortem penetration. The vaginal mucosa was severely extended, and I found small lacerations around the introitus."

My body stiffened in rage. *"She was raped."*

*"If* she was raped," Claire replied, "it was a very bad deal. The vaginal cavity was as wide as I've ever seen it. Honestly, I don't think we're talking penile entry at all."

"Blunt instrument?" Raleigh said.

"Certainly wide enough . . . but there are abrasions along the vaginal walls consistent with some kind of ring." Claire took in a breath. "Personally, I'd go with a fist."

The angry, shocking nature of Melanie Brandt's death shivered me again. She had been mutilated, defiled. A fist. It had a blunt, savage finality to it. Her assailant wasn't just trying to act out his nightmare but wanted to shame her as well. *Why?*

"If you can handle one more thing, follow me," Claire said.

She led us out through a swinging door into an adjoining lab.

On an apron of white sterile paper lay the blood-smeared tuxedo jacket we had found next to the groom.

Claire picked it up by the collar. "Clapper loaned it to me. Of course, the obvious thing was to confirm whose blood was actually on it."

The left front panel was slashed through with the fatal incision and sprayed with dark blotches of blood. "Where this starts to get really interesting," said Claire "is that it wasn't just David Brandt's blood that I found on the front of the jacket."

Raleigh and I gaped in surprise.

"The killer's?" he said, wide-eyed.

She shook her head. "No, *the bride's.*"

I made a fast recollection of the crime scene. The groom had been killed at the door; his wife, thirty feet away in the master bedroom.

"How could the bride's blood get on his jacket?" I said, confused.

"I struggled with the same thing. So I went back and lined up the jacket against the groom's torso. The slash mark didn't quite match up with his wound. Look, the groom's wound was here. Fourth rib. The slash marks on the jacket are three inches higher. Checking further, the damned jacket isn't even the same brand as the pants. This is Joseph Abboud."

Claire winked, seeing the gears of my brain shift into place.

The jacket wasn't the groom's. It belonged to the man who had killed him.

Claire rounded her eyes. "Ain't no professional I know would leave that behind."

"He could've been just trying to utilize the wedding as a cover," Raleigh replied.

An even more chilling possibility had already struck me.

"He could have been a guest."

# Chapter 15

At the offices of the *San Francisco Chronicle,* Cindy Thomas's frantic brain was just barely staying ahead of her fingers.

The afternoon deadline was barely an hour away.

From a bellhop at the Hyatt, she had been able to obtain the names of two guests who had attended the Brandt wedding and who were still at the hotel. After running down there again last night, she had been able to put together a heart-wrenching, tragic picture — complete with vows, toasts, and a romantic last dance — of the bride and groom's final moments.

All the other reporters were still piecing together the sparse details released by the police. She was ahead so far. She was winning, and it felt great. She was also certain this was the best writing she'd done since arriving at the *Chronicle,* and maybe since she'd been an undergraduate at Michigan.

At the paper, Cindy's coup at the Hyatt had turned her into an instant celebrity. People she scarcely knew were suddenly stopping and congratulating her. Even the publisher, whom she rarely saw on the Metro floor, came down to find out who she was.

Metro was covering some demonstration in Mill Valley about a construction rerouting that had built up traffic near a school zone.

She was writing page one.

As she typed, she noticed Sidney Glass, her city editor, coming up to her desk. Glass was known at the newspaper as El Sid. He parked himself across from her with a stiff sigh. "We need to talk."

Her fingers slowly settled to a halt as she looked up.

"I've got two very pissed-off senior crime reporters itching to get into this. Suzy's at City Hall awaiting a statement by the police chief and the mayor. Stone's put together profiles on both families. They have twenty years and two Pulitzers between them. And it is their beat."

Cindy felt her heart nearly come to a stop. "What did you tell them?" she asked.

In El Sid's hardened eyes, she could see the greedy first-team crime staff, senior reporters with their own researchers, trying to hack their way in and carve this story up. *Her* story.

"Show me what you've got," the city editor finally said. He came around, peered over her shoulder, read a few lines off the computer screen. "A lot of it's okay. You probably know that. 'Anguished' belongs over here," he said, pointing at the screen. "It modifies 'bride's father.' Nothing pisses Ida Morris off like misplaced modifiers and inversions."

Cindy could feel herself blushing. "I know, I know. I'm trying to get this in. Deadline's at . . ."

"I know when deadline is." The editor glowered. "But down here, if you can get it in, you can get it in right."

He studied Cindy for what seemed an interminable duration, a deep, assessing stare that kept her on edge.

"Especially if you intend to stay on this thing." Glass's generally implacable face twitched, and he *almost* smiled at her. "I told them it was yours, Thomas."

Cindy repressed an urge to hug the cranky, domineering editor right on the bull pen floor. "You want me at City Hall?" she asked.

"The real story's in that hotel suite. Go back to the Hyatt."

El Sid began to walk away with his hands, as always, thrust into his trouser pockets.

But a moment later, he turned back. "Course, if you intend to stay on this story, you'd better find a police source on the inside — and quick."

# Chapter 16

After leaving the morgue, Raleigh and I walked back to the office, mostly in silence. Lots of details about the murders were bothering me. Why would the killer take away the victim's jacket? Why leave the champagne bottle? It made no sense.

"We've got a sex crime now. Bad one." I finally turned to him on the asphalt walkway leading to the Hall. "I want to run the autopsy results through Milt Fanning and the FBI computers. We also need to meet with the bride's parents. We'll need a history on anyone she may have been involved with before David. And a list of everyone at that wedding."

"Why don't we wait for some confirmation on that one," my new partner said, "before we go all out on that angle."

I stopped walking and stared at him. "You want to see if anybody checked in for a bloody jacket with the lost and found? I don't understand. What's your concern?"

"My concern," Raleigh said, "is that I don't want the department intruding on the grief of the families with a lot of hypotheticals until we have more to go on. We may or may not have the killer's jacket. He may or may not have been a guest."

"Who do you think it belonged to, the rabbi?"

He flashed me a quick smile. "It could've been left there to set us off."

His tone seemed suddenly different. "You're backing off?" I asked him.

"I'm not backing off," he said. "Until we have something firm, every old boyfriend of the bride or casualty of some corporate downsizing Gerald Brandt had a hand in could be rolled out as a possible suspect. I'd rather the spotlight wasn't aimed back at them unless we have something firm to go on."

Here it was. The spiel. Packaging, containment. Brandt and Chancellor Weil, the bride's father, were VIPs. Find us the bad guys, Lindsay. Just don't put the department at any risk along the way.

I chuffed back, "I thought the possibility that the killer could've been at that wedding *was* what we had to go on."

"All I'm suggesting, Lindsay, is let's get some confirmation before we begin ripping into the sex life of the best man."

I nodded, all the while fixing in on his eyes. "In the meantime, *Chris,* we'll just follow up on our *other* really strong leads."

We stood there in edgy silence.

"All right, why do you think the killer changed jackets with the groom?" I asked him.

He leaned back against the edge of a cement retaining wall. "My guess is that he was wearing it when he killed them. It was covered with blood. He had to get out undetected. The groom's jacket was lying around. So he just switched."

"So you figure he went to all that trouble

making the slash mark and all, thinking no one would notice. Different size, different maker. That it would just slip by. Raleigh, *why did he leave it behind?* Why wouldn't he stuff the bloody jacket into a bag? Or roll it under his new jacket?"

"Okay," Raleigh conceded, "I don't know. Your guess is?"

I didn't know why he had left it behind, but a chilling possibility was beginning to form in my mind. "Possibility one," I answered, "he panicked. Maybe the phone rang or someone knocked at the door."

"On their wedding night?"

"You're starting to sound like my ex-partner."

I started toward the Hall, and he caught up. He held the glass doors open for me. As I walked through, he took my arm. "And number two?"

I stood there, looking squarely into his eyes, trying to assess just how far I could go with him. "What's your real expertise here, anyway?" I asked.

He smiled, his look confident and secure. "I used to be married."

I didn't reply. Possibility two: A fear was building inside me. The killer was signing his murders? He was toying with us? Purposely leaving clues? One-time crime-of-passion killers didn't leave clues like the jacket. Professionals didn't, either.

Serials left clues.

# Chapter 17

The window that Phillip Campbell was staring out had a startling view of the bay, but he didn't really notice the sights. He was lost in his thoughts.

It's finally started. Everything is in play, he was thinking. The City on the Bay will never be the same, will it? I will never be the same. This was complicated — not what it seemed to be but beautiful in its own way.

He had closed his office door, as he always did when he was absorbed in research. Lately, he had stopped catching lunch with his coworkers. They bored him. Their lives were filled with petty concerns.

The stock market. The Giants and the 49ers. Where they were headed on vacation. They had such shallow, simple, middle-class dreams. His were soaring. He was like the moguls thinking up their new, new things over in Silicon Valley.

Anyway, that was all in the past. Now he had a secret. The biggest secret in the world.

He pushed his business papers to the corner of his desk. This is the old world, he thought. The old me. *The bore. The worker bee.*

He unlocked the top left drawer of his desk. Behind the usual personal clutter was a small gray lockbox. It was barely large enough to hold a packet of three-by-five-inch cards.

This is my world now.

He thought back to the Hyatt. The bride's beautiful porcelain face, the blossoms of blood on her chest. He still couldn't believe what had taken place. The sharp *crack* of the knife ripping through cartilage. The gasp of her last breath. And his, of course.

What were their names? Oh, Jesus Christ, he'd forgotten. No, he hadn't! The

Brandts. They were all over the newspapers and the TV news.

With a key from his chain, he opened the small box. What spilled out into the room was the intoxicating spell of his dreams.

A stack of index cards. Neat and orderly. Alphabetically arranged. One by one, he skimmed through them. New names . . . *King . . . Merced . . . Passeneau . . . Peterson.*

All the brides and grooms.

# Chapter 18

Several urgent messages were on my desk when I got back from the morgue. *Good* — urgent was appropriate.

Charlie Clapper from CSU. Preliminary report in. Some reporters: from the AP, local television stations. Even the woman from the *Chronicle* who had left me her card.

I picked at a grilled chicken and pear salad I had brought up as I dialed Clapper back. "Only good news," I joked, as his voice came on the phone.

"In that case, I can give you a nine hundred number. For two bucks a minute they'll tell you anything you want to hear."

I could hear it in the tone of his voice. "You got nothing?"

"Tons of partials, Lindsay," the CSU chief replied, meaning inconclusive prints his team had lifted from the room. "The bride's, the groom's, the assistant manager's, housekeeping's."

"You dusted the bodies?" I pressed. The killer had pulled Melanie Brandt up off the floor. "And the box of champagne?"

"Of course. Nothing. Somebody was careful."

"What about off the floor? Fibers, shoeprints."

"Besides the pee." Clapper laughed. "You think I'm holding out on you? You're cute, Lindsay, but I get off on bagging killers more. Meanwhile, I've got someone running that tux jacket under the microscope. I'll let you know. Roger wilco."

"Thanks, Charlie," I muttered disappointedly.

As I flipped further through my stack of messages, Cindy Thomas's name came to the top.

Normally, I wasn't in the habit of phoning back reporters in the middle of an ongoing investigation. But this one had been smart and cool making her way up to the crime scene, yet kind in backing off when she had me cornered in the bathroom.

I found her at her desk. "Thanks for calling me back, Inspector," she said in an appreciative tone.

"I owed you, I guess. Thanks for cutting me some slack at the hotel."

"Happens to us all. But I have to ask: Do you always react so personally at a crime scene? You're a homicide detective, right?"

I didn't have the time or heart to get into a battle of wits, so I used Jacobi's line. "It was a wedding. I always cry at them. What can I do for you, Ms. Thomas?"

"Cindy. . . . I'm going to do you a favor. When I reach five, maybe you'll do one for me."

"We have a homicide, a very bad one. We're not going to play Let's Make a Deal. And if we meet again, you'll find I'm not my cheeriest when I feel indebted."

"I guess what I was hoping for," she said, "was to hear your spin on the bride and groom."

"Doesn't Tom Stone cover homicide for the *Chronicle*?" I asked.

I heard her take in a breath. "I won't lie to

you. I normally handle local interest out of Metro."

"Well, you got yourself a real story now. 'Marriage Made in Heaven Ends Up in Hell.' You're quick out of the gate."

"Truth is, Inspector," — her voice grew softer — "I'd never seen anything like that before. Seeing David Brandt lying there . . . on his wedding night. I know what you must think, but it's not just about the story. I'd like to help any way I can."

"I appreciate that, but since we've got all these eager people with badges walking around here. We ought to give them a shot? Anyway, you should know that you sneaking your way up to the thirtieth floor didn't exactly get me invited to the commissioner's for brunch. I had tactical responsibility at the crime scene."

"I never thought I'd actually make it through."

"So we've established we don't know who owes whom here. But since it's my dime . . ."

The reporter's voice went back to a peremptory tone. "I called to get your reaction to a story we're going to break later today. You know the groom's father runs a buyout firm. Our business editor pulled off Bloomberg that they backed out of a proposed agreement at the last minute with the third-largest Russian automaker, Kolya-Novgorod. Brandt was providing up to two hundred million dollars for a significant stake. Kolya's one of those Russian conglomerates taken over by a new branch of black-market capitalists. Without the cash, I'm told it's virtually bankrupt. My source tells me the mood got very fractious."

I laughed. "Fractious, Ms. Thomas? I might be getting a little fractious myself."

"Apparently, some of the Russians were left hanging with their Uncle Vanyas out."

I laughed again. "Conspiracy to commit murder is a federal crime," I told her. "If there's something to it, you should make the call to Justice."

"I just thought I'd let you know. In the meantime, you want to throw me a comment on any other possibilities you're looking into?"

"Sure. I'd feel safe in saying that they're 'ongoing.'"

"Thanks." She sighed. "Have you narrowed in on any suspects yet?"

"This is what they tell you to ask at the *Chronicle*? You know I can't divulge that."

"Off the record. No attribution. As a friend."

As I listened, I remembered when I was a recruit trying to elbow my way in. How the police world had been barred, closed off, until someone had opened up the tiniest crack to let me crawl through. "Like I said, Ms. Thomas," my tone starting to soften, "no promises."

"Cindy," the reporter said. "At least call me Cindy. For the next time you get cornered in the bathroom with your guard down."

"Okay, *Cindy.* I'll be sure to keep you in mind."

# Chapter 19

I didn't want to go home. And I knew I couldn't stay at the Hall any longer.

I grabbed my bag, rushed down to the underground garage, and started up my trusty-dusty Bronco without a clear sense of where I was headed.

I just drove — Fourth, Third, onto Mission, past the Moscone Center — cafés, closed-up shops. All the way down toward the Embarcadero.

I wrapped around Battery, heading away from the bay. I had nowhere to go, but my hands seemed to act on their own, leading me somewhere. Flashes of the murdered bride and groom flickered in my head. Echoes of Orenthaler. I had finally called Dr. Medved, the hematologist, for an appointment.

I was approaching Sutter, and I turned. Suddenly, I knew where I was heading.

I pulled into Union Square. Without even trying, I found myself in front of the brightly lit entrance of the Hyatt.

I badged the manager and took the elevator up to the thirtieth floor.

A single uniformed guard sat in front of the Mandarin Suite. I recognized him, David Hale out of Central. He stood up as he saw me approach. "Nowhere to go, Inspector?"

A crisscrossing barrier of yellow tape blocked the entrance to the Mandarin Suite. Hale gave me the key. I peeled off a band or two of tape and slipped under the rest. I turned the lock and I was inside.

If you've never wandered alone at the site of a freshly committed murder, you don't really know the feeling of restless unease. I felt the dark ghosts of David and Melanie Brandt were still in the room.

I was sure I had missed something. I was also sure it was here. *What?*

The suite was pretty much as I had left it.

The Oriental carpet in the living room had gone to Clapper's lab. But body positions and blood sites were clearly marked out with blue chalk.

I looked at the spot where David Brandt had died. In my mind, I retraced what had likely taken place.

They are toasting each other. (I knew that from the half-filled champagne glasses on a table near the terrace.) Maybe he just gave her the earrings. (The open box was on the master bathroom counter.)

There's a knock. David Brandt goes to answer. It was as if secrets were buzzing in the thick air, alive with whispers.

The killer comes in, carrying the champagne box. Maybe David knows him. Maybe he just left him an hour before at the reception. The knife comes out. Only one thrust. The groom is pinned against the door, apoplectic. It happens so fast that he cannot scream. "Poor man went in his pants," Claire had said.

The bride doesn't scream? Maybe she's in the bathroom. (The jewelry box.) Maybe she went in there to put on the earrings.

The killer hunts through the suite. He in-

tercepts the bride, coming out unsuspect-
ingly.

I envision Melanie Brandt — radiant, full
of joy. He sees it, too. Was he someone she
knew? Had she just left him? Did Melanie
know her killer?

There's a Navajo saying, "Even the still
wind has a voice." In the quiet, confessing
hotel room, I listen.

Tell me, Melanie. *I am here for you.* I'm listening.

My skin tingles with the chill of resurrect-
ing each detail of the murder. She fights,
tries to run away. (The bruises and small
abrasions on her arms and neck.) The killer
stabs her at the foot of the bed. He is horrified, yet wildly excited about what he has
done. She doesn't die immediately. He has
to stab her again. And once more.

When he is finished, he carries her to the
bed. (Not drags. There is no sign of blood
trailing behind.) This is important. He is gentle with her. It makes me think he knows her.

Maybe he once loved Melanie? He folds
her arms on her waist in a restful pose. A
princess sleeping. Maybe he pretends that
what has taken place is only a bad dream.

Nowhere in the room do I feel the clinical

pattern of professionals or hired killers. Or even someone who has killed before.

I'm listening.

A ferocious anger rises up in his blood. He realizes he will never see her again. His princess . . .

He's so angry. He wants to lie down with her this one time. Feel her.

But he cannot. That would defile her. But he must have her. So he lifts her dress. Uses his fist.

It is all screaming at me. I'm sure there is one last thing I am not seeing. Unrevealed. What am I missing? What has everyone missed so far?

I step over to the bed. I envision Melanie, her horrifying stab wounds, but her face is calm, unaccusing. He leaves her like that. He doesn't take the earrings. He doesn't take the huge diamond ring.

Then it hit me with the power of a train exploding from a dark tunnel. What was missing. What I hadn't seen. Jesus Christ, Lindsay.

Rings!

I ran my mind over the image of her lying there. Her delicate, blood-smeared hands.

*The diamond was still there, but . . . Jesus! Is it possible?*

I ran back to the foyer and brought to mind the crumpled body of the groom.

They had been married just a few hours before. They had just completed their vows. But they weren't wearing gold bands.

Wedding rings.

The killer doesn't take the earrings, I realized.

He takes the rings.

# Chapter 20

Nine the next morning, I was in the office of Dr. Victor Medved, a pleasant, smallish man with a narrow, chiseled face, who, with a trace of an Eastern European accent, scared the hell out of me.

"Negli's is a killer," he stated evenly. "It robs the body of its ability to transport oxygen.

"In the beginning, the symptoms are list-lessness, a weakening of the immune system, and some light-headedness. Ulti-mately, you may experience similar brain dysfunction to a stroke and begin to lose mental capacity as well."

He got up, walked over to me, cradled my face in his gentle hands. He stared at me through thick glasses. "You're already peaked," he said, pressing my cheeks with his thumbs.

"Always takes me a while for the blood to get hopping in the mornings," I said with a smile, trying to mask the fear in my heart.

"Well, in three months," Dr. Medved said, "unless we reverse it, you will look like a ghost. A pretty ghost, but a ghost all the same."

He went back to his desk and picked up my chart. "I see you are a police detective."

"Homicide," I told him.

"Then there should be no reason to go forward under any delusions. I don't mean to upset you. Aplastic anemia can be reversed. Up to thirty percent of patients respond to a regimen of biweekly transfusions of packed red blood cells. Of those who do not respond, a similar percentage can be ultimately treated through a bone marrow transplant. But this involves a painful process of chemotherapy first in order to boost up the white cells."

I stiffened. Orenthaler's nightmarish predictions were coming true. "Is there any way to know who responds to the treatment?"

Medved clasped his palms together and shook his head. "The only way is to begin. Then we see."

"I'm on an important case. Dr. Orenthaler said I could continue to work."

Medved pursed his lips skeptically. "You may continue as long as you feel the strength."

I meted out a slow, painful breath. How long could I hide this? Who could I tell? "If it works, how long before we see improvement?" I asked with some hope.

He frowned. "This is not like popping aspirin for a headache. I'm afraid we're in this for the long haul."

The long haul. I thought of Roth's likely response. My chances at lieutenant.

This is it, Lindsay. This is the greatest challenge of your life.

"And if it doesn't work, how long . . . before things start to . . ."

"Start to get worse? Let us attack this with optimism and hope. We'll discuss that as we go along."

Everything was thrown open now. The case, my career, all the goals of my life. The stakes had changed. I was walking around with a time bomb ticking in my chest, tightly wound, incendiary. And the slow, disappearing fuse was all that I thought I might be.

I asked quietly, "When do we start?"

He scribbled out the location of an office in the same building. Third floor. Moffett Outpatient Services. There was no date.

"If it's all the same to you, I'd like to start right now."

## Chapter 21

The story about Gerald Brandt's business deal with the Russians had broken. It was on every newsstand: bold headline reading, "GROOM'S FATHER MAY HAVE TRIGGERED RUSSIAN WRATH."

The *Chronicle* reported that the FBI was seriously looking into the matter. *Great.*

Two half-liter bags of hemoglobin-enriched blood were pumping through me as I finally reached my desk at about ten-thirty. It took everything I had to push from my mind the image of the thick, crimson blood slowly dripping into my vein.

Roth called my name — the usual disgruntled glower was all over his face. *"Chronicle* says it's the Russians. The FBI seems to agree," he said as he leaned over my desk. He pushed a copy of the morning's paper at me.

"I saw it. Don't let the FBI in on this," I said. "This is our case."

I told him about last night, my going back to the crime scene. How I was pretty sure the sexual assault on the corpse, the bloody jacket, the missing rings, added up to a single, obsessed killer.

"It's not some Russian professional. He put his fist inside her," I reminded him. "He did this on her wedding night."

"You want me to tell the Feds to back off," Roth said, "because you have *strong feelings* about the case?"

"This is a *murder* case. A kinky, very nasty sex crime, not some international conspiracy."

"Maybe the Russian killer needed proof. Or maybe he *was* a sex maniac."

"Proof of what? Every paper and TV station in the country carried the story. Anyway, don't the Russki hitters usually cut off a finger, too?"

Roth rattled a frustrated sigh. His face showed more than its usual tic of agitation.

"I've got to run," I said. I shot my fist in the air and hoped that Roth got the joke.

Gerald Brandt was still at the Hyatt, waiting for his son's body to be released. I went to his suite and found him there alone.

"You see the papers?" I asked him as we sat at the umbrellaed table on the terrace.

"The papers, Bloomberg, some woman reporter from the *Chronicle* calling all night. What they're suggesting is total madness," he said.

"Your son's death was an act of madness, Mr. Brandt. You want me to be straight with you when it comes to the investigation?"

"What do you mean, Detective?"

"You were asked the other day if you knew anyone who might want to cause you harm —"

"And I told your detective, *not in this way.*"

"You don't think certain factions in Russia might be a *little* angry at you for pulling out of their deal?"

"We don't deal with factions, Ms. Boxer. Kolya's shareholders include some of the most powerful men in this country. Anyway, you make me seem like I'm a suspect. It was business. Negotiations. In what we do, we deal with this sort of thing every week. David's death has nothing to do with Kolya."

"Mr. Brandt, how can you be so sure? Your son and his wife are dead."

"Because negotiations *never broke off,* Detective. That was a ruse we used for the media. We closed on the deal last night."

He stood up, and I knew my interview was over.

My next call was to Claire. I ached to talk to her anyway. I craved my daily Claire fix. I also needed help on the case.

Her secretary said she was in the middle of a conference call when my call came in. She told me to hold on.

"Forensic specialists," Claire grumbled as she came on the line. "Listen to this. . . . Some guy's driving sixty in a thirty-five zone, rams into an elderly man in his Lexus, double-parked, waiting for his wife. DOA. Now the driver's tying up the guy's estate with a suit that the victim was illegally parked. All each side wants is to grab a piece of the estate, experts included. Righetti's pushing me in 'cause the case's being written up in an AAFS journal. Some of these bastards, you give them a penny for their thoughts, you know what you get?"

"Change," I answered with a smile. Claire *was* funny.

"You got it. I've got about thirty-one seconds. How you doing?" she inquired. "I love you, sweetheart. I miss you. What do you *want,* Lindsay?"

I hesitated, part of me wishing I could let the whole thing burst out, but all I asked was if the Brandts were wearing any wedding bands when they were brought in.

"To my knowledge, no," she replied. "We inventoried earrings and a diamond as large as an eyeball. But no wedding bands. I noticed that myself. In fact, that's why I was calling you last night."

"Great minds think alike," I said.

"Busy minds, at least," she countered. "How's your grisly, godawful case coming?"

I sighed. "I don't know. Next thing we have to do is go through three hundred guests to see if any might've been carrying any special grudges. You saw how this is being played up in the press. Russian revenge. The FBI's creeping around, and Chief Mercer's barking in Roth's ear to put a *real* detective on it. Speaking of which, I have Jacobi out trying to trace down the jacket. Other than that, the case is moving along smoothly."

Claire laughed. "Stick with it, sweetie. If anyone can solve these murders, it's you."

"I wish it were only that. . . ." I let my voice drop.

"Is everything all right?" Claire came back. "You don't sound your usual chatty, irreverent self."

"Actually, I need to talk with you. Maybe we can get together Saturday?"

"Sure," Claire said. "Oh, damn . . . we've got Reggie's graduation party. Can it keep a day? I could drive in for brunch on Sunday."

"Of course it can hold," I said, swallowing my disappointment. "Sunday would be great. I'd like that."

I hung up with a smile. For a moment, I actually felt better about things. Just making the date with Claire made it seem as if weights had been lifted off my shoulders. Sunday would give me some time to prepare. About how I was going to deal with the treatment, and my job.

Raleigh wandered up. "You want to grab a coffee?"

I thought he was needling me about what time I'd come in. He must have sensed my resentment.

He wagged a legal-size manila envelope in my face and shrugged. "It's the Brandts' wedding guest list. I thought you'd want to see who made the cut."

# Chapter 22

We went down to Roma's, one of those stucco-on-stucco, high-ceilinged, Euro-style coffee joints, across the street from the Hall. I prefer Peet's, but Roma's is closer.

I ordered a tea, and Raleigh came back with some fancy mocha latte and a slice of fresh pumpkin bread that he put in front of me.

"You ever wonder how these places make any money?" he asked.

"What?" I looked at him.

"There's one on every corner. They all serve the same thing, and their average sale's gotta be, what . . . two dollars and thirty-five cents?"

"This isn't a *date,* Raleigh," I snapped. "Let's go through the list."

"Maybe closer to three or three-fifty. Lucky if the places *gross* four hundred thousand."

"Raleigh, please," I said, losing patience.

He pushed the envelope toward me.

I opened it and fanned out eight or nine pages of names and addresses bearing Gerald Brandt's office crest. I recognized some of the guests on the groom's side immediately. Bert Rosen, former secretary of the treasury of the United States. Sumner Smith, some billionaire who had made his money in the eighties through big-time LBOs. Chip Stein, of E-flix, Spielberg's buddy; Maggie Sontero, the hot SoHo designer from New York. Lots of big names and big trouble.

On the bride's side, there were several prominent names from the San Francisco area. Mayor Fernandez for me. Arthur Abrams, the prominent local attorney. I had gone up against his firm once or twice in the witness box, testifying in homicide cases.

Willie Upton, superintendent of public schools.

Raleigh pulled his seat over to me. Side by side we scanned the rest of the list. Columns of impressive-sounding couples with Doctor or Honorable in front of their names.

It was a long, unrevealing, seemingly impenetrable list.

I don't know what I expected — just *something* to jump out at me. Some flashing name resonating with a culpability even the families didn't recognize.

Raleigh let out a worried breath. "This list is *scary.* You take fifty, I'll take fifty, and we'll give the balance to Jacobi. We'll all meet back here in two weeks and see what we've got."

The prospect of hammering away at these people — each one horrified and indignant at the prospect of why we were looking into them — didn't fill me with joy or high hopes.

"You think Mayor Fernandez might be a sex killer?" I muttered. "I do."

What came out of me next was a complete surprise. "So you said you were married?"

If we were going to be thrown together, we might as well get it out. And the truth was, I was curious.

Raleigh nodded after a short pause. I thought I saw pain in his eyes. "Actually, I still am. Our divorce is coming up next month. Seventeen years."

I flashed him a sympathetic wag of my eyes. "I'm sorry. Let's stop the Q and A."

"It's okay. Things happen. Suddenly, it seemed we were just traveling in different circles. To be more precise, Marion fell in love with the guy who owned the real estate office where she worked. It's an old story. I guess I never quite learned which fork to use."

"I could've saved you some pain," I said. "It goes left to right. Are there kids?"

"Two great boys. Fourteen and twelve. Jason is the jock. Teddy's the brain. Set up a home page for his sixth-grade class. I get them every other weekend. Lights of my life, Lindsay."

I could actually see Raleigh as superdad. Kicking the ball around on Saturdays, installing the computer in the den. On top of it, the guy did have affectionate eyes. It was gradually dawning on me that he wasn't the enemy.

"I guess —" he grinned at me — "getting the order of forks right didn't exactly help you, though. You're divorced, right?"

"Oohh. Somebody's been checking around," I said. "I was just out of the police academy. Tom was in his second year of law school at Berkeley. At first, he was going to go criminal. We had sort of a Carville-and-Matalin thing going. I imagined me testifying, Tom Terrific socking it to me on the cross. Ultimately, he opted for corporate."

"And?"

"It was his picture, not mine. I wasn't ready for the country club. It's an old story, right?" I smiled. "The *truth:* He walked out on me. Kind of broke my heart into tiny pieces."

"Sounds like we've got some things in common," Raleigh said gently. He did have nice eyes. *Stop it, Lindsay.*

"If you must know," I replied, deadpan, "for the past six months I've been having this torrid affair with Warren Jacobi."

Raleigh laughed and pretended to look surprised. "Geez, Jacobi doesn't seem like your type. What's the fatal attraction?"

I thought of my ex-husband, Tom, then one other man I had been sort of serious about. What always attracted me when I let someone get close. "Soft hands. And, I guess, a soft heart."

"So what ya think?" Raleigh said. "You put a few homemade jams on the shelves. Give the coffees some sexier names. Arabian Breeze, Sirocco. You think we can hike up the average sale?"

"Why are you going through this, Raleigh?"

He gave me a look that was sort of between an embarrassed grin and a sparkle in his clear blue eyes. "I've been doing police work for sixteen years. So you get to thinking. . . . I have this favorite place. Up in Tahoe. Maybe one of these franchises . . ."

"Sorry, I don't see you behind the counter picking out the muffins."

"Nicest thing you've said to me so far."

I got up, tucked the envelope under my arm, and headed toward the door. "On second thought, you might make a better baker than a cop."

"That's my girl." He smiled. "Wise-guy answer for everything. Keep those defenses up."

As we left the shop, I softened and said to him, "I have this favorite place, too."

"Maybe you'll show me one day."

"Maybe I will."

I was surprised by Raleigh — live and learn. He was actually a nice guy. I wondered if he had soft hands.

# Chapter 23

When Rebecca Passeneau looked at herself in the full splendor of her wedding dress, she knew that she was no longer her mother's little girl.

*You're my baby.* She had heard those words from her very first days on the planet.

With three older brothers, it wasn't so hard to imagine why. Her mother had always wanted a girl. Daddy, too; but as the years went on they had assumed their time had passed. The oldest — Ben, the daredevil — had been killed before she was born. Her parents were crushed. They couldn't even think of more children. Then, miraculously, Becky came.

*"My baby,"* she heard her mother exclaim from where she stood behind Becky.

"Oh, Mom." Becky sighed, but she also smiled.

She continued to look at herself. She was beautiful. In her long, white, strapless dress, an avalanche of tulle, she shone like the most lovely and beautiful thing in the world. Michael would be so happy. With all the arrangements — the hotel in Napa, the flowers, the last-minute alterations to the dress — she had thought the day would never actually come. But now it was almost here. *Friday.*

Ms. Perkins, the saleswoman at Saks, could only stand and admire. "You're gonna knock 'em dead, sweetheart."

Becky spun around, catching herself in every view of the three-paneled mirror. She grinned. "I will, won't I?"

"Your father and I want you to have something," her mother said.

She reached into her purse and pulled out a small suede jewelry pouch. In it was her diamond brooch, a four-carat oval on a string of pearls, passed on from her own mother.

She stepped closer to Becky, clasped the strand around her neck.

"It's gorgeous." Becky gasped. "Oh, *Mom.*"

"It was given to me on my wedding day," her mother said. "It has brought me a beautiful life. Now it's for you."

Becky Passeneau stood there in the spell of the mirror. The glorious dress, the diamond in the hollow of her throat.

She finally stepped off the alteration platform and hugged her mother. "I love you, Mom. You're the best."

"Now it's complete," her mother said, with a tear in her eye.

"No, not quite," said Ms. Perkins. She ran into the back and hurriedly returned with a bouquet of flowers. Imitations, sales accessories, but at the moment they looked like the most resplendent blossoms in the world.

She gave them to Becky, who stepped back up onto the platform, hugging them to herself. She saw her beaming smile reflected three times. They all stood back and admired.

"Now you are complete," Ms. Perkins said.

Standing nearby in Saks, watching Becky model her stunning dress, Phillip Campbell couldn't have agreed more.

"Your big day is almost here," he whispered softly. "You look beautiful."

# Chapter 24

The following morning, Milt Fanning from the FBI Sex Crimes Unit reported in. His computer had popped up a handful of related crimes, but he was letting me know that none of them was a strong lead.

They had started by plugging in fists used in the act of sexual assault, and that produced several cases, mostly gay crimes. One was in connection with a couple of murdered prostitutes in Compton that dated back to 1992, but Nicholas Chito was serving twenty-five years to life in San Quentin for that.

There had been several hotel murders,

even one involving newlyweds in Ohio, in which the groom had opened up the womb of his beloved with a 30-30 when he discovered he wasn't the first. But there was nothing local or still outstanding, nothing tangible to give us a direction.

I was disappointed but not surprised. Everything we had uncovered so far convinced me that when David and Melanie Brandt ran into their killer at the Hyatt, it wasn't the first time they had met.

I saw Jacobi wandering in from outside. For two days, he had been avoiding me — running down his assignments, specifically the searches for the champagne and the jacket.

After two years, I knew that when Jacobi wasn't needling me, he wasn't happy.

"How's the search going?" I asked.

He flashed me a tight-lipped smirk. "Chin and Murphy are calling every fricking wine store in a forty-mile radius. You think any of these guys keep track of this sort of thing? They all tell me that bottle could've been ordered from anywhere in the country. Then there's mail order to consider. The Internet. Cripes!"

I knew it was a long shot. But how many

people pay two hundred bucks for a bottle of champagne?

"Still," — he finally faced me with a self-satisfied smile — "we came up with some names."

As if to torture me, Jacobi leafed through his notepad to what must've been page thirty. Then he squinted, cleared his throat, saying, "Yeah, here we go . . . Golden State Wine Shop, on Crescent. *Krug. Clos du Mesnil,*" he pronounced, bludgeoning the French. "Nineteen eighty-nine. Someone ordered a case of the stuff last March. Name of Roy C. Shoen."

"You check him out?"

He nodded. "Never heard of any Brandt. He's a dentist. I guess rich dentists like fancy wine, too." He flipped over the page. "Then there's Vineyard Wines in Mill Valley. Murphy handled it." For the first time in a couple of days he really smiled at me. "The guy who bought the wine was named Murphy, too. Regular customer there. Threw a dinner party for his wife's birthday. You want to give me a morning off I'll check him out, but I thought I'd send Murphy himself. Just for the laugh."

"Any luck with the tuxedo jacket?"

"We called the manufacturer. Fifteen stores in the area sell this brand. If it even came from around here. We're bringing in their local rep. Tracking down the owner of this thing . . . it ain't gonna be easy."

"While you're out there, Warren," I teased, "see if you can pick yourself up a decent tie."

"Ho ho. So how you getting along without me?" Jacobi asked, facing me. He flattened his lips, and I could see the disappointment all over his face. Made me feel bad.

"I'm coping." Then, seriously, "I'm sorry, Warren. You know that I didn't ask for this guy."

He nodded self-consciously.

"You want me to check out everyone we dig up who's into fancy champagne?"

I shook my head. I got up, dropped a copy of the Brandt wedding list on his desk. "What I want you to do is check and see if they match against this list."

He leafed through the lists, whistling at a few of the more prominent names. "Too bad, Boxer. No Shoen or Murphy. Maybe we'll just have to wait and take a shot at couple number two."

"What makes you say that?" I asked. Jacobi was a pain in the ass, but he was a good cop with a good nose for sniffing out a pattern.

"We're looking for a spiffy dresser who likes to get dirty with dead brides, right?"

I nodded. I remembered something my first partner had told me. Never wrestle with a pig, Lindsay. You both get dirty. The pig likes it.

"I figure it's gotta be hard for a guy like that to find a date," said Jacobi.

# Chapter 25

The first week of the bride and groom investigation was gone. Unbelievable.

Jacobi's team had pounded the jacket-and-champagne search, but so far they had come up empty. Raleigh and I had spoken to twenty wedding guests, from the mayor to the groom's best friend. All of them were numb and sickened, but unable to put a finger on any one thing that might move us along.

All I could focus on was that we needed something firm — fast — before this guy who took the rings killed again.

I underwent my second transfusion. I

watched the thick red blood drip into my vein. I prayed it was making me stronger, but I didn't know. It had the slow, steady beat of a ticking clock.

And the clock *was* ticking. Mine, Chief Mercer's.

Saturday at six, Jacobi closed his pad, put on his sport jacket, and tucked his gun into his belt. "See ya, Boxer," he said.

Raleigh stopped by before heading out. "I owe you a beer. You want to collect?"

A beer would be nice, I thought. I was even growing used to Raleigh's company. But something told me that if I went with him now, I'd let everything out: Negli's, my treatments, the fear in my heart.

I shook my head. "Think I'll stick around," I said with a polite shrug.

"You got plans tomorrow?"

"Yeah. I'm meeting Claire. Then I'll come in here. What about you?"

"Jason's in a soccer tournament in Palo Alto. I'm taking both boys down."

"Sounds nice." It did sound nice. It had the ring of something I might miss out on in life.

"I'll be back tomorrow evening." He had given me his beeper the first day we hooked up. "I'm an hour away. Call if anything comes up."

With Raleigh gone, my corner of the squad room became shrouded in silence. The investigation was shut down for the night. One or two of the night staff were chatting out in the hall.

I had never felt so lonely. I knew that if I went home now I'd be leaving behind some vital nexus to the case. Failing some unsaid promise I had made to Melanie. One more look, I said. One more pass.

*Why would the killer take the rings?*

A wave of exhaustion washed through my veins. My new fighting cells were sapping my strength even as they defended me, multiplied. The cavalry, charging in to the rescue. Hope attacking doubt. It seemed crazy.

I had to let David and Melanie sleep for the night. I bound the thick crime file up in its elastic cord and placed it in the gray bin marked "Open Cases." Next to similar files, with similar names.

Then I sat at my desk in the dark squad room for a couple of minutes more. I started to cry.

# Book Two

## THE WOMEN'S MURDER CLUB

# Chapter 26

Becky DeGeorge, in the bloom of her first full day as Michael's wife, walked out of the hotel lobby holding her husband's hand. She breathed in the cool night air, the first fresh air she had inhaled all day.

In the brief span of their marriage, she and Michael had made love several times and taken two steamy showers together. They had poked their heads out for an obligatory but, at last, final brunch with the families. They had begged off the trip to Opus One, scurried back upstairs, and popped a last bottle of champagne. Michael had put on a sex video and as they watched the film they played out some unusual and exciting roles. He seemed to have several fantasies about wearing women's clothes.

Tomorrow, they'd be off to Mazatlan, for a heavenly week exploring all those sexy spots on his body she had yet to find. Maybe they'd even come out once or twice to see the dolphins.

So far, she decided, things were going very well.

Tonight, they were headed to the French Laundry, the finest restaurant in Napa. Everyone said it was *the* place to eat, and they had booked the reservation almost six months in advance. Becky's mouth watered as she dreamed of some fabulous sequence of tastes: foie gras, wild-berry duck, all washed down with an expensive champagne.

On the short walk to the car, a black limo pulled up alongside them. The passenger window opened, and a uniformed driver stuck his head out. "Mr. and Mrs. DeGeorge?"

They looked at each other, puzzled, then smiled. "That's us."

"I'm at your service," the driver announced. "Compliments of the hotel."

Becky was ecstatic. "You mean for us?" Once, in her job as a legal secretary, at a big closing, she had ridden in a fabulous stretch; but she had been jammed in the backseat with four preoccupied lawyers.

"Booked and paid for the night," the driver said, and winked.

The newlyweds exchanged a bright, exclamatory look.

"No one mentioned anything about this," said Michael, who seemed pleased with the notion that he was thought of as a VIP.

Becky peeked inside. "Oh, Michael." There were lush leather seats and a polished mahogany bar with crystal glasses. The lights were dimmed to a romantic glow. There was even a bottle of chardonnay on ice. She thought of pulling up to the most fashionable restaurant in Napa in this wonderful car.

"C'mon, Michael." She laughed, almost pulling him in. "It'll be a trip."

"I can be waiting at the restaurant when you come out," the driver said, "and as it happens, you're talking to someone who happens to know the most scenic routes through Napa."

She saw Michael's mild hesitation begin

to crack. "Don't you want to take your princess in style?"

Just as he had when she first smiled his way in the office, just as he had in bed last night, she saw him slowly come around. He was a little cautious sometimes. Accountants often were. But she'd always found ways of loosening him up.

"Whatever Becky wants," Michael finally said.

# Chapter 27

"Just married?" Phillip Campbell asked, his heart jumping.

The bright lights of oncoming cars shot through him like X rays, exposing innermost desires.

"Twenty-six hours, twenty-two minutes, and . . . forty-five seconds," Becky chirped.

Campbell's heart pounded loudly. She was perfect. They were perfect together. *Even better than he had hoped.*

The road was blank and seemed directionless, but he knew where he was going. "Help yourself to a drink. That's a Palmeyer in the bucket. Some people think it's the best in the valley."

As he drove, the killer's nerves were taut and excited. *What is the worst thing anyone has ever done? Can I do it again? More to the point, can I ever stop doing it?*

He glanced back and saw Becky and Michael pouring the Palmeyer wine. He heard the clink of raised glasses, then something about years of good luck. With a chill in his heart, he watched them kiss.

He hated every smug, deluded pore in their bodies. *Don't you want to take your princess in style?* He fingered the gun resting in his lap. He was changing murder weapons.

After a while, Campbell turned the limo up a steep hill off the main road.

"Where're we heading, driver?" the husband's voice came from the back.

He glanced in the mirror and smiled confidently at the DeGeorges. "I thought I'd take you the scenic way. Best views in the valley. And I'll still have you to the restaurant by eight."

"We don't want to be late," the groom warned sheepishly. "These reservations were harder to get than the damn hotel."

"Oh, c'mon, honey," Becky chimed in with perfect timing.

"Things start to open up just ahead," he told them. "Real pretty. In the meantime, relax. Put on some music. I'll show you the best views. Very romantic."

He pushed a button, and a thin band of pulsing lights began to shoot around the roof of the back compartment, a soft, romantic light show.

"Oooh," Becky said as the lights came on. "This is so great."

"I'll put up the privacy screen for the rest of the trip. You're only newlyweds once. Feel free to do whatever. Just look at it as your night."

He left the screen slightly open, so he could still see and hear them as he drove deeper into the hills. They were nuzzling now, sharing kisses. The groom's hand was moving up Becky's thigh. She pushed her pelvis into him.

The road became bumpy, and at intermittent points the rough, split concrete gave way to gravelly dirt. They were climbing. On both sides, the slopes were patterned with grids of darkened vines.

Becky's teasing laughter gave way to a

steady rhythm of deep-throated sighs. Phillip Campbell's breath began to race. Only inches away, he could hear her panting. A warm, velvety sensation began to burn in his thighs, as it had a week ago at the Grand Hyatt. Michael was entering Becky, and she moaned.

*What is the worst thing*?

At a clearing, he pulled the car to a stop, turned the headlights off. He took the gun and pulled back the double-clicking action.

Then he lowered the privacy screen.

In the ambient light, there was Becky, her black cocktail dress pulled up around her waist.

"Bravo!" he exclaimed.

They looked up, startled.

He saw a flicker of fear in the bride's eyes. She tried to cover herself.

Only then did the killer recognize that the warm flood burning his thighs and his knees was his own urine.

He emptied the gun into Becky and Michael DeGeorge.

# Chapter 28

That Sunday morning, I woke for the first time all week with a sense of hopefulness. It's the way I am . . . or *was.*

It was clear and beautiful outside; the bay was shimmering as if it were thrilled, too. And it was the day of my brunch with Claire. My confession to her.

Sunday mornings I had this place I always went to. My favorite place, I had told Raleigh.

First I drove downtown, to the Marina Green, in my tights, and jogged in the shadow of the bridge.

Mornings like this, I felt infused with

everything that was beautiful about living in San Francisco. The brown coast of Marin, the noises of the bay, even Alcatraz, standing guard.

I ran my usual three-plus miles south on the harbor, then up the two hundred and twelve stone stairs into Fort Mason Park.

Even with Negli's I could still do it. This morning it seemed to be letting me free.

I jogged past yelping dogs running loose, lovers on a morning walk, gray-clad, bald-headed Chinese men bickering over mah-jongg. Always to the same spot, high on the cliff, looking east over the bay. It was 7:45.

No one knew I came here. Or why. Like every Sunday, I came upon a small group practicing their tai chi. They were mostly Chinese, led, as every week, by the same old man in a gray knit cap and sweater vest.

I huffed to a stop and joined in, as I had every Sunday for the past ten years, since my mother died.

They didn't know me. What I did. Who I was. I didn't know them. The old man gave me the same quick, welcoming nod he always did.

There's a passage in Thoreau: "Time is but the stream I go a-fishing in. I drink at it, but while I drink, I see the sandy bottom and detect how shallow it is. Its current slides away, but eternity remains. I would drink deeper, fish in the sky, whose bottom is pebbly with stars."

I guess I've read that a hundred times. It's the way I feel up here. Part of the stream.

No Negli's.

No crimes, no faces twisted in death.

No bride and groom murders.

I did my Morning Swan, my Dragon, and I felt as light and free as I had before Orenthaler first dropped the news on me.

The leader nodded. No one asked me if I was well. Or how the week was.

I just welcomed the day, and knew that I was lucky to have it.

My favorite place.

I got home just before eleven, a half-finished coffee and the Sunday *Chronicle* in my hands. I figured I'd poke through the Metro section, see if there was anything on the case from my new best friend Cindy Thomas, shower, and be ready to meet Claire at one.

It was 11:25 when the phone rang. To my surprise, the voice on the line was Raleigh's.

"You dressed?" he asked.

"Sort of. Why? I have plans."

"Cancel them. I'm picking you up. We're going to Napa."

"Napa?" There was no trace of anything light or playful in his voice. "What's up?"

"I went into the office this morning just to check. While I was there, someone named Hartwig got transferred from Central Dispatch. He's a lieutenant in Napa. He's got some couple out there who are missing. They're newlyweds on their honeymoon."

# Chapter 29

By the time I had called Claire to cancel, showered, put my wet hair under a turned-back Giants cap, and thrown on some clothes, Raleigh's white Explorer was beeping me from below.

When I got downstairs, I couldn't help but notice him looking me over — wet hair, jeans, black leather jacket. "You look nice, Boxer," he said. He smiled as he put the car in gear.

He was casually dressed, in crumpled khakis and a faded blue polo shirt. He looked nice, too, but I wasn't going to say it.

"This isn't a date, Raleigh," I told him.

"You keep saying that," he said with a shrug, then stepped down on the gas.

We pulled up to the Napa Highlands Inn an hour and fifteen minutes later, the exact time, I noted, I was supposed to be pouring my heart out to Claire.

The inn turned out to be one of those fancy, high-end spas I always dreamed about going to. It was tucked into the mountains on Stag's Leap Road. By the looks of it, with its main lodge built of stacked giant redwoods and arcing windows of tempered glass, the guests here were not exactly into self-denial.

Two green-and-white police units were parked along the rotary outside the hotel's entrance. In the lobby, we were directed to the manager's office, where a nervous, red-haired management type, who seemed just a few days out of the training program, was standing with a couple of local cops.

"I'm Hartwig," said a tall, lanky man in street clothes. He was holding a paper cup from Starbucks. "Sorry to bust up your weekend," he apologized in a friendly drawl.

He passed us a wedding photo of the missing couple. It was enclosed in one of those Plexiglas "shaky toys" with the

Golden Gate Bridge in the foreground. "Party favor," he acknowledged. "Mr. and Mrs. Michael DeGeorge. From down your way. They both worked in the city at a large accounting firm. Married on Friday night."

Actually, it was a sweet photo. She, bright-eyed, with thick brown hair; he, ruddy and serious looking, wire-rimmed glasses. *Oh, God, not them. Not again.*

"So when were they last seen?" I asked.

"Seven-fifteen last night. Hotel staff saw them come down on their way to dinner. French Laundry," Hartwig said. "The concierge wrote them out directions, but they never showed."

"They drove off to go to dinner and were never heard from again?"

Hartwig kept rubbing the side of his face. "The manager said they checked in the day before in a gold Lexus. Door staff confirms they drove it briefly that afternoon."

"Yeah?" I nodded, fast-forwarding him.

"Car's still in the lot."

I asked, "Any messages from the outside we should know about?"

Hartwig went back to a desk and handed me a small stack of slips. I skipped through them. *Mom. Dad. Julie and Sam. Vicki and Don. Bon voyage.*

"We thoroughly searched the grounds around the property. Then we widened the search. It's sort of like your murders down there. Big wedding, celebration. Then *poof,* they're gone."

"Sort of like our thing," I said. "Except we had *bodies.*"

The Napa cop's face tightened. "Believe me, I didn't call you guys all the way out here just to help us with the missing-persons forms."

"What makes you so sure?" Raleigh asked.

"'Cause the concierge did receive one call last night. It was from the restaurant, confirming their reservations."

"So?"

Hartwig took a sip of his coffee before he met our eyes. "No one at the restaurant ever called them."

# Chapter 30

The honeymoon couple had received no unusual visitors, scheduled no conflicting side trips. The reservation at the French Laundry had been for just two.

What made this all the more grave was that they had missed their scheduled flight to Mexico.

While Raleigh poked around outside, I made a quick check of their room. There was this enormous redwood bed neatly turned down, a suitcase laid out, clothes stacked, toiletries. Lots of flowers — mostly roses. Maybe Becky DeGeorge had brought them from the reception.

There was nothing to indicate that the De-Georges weren't set to board that plane the next morning.

I caught up with Raleigh outside. He was talking with a bellhop who was apparently the last person who saw the DeGeorges leaving.

When it was just the two of us, Raleigh said, "Two of the local guys and I swept a hundred yards into the woods." He shook his head in exasperation. "Not even a foot-print. I looked around the car, too. It's locked. No blood, no sign of a struggle. But *something* happens to them out here. Someone accosts them. Twenty, thirty yards from the hotel."

I took a frustrated 360-degree scan of the driveway and the nearby parking lot. A local police cruiser was set up outside the prop-erty gate. "Not accosts them. Too risky. It's in plain view. Maybe someone picked them up."

"Reservations were only for two," he countered. "And the guy at the front door insists they were headed to their car."

"Then they *vanish?*"

Our attention was diverted by the swoosh of a long black limousine turning into the resort's pebbly driveway. It pulled up under the redwood overhang in front of the entrance.

Raleigh and I watched the hotel door open and the doorman emerge rolling a trolley of bags out. The driver of the limo hopped out to open the trunk.

It hit us both at the same time.

"It's a long shot," said Raleigh, meeting my eyes.

"Maybe," I agreed, "but it would explain how someone gained access without attracting anyone's attention. I think we should check if any limos have been reported stolen lately in the Bay Area."

Another car turned into the driveway, a silver Mazda, and parked near the far end of the circle. To my dismay, a woman in cargo pants and a University of Michigan sweatshirt jumped out.

"Raleigh, you said one of your particular skills was containment, didn't you?"

He looked at me as if I had asked Dr. Kevorkian, *You're sort of good at mixing chemicals, aren't you?*

"Okay," I said, eyeing the approaching figure, "contain this."

Walking up to us was Cindy Thomas.

# Chapter 31

"Either you've got the sharpest nose for a story I've ever seen," I said to Cindy Thomas angrily, "or I may start to think of you as a murder suspect."

This was the second time she had intruded in the middle of a possible crime scene.

"Don't tell me I'm stepping on some interoffice romance?" she quipped.

That made me steaming mad. We had a developing situation here. If it got in the news prematurely, it would hurt any chance the department had to control this case. I could just imagine the nightmare headlines:

BRIDE AND GROOM KILLER STRIKES AGAIN. And Roth would be livid. This would be the second time I had failed to control the crime scene with the same reporter.

"Who's your friend?" Raleigh asked.

"Cindy Thomas," she announced, extending her hand. "And you?"

"Cindy's with the *Chronicle,*" I alerted him.

Raleigh did a startled double take, left in midshake like a fired worker holding the hand of his replacement.

"Listen very clearly, Ms. Thomas," I said firmly. "I don't know if you've been around long enough to develop a sense for how this is supposed to work. But if you're planning on doing anything besides telling me why you're here and then packing up your little reporter's kit and driving away, you're definitely gonna make the department's shit list in a hurry."

"*Cindy,*" she reminded me. "But first, the much more interesting question is, why am I bumping into you out here?"

Raleigh and I both glared at her with deepening impatience. "Answer my question," I pressed.

"All right." She pursed her lips. "You two

shooting up here on a Sunday, Captain Raleigh kicking around the woods and the parking lot, your grilling the hotel staff, both of you looking stumped. I have to figure it all starts to add up. Like the fact that the place hasn't been cordoned off, so no crime's been committed yet. That someone could be missing. Since we all know what you two are working on, it's not a far reach to assume it might be a couple who just got married. Possibly, that our bride and groom killer found himself number two."

My eyes were wide, worried.

"Either that" — she smiled — "or I've grossly misjudged things and you guys are just here zin-tasting for the department's wine club."

"You picked up all that from watching us?" I asked her.

"Honestly, *no.*" She nodded toward the hotel gate. "Most of it was from the big-mouth local cop I was yapping with out there."

Without meaning to, I started to smile.

"Seriously, you realize you can't run with anything here," Raleigh said.

"Another dead bride and groom? Same

M.O.?" She snorted with resolve. "Damn right I'm going to run with it."

I was starting to see the situation going straight downhill. "One thing I'd *strongly* consider would be to get in your car and just drive back into town."

"Would you say that to Fitzpatrick or Stone?"

"If you went back to town, then I really *would* owe you one."

She smiled thinly. "You're kidding, aren't you? Just walk away?"

"Yeah, just walk away."

Cindy shook her head. "Sorry. One, I'd probably get fired, and two, there's just no way I can let this pass."

"What if I drove back with you?" I said, spur of the moment. "What if you can have pretty much what you're looking for, be on the inside, and give me some consideration at the same time?"

Raleigh's eyes almost bulged out of his head, but I gave him my best let-me-handle-this expression.

"When this story does break," Cindy insisted, "it's gonna be larger than any of us can control."

"And when it does, it'll be *yours.*"

Her eyes narrowed. She was rolling around in her head whether she could trust me. "You mean from you, exclusive?"

I waited for Raleigh to object. To my amazement, he went along.

"Chief Mercer handling all the releases?" Cindy asked.

"He is. All the *public* ones."

I looked at Raleigh with my nerves jumping around like Mexican jumping beans. If I couldn't trust him, then when we got back to town, I could be facing maximum rebuke. I would have Roth at my desk, or worse, Mercer. But I already felt I could trust him.

"So *I'm* gonna catch a ride back to town with Ms. Thomas," I said, waiting for his response.

*"Cindy,"* the reporter said with renewed determination.

Raleigh began to nod in a gradual, acquiescent way. "I'll finish up with Hartwig. I'll talk to you soon. Ms. Thomas, an unexpected pleasure."

I shot him a grateful smile. Then I took the reporter by the arm and said, "C'mon, *Cindy,* I'm gonna explain the rules along the way."

# Chapter 32

I don't know why I did it.

It was risky and rash, precisely the opposite of whatever had gotten me as far as I was.

Maybe I just wanted to say *screw it* in the face of authority. To Roth, Mercer. To play things my own way.

Maybe the case was widening, and I just wanted to keep the illusion that it was in my control.

Or maybe all I wanted to do was let someone else in.

"Before we go anywhere," I said, grasping Cindy's wrist as she started up the car,

"I need to know something. How did you find out about what was going on down here?"

She took a deep breath. "So far, all that's happened is you've pushed me away from the story of my career. Now I have to give up my sources, too?"

"*Anything* we do from here on is dependent on it."

"I'd kind of prefer it if I can keep you guessing," Cindy said.

"If this is gonna work, it's gotta be based on trust."

"Then trust goes two ways, doesn't it, Inspector?"

We sat there, baking in the hot Mazda littered with empty fast-food drink cups, sort of squaring off.

"Okay," I finally relented. I gave her what little we knew about why we were in Napa that afternoon. The DeGeorges missing in action. That they had been married Friday night. The possibility that they were couple number two. "None of this goes to print," I insisted, "until we have confirmation. I give you the okay."

Her eyes beamed with her suppositions suddenly confirmed.

"Now it's your turn. There was *no* press here. Even local. How did you get onto this?"

Cindy put the Mazda in gear. "I told you I was from Metro," she said, as the car putted out onto the main road, "and I've been fighting to stay on this story. My boss gave me the weekend to come up with something solid on this biggie. You had already brushed me off, so I parked myself down your street since yesterday and waited for something to turn up."

"You followed me?"

"Pretty desperate, huh? But effective."

I scrolled back over the past two days. "To the movies? To the marina this morning?"

She blushed slightly. "I was about to call it quits when your partner came by. I just tagged along for the ride."

I pressed myself back in my seat and started to laugh. "Not so desperate," I muttered. "Bad guys've been falling for it for years." I was both embarrassed and relieved.

On the drive back to town, I fleshed out the rules of our agreement. I had done this before when a reporter got too close on a story and threatened an investigation. She couldn't go out with this story until we had confirmation. When we did, I'd make sure she had it first. I'd keep her ahead of the story, but just slightly ahead.

"There's a catch," I said firmly. "What we have now is what you call a prioritized relationship. It goes past anything you already have — with your boyfriend or someone at work. Even your boss. Anything I give you is totally between us, and it stays with us, until I give you the okay to run with it."

Cindy nodded, but I wanted to make sure she understood.

"Your boss asks you where any of this comes from, you just shrug. Some big shot in the department — I don't care if it's Chief Mercer himself — parks his limo outside your door and calls you in about some leak, you say, Thanks for the ride. The district attorney's office calls you down to a grand jury, asks you to give up your sources, and a judge slaps you into a cell — you just make sure you bring enough reading material to fill the time."

"I understand," Cindy said. I could see in her eyes that she did.

The rest of the trip we talked about ourselves, our jobs and hobbies, and an unexpected development began to take shape. I started to like Cindy.

She asked me how long I'd been a cop, and I took her through more of the story than I had planned to. How my father was one, and how he'd left when I was thirteen. How I was sociology at SF State. How I wanted to prove I could make a difference in a man's world. How a lot of who I was and what I did was simply trying to prove I belonged.

She came back that she was sociology, too, at Michigan. And before we even hit Marin, we had discovered a few other startling things we had in common.

Her younger brother was born on my birthday, October 5. She was also into yoga, and the woman who had first taught me, years before in South San Francisco, was now instructing her in Corte Madera. We both liked to read travel books and mysteries — Sue Grafton, Patricia Cornwell, Elizabeth George. We *loved* Gordon's *House of Fine Eats.*

Cindy's father had died early — some seventeen years ago — eerily, when she was only thirteen, too.

But the most chilling coincidence — the one that gave me an eerie feeling — was that he died of leukemia, cousin of the same degenerative disease that was coursing through me.

I thought of telling her my secret, but I stopped short. That was Claire's to hear. But as we drew close to the Golden Gate, I had a premonition that I was riding with someone I was meant to be with, and definitely someone I liked to be with.

Approaching the city, I called Claire. It was hours after we were supposed to meet, but she still seemed eager to get together — and I had a lot to share.

We arranged to keep our date at Susie's, this time for an early dinner instead of a brunch. She pressed me for what I had found during the day. "I'll fill you in when I get there," I told her.

Then I did the second thing that surprised me that day.

I asked, "Do you mind if I bring a friend?"

# Chapter 33

Cindy and I were already into our second margarita by the time Claire walked in. From ten feet away, her smile seemed to brighten the entire room. I stood up and gave her a big hug.

"Couldn't wait for the old mom?" she said, eyeing the array of empty glasses.

"It's been a long day," I explained. "Say hey to Cindy."

"Pleasure," said Claire brightly, grasping Cindy's hand. Though the date had been planned for just her and me, Claire was one of those people who rolled easily with whatever came up.

"Lindsay's been telling me all about you," Cindy said over the din.

"Most of it's true, unless she's been saying I'm some kind of crackerjack forensic pathologist," Claire said, grinning.

"Actually, all she's been saying is that you're a real good friend."

Susie's was a bright, festive café with faux-painted walls and pretty good Caribbean food. They played a little reggae, a little jazz. It was a place where you could kick back, talk, shout, even shoot a rack of pool.

Our regular waitress, Loretta, came up, and we swayed Claire into a margarita for herself and ordered another round of spicy jerked wings.

"Tell me about Reggie's graduation," I said.

Claire stole a wing from our bowl and wistfully shook her head. "It's nice to know after all those years of school, they can actually say a few words that aren't 'phat' or 'it's the bomb.' They looked like a bunch of street-struttin' kids auditioning for the Grammys, but the principal swears they'll come out of it eventually."

"If they don't, there's always the Academy." I grinned, feeling light-headed.

Claire smiled. "I'm glad to see *you* looking up. When we spoke the other day, it sounded like Cheery was pressing those big, ugly shoes of his all over your toes."

"Cheery?" asked Cindy.

"My boss. We call him Cheery 'cause he inspires us with his humanistic concern for those entrusted to his command."

"Oh, I thought you were talking about my city editor." Cindy snickered. "The guy's only truly happy when he can threaten someone with their benefits. He has *no clue* how demeaning and condescending he is."

"Cindy's with the *Chronicle,*" I said to Claire, seeing her react with surprise. There was an undeclared no-fly zone between the force and the press. To cross it, as a reporter, you had to earn your place.

"Writing your memoirs, child?" Claire asked me with a guarded smile.

"Maybe." The short version. But with lots to tell.

Claire's margarita arrived, and we raised our glasses.

"To the powers that be," I toasted.

Cindy laughed. "Powers that be full of shit, powers that be pompous jerks, powers that be trying to keep you down."

Claire yelped in approval, and we all clinked glasses as if we were old friends.

"Y'know, when I first came to the paper," Cindy said, nibbling a wing, "one of the senior guys told me it was this particular editor's birthday. So I e-mail him this happy birthday message. I figure, him being my boss and all, it's a way to break the ice, maybe get a smile out of him. Later that day, the jerk calls me in. He's all polite and smiley. He's got bushy eyebrows as big as squirrels' tails. He nods me into the seat across from him. I'm thinking, Hey . . . the guy's human like everybody else."

Claire smiled. Enthusiastically, I drained the last of my second drink.

"So then the bastard narrows his eyes and says, 'Thomas, in the next hour and a half, I have sixty reporters trying to take everything that doesn't make sense in this fucking world and somehow cram it into forty pages. But it's reassuring to know that while everyone else is madly rushing against the clock, you've got the time to paste a happy little smiley face on my day.' He ended up assigning me a week of picking a winner from a fifth-grade 'Why I Want to Be an Editor for a Day' contest."

I laughed and coughed up a little of my drink. "Goes under the heading of 'No Good Deed Goes Unpunished.' What did you do?"

Cindy had a great smile. "E-mail it was the boss's birthday to every guy in the department. Jerks were slumping out of his office with their faces white all day."

Loretta came around again, and we ordered meals: chicken in a hot sauce, fajitas, and a large salad to share. Three Dos Equis to go with them. We poured this lethal Jamaican hot sauce, Toasty Lady, on our wings and watched Cindy's eyes glaze over from the first fiery blast.

"Rite of initiation." I grinned. "Now you're one of the girls."

"It's either the hot sauce or a tattoo," Claire announced, straight-faced.

Cindy scrunched up her eyes in an evaluating sort of way, then turned around and rolled up a sleeve of her T-shirt. She exposed two small G clefs etched on the back of her shoulder. "The downside of a classical education," she said with a crooked smile.

My eyes met Claire's — and both of us hooted with approval.

Then Claire yanked up her own shirt with a blush. Just below her ample brown waist, she revealed the outline of a tiny butterfly.

"Lindsay dared me one day," she admitted. "After you broke up with that prosecutor from San Jose. We went down to Big Sur overnight. Just the girls. To let off some steam. Ended up coming back with these."

"So where's yours?" Cindy turned to me and asked.

"Can't show you." I shook my head.

"C'mon," she pressed. "Let's see it."

With a sigh, I rolled onto my left buttock and patted my right. "It's a one-inch gecko. With this really cute little tail. When some suspect's giving me a hard time, I push him up against a wall and I tell him I'll stick it in his face so tight it's gonna look as large as Godzilla."

A warm silence fell over us. For a moment, the faces of David and Melanie Brandt, even Negli's, seemed a million miles away. We were just having fun.

I felt something happening, something that hadn't happened in a long time, that I desperately needed.

I felt connected.

# Chapter 34

"So now that we're all friends . . . ," said Claire, after we had eaten, "how'd the two of you meet up, anyway? Last I heard, you were going out to Napa to check on some missing newlyweds."

Michael and Becky DeGeorge, who a moment ago had seemed so far away, came hurtling back with a crash.

I had so much to tell her, but the day had changed so subtly from what I had planned. I almost felt deceitful, withholding, filling her in on what had taken place in Napa yet leaving out the important development that was going on inside of me.

Claire took it in, digesting it all with that sharp mind of hers. She had consulted on several serial-homicide cases, both as a lead examiner and an expert witness.

An idea was rolling through my head. In my weakened condition, I didn't relish the responsibility of running a media-intensive investigation into multiple homicides alone. What I came back with surprised even me.

"How'd you like to lend me some help?"

"Help?" Claire blinked with surprise. "How?"

"This thing is about to explode, Claire," I said. "If there's a bride and groom killer out there, the attention will be national. We all have an interest in this case. Maybe we could meet like this. The three of us . . . off the record."

Claire looked at me warily. "You're suggesting we do this on our own?"

"We've got the top guns of the M.E.'s office, Homicide, even the press, eye-deep in margaritas at this table." The more I thought it out, the more I knew it could work.

We could reassemble whatever clues came out of the official investigation, share what we had, cut through the political cover-your-ass and the bureaucracy. Three women, who would get a kick out of showing up the male orthodoxy. More important, we shared a heartfelt empathy for the victims.

Suddenly, the idea seemed lit with brilliance.

Claire shook her head in an incredulous way.

"C'mon," I pressed, "you don't think it would work? You don't think we'd be good at this?"

"That's not it at all," she replied. "It's that I've known you for ten years, and *never once,* on *anything,* have I ever heard you ask for help."

"Then *surprise,*" I said, looking straight into her eyes. "'Cause I'm asking now."

I tried to let her see that something was troubling me, something maybe larger than the case. That I wasn't sure I could handle it. That I could use the help. That there was more to it.

Claire gradually broke into the slimmest acquiescent grin. "In margaritas veritas. I'm in."

I beamed back, grateful, then turned to Cindy.

"How about you? You in?"

She stammered, "I-I have no idea what Sid Glass would say — but fuck him. I'm in."

We clinked glasses.

The Women's Murder Club was born.

# Chapter 35

The next morning, I arrived at the office straight from an eight o'clock transfusion, feeling light-headed, slightly woozy. First thing I did was scan the morning *Chronicle.* To my relief, there was nothing on the front page about anything relating to the disappearance in Napa. Cindy had kept her word.

I noticed Raleigh coming out of Roth's office. His sleeves were rolled up, exposing his thick forearms.

He gave me a guarded smile — one that told me of his discomfort at my cutting a deal yesterday with Cindy. With a flick of his blue eyes, he motioned me outside to the corridor.

"We have to talk," he said, as we huddled near the staircase.

"Listen, Raleigh," I said. "I'm really sorry about yesterday. I thought it would buy us some time."

His dark eyes smoldered. "Maybe you should tell me why she was worth compromising control of this case."

I shrugged. "You see anything about Napa in the papers this morning?"

"You contramanded a direct order from the chief of police. If that doesn't leave you in a hole, it sure digs one for me."

"So you'd rather be digging out of a story in the *Chronicle* about a serial killer?"

He backed against the wall. "That's Mercer's call."

A policeman I knew skipped up the stairs past us, grunting hello. I barely nodded back.

"Okay," I said, "so how do you want to play it? You want me to go in and spill my guts to Sam Roth? I will."

He hesitated. I could see he was torn, clicking through the consequences. After what seemed like a minute, he shook his head. "What's the point? Now."

I felt a wave of relief. I touched his arm and smiled at him for a couple of long beats. "Thanks."

"Lindsay," he added, "I checked with the state highway patrol. No record of any limos reported stolen in the past week."

That news, the dead end that it represented, discouraged me.

A voice shouted out from the squad room. "Boxer out there?"

"I'm here," I hollered back.

It was Paul Chin, one of the bright, efficient junior grades assigned to our team. "There's a Lieutenant Frank Hartwig on the line. Says you know him."

I ran back in, grabbed the phone on our civilian clerk's desk. "This is Lindsay Boxer."

"We found them, Inspector," Hartwig said.

# Chapter 36

"Caretaker discovered them," Hartwig muttered with a grim shake of his head. We were walking up a dirt path leading to a small Napa winery. "I hope you're ready for this. It's the worst thing I've ever seen. They were killed making love."

Raleigh and I had rushed up to St. Helena, turning east off 29, "the wine road," onto Hawk Crest Road until it wound high into the mountains, no longer paved. We had finally come upon an obscure wooden sign: Sparrow Ridge.

"Caretaker comes up here twice a week.

Found them at seven this morning. The place's no longer in regular use," Hartwig continued. I could tell he was nervous, shook up.

The winery was barely more than a large corrugated shed filled with shiny, state-of-the-art equipment: crushers, fermenting tanks, staggered rows of stacked, aging barrels.

"You're probably used to this sort of homicide," Hartwig said as we walked in. The sharp, rancid smell hit our nostrils. My stomach rolled. You never get used to homicide scenes.

*They were killed making love.*

Several members of the local SCU team were huddled over the open bay of a large, stainless grape presser. They were inspecting two splattered mounds. The mounds were the bodies of Michael and Becky DeGeorge.

"Awhh, shit, Lindsay," Raleigh muttered.

The husband, in a blazer and khakis, stared up at us. A dime-sized penetration cut the center of his forehead. His wife, whose black dress was pushed up to her neck, was on top of him. White-eyed fear was frozen on her face. Her bra was pulled down to her waist, and I could see blood-spattered breasts. Her panties were down to her knees.

It was an ugly, nauseating sight. "You have an approximate time?" I asked Hartwig. He looked close to being sick.

"From the degeneration of the wounds, the M.E. thinks they've been dead twenty-four to thirty-six hours. They were killed the same night they disappeared. Jesus, they were just kids."

I stared at the sad, bloodied body of the wife, and my eyes fell to her hands.

*Nothing there. No wedding band.*

"You said they were killed in the act?" I asked. "You're sure about that?"

Hartwig nodded to the assistant medical examiner. He gently rolled Becky DeGeorge's body off her husband's.

Sticking out of Michael DeGeorge's unfastened khakis was the perfectly preserved remainder of his final erection.

A smoldering rage ripped through me. The DeGeorges *were* just kids. Both were in their twenties, like the Brandts. Who would do such a terrible thing?

"You can see over here how they were

dragged," Hartwig said, pointing to smears of dried blood visible on the pitched concrete floor. The smears led to car tracks that were clearly delineated in the sparsely traveled soil. A couple of sheriff's men were marking off the tracks in yellow tape.

Raleigh bent down and studied them. "Wide wheel base, but fourteen-inch tires. The tread is good, kept up. An SUV would have sixteen-inch wheels. I would guess some kind of large luxury sedan."

"I thought you were just a desk cop," I said to him.

He grinned. "I spent a summer in college working in the pit crew on the NASCAR circuit. I can change a tire faster than a beer man at 3Com can change a twenty. My guess would be a Caddy. Or a Lincoln." *Limo,* his eyes were saying.

My own mind was racing through something Claire had once said. *Link the crimes.*

It was uncommon for a pattern killer to switch methods. Sexual killers liked closeness to their victims: strangulation, bludgeoning, knives. They wanted to feel their victims struggle, expire. They liked to invade a victim's home. Shooting was detached, clinical. It provided no thrill.

For a moment, I wondered if there were two murderers. Copycat killers. It couldn't be.

*No one else knew about the rings.*

I went over to Becky DeGeorge as the doctor was zipping her into a body bag. I gazed down into her eyes. They were making love. *Did he force them? Did he surprise them?*

*A sexual psycho who changes his methods. A killer who leaves clues.*

*What did he leave here?*

*What were we missing?*

# Chapter 37

Fresh air filled my lungs as soon as we stepped outside. Chris Raleigh, Hartwig, and I walked down the dirt road. The grid of the valley floor stretched out below us. Rows of fallow grapes hugged each side. We were silent. Shell-shocked.

A scary idea shot through me. We were a thousand feet up, totally isolated. Something didn't sit right. "Why *here,* Hartwig?"

"How about, it's remote and no one ever comes up here."

"What I meant," I said, "is why *here?* This particular spot. Who knows about this place?"

"There's isolated property all up and down these slopes. The consortiums have eaten up the valley floor. These properties take more work than capital. Labors of love. Check the listings. Dozens of them dry up every season. Anyone around here knows places like this."

"The first killings were in the city. Yet he knew exactly where to come. Who owns this plot?"

Hartwig shook his head. "Dunno."

"I'd find out. And I would also make another pass through their room. Someone had them targeted. Knew all their plans. Travel brochures, business cards, see if there's anything from any limousine services."

From below, I heard the sound of a large vehicle climbing up the dirt road. I caught sight of a white San Francisco Medical Examiner's Bronco pulling to a stop.

Claire Washburn was behind the wheel. I had asked her to come — in the hope of matching evidence from both crime scenes.

I opened her door and said gratefully, "Thanks for coming, sweetie."

Claire solemnly shook her head. "I only wish they had turned up differently. It's a call

I never like to receive." She pulled her heavy frame out of the car with surprising ease. "I have a meeting later back in town, but I thought I'd look over the crime scene, introduce myself to the presiding on-site."

I introduced Claire to Frank Hartwig. "Your M.E.'s Bill Toll, isn't he?" she asked with authority.

He blinked warily, clearly nervous. First, he had Raleigh and me here as consults. But he had asked us in. Now the San Francisco M.E. pulls up.

"Relax, I already patched through to his cell phone," Claire said. "He's expecting me." She spotted the medical team standing over the yellow bags. "Why don't I go take a look."

Trying to hold on to some sense of order, Hartwig followed close behind.

Raleigh came and stood next to me. He looked tired.

"You okay?" I asked.

He shook his head. He kept his eyes fixed on the shed where the bodies had been dumped.

I remembered how he had steadied me at the morgue. "Been a while since you took in a really bad one?"

"That's not it," he said, with the same un-settled look. "I want you to know . . . that wherever this leads, it's not about interfac-ing with City Hall. Or containment, Lindsay. I want this guy."

I was already there in my head. This wasn't about the big collar. Or my shot at lieutenant. Or even fighting Negli's.

We stood there side by side for a while.

"Not that either of us," he finally said, breaking the silence, "is in much of a posi-tion to be the last line of defense for the in-stitution of marriage."

# Chapter 38

Phillip Campbell had driven since the first light of dawn, setting out in the bulky rented stretch limo. He was nervous, wired — and he absolutely loved it.

He chewed up the miles in a steady, purposeful daze, crossing the Bay Bridge and continuing east on 80. He finally broke free of the morning traffic near Vallejo and maintained a vigilant sixty on the speedometer as he headed east.

He didn't want to be stopped.

The papers called him a monster. Psychotic, sociopathic. Expert witnesses on TV analyzed his motives, his past, his possible future murders.

*They know nothing. They are all wrong. They'll find what I want them to find. They only see what I want them to see.*

From the Nevada border it was a short drive down into Reno, which he considered a vulgar, aging cowboy town. He stayed on the highway, avoiding the Strip. Wide, stucco-lined boulevards of gas stations, gun dealerships, pawnshops. You could get anything here without a lot of questions. It was the place to come to buy a gun, or unload a car, or both.

Out by the convention center, he turned into Lumpy's. He pulled the car up to an open area in the lot, opened the glove compartment, recovered the folded paperwork, breathed a sigh of relief.

The limo was perfectly clean. Spotless. There were no ghosts whispering. All day yesterday, he had cleaned and polished, scrubbing out the bloodstains until the last trace of evidence was gone. Now the car was silent, as unconfiding as the day he had picked it up.

He breathed easier. It was as if Michael and Becky DeGeorge had never existed.

In minutes he had paid for the car and called a cab to take him to the airport.

At the airport, he checked in, looked through a San Francisco paper at a newsstand. Nothing about Becky and Michael. He made his way to the gate.

He bought a bottle of Fruitopia apricot drink and a vegetarian wrap at a fast-food counter.

He checked in at Gate 31, Reno Air to San Francisco. He took a seat and started eating his lunch.

An attractive young woman sat next to him. Blond hair, tight ass, just tawdry-looking enough to attract his eye. She wore a gold chain around her neck with her name on it in script: Brandee. A tiny diamond ring.

He smiled a quick, inadvertent greeting.

She pulled out a Kipling knapsack, took a swig from a plastic water bottle, and took out a paperback, *Memoirs of a Geisha.* It interested him that of all things, she was reading about a woman in bondage. These were signs.

"Good book?" He smiled her way.

"That's what everyone says," she replied. "I'm just starting."

He leaned over and breathed in the cheap, citrusy scent of her perfume.

"Hard to believe," he went on, "it was written by a man."

"I'll let you know." She flipped a few pages, then added. "My fiancé gave it to me."

Phillip Campbell felt the short, thin hairs on his arms stand up.

His heart began to throb. He ran a tremulous finger along the edge of his goatee.

"Oh — when's the big day?"

# Chapter 39

Raleigh drove back to town in our car. I hung around and caught a ride with Claire. I needed to tell her what was going on with me. Claire and I have been best friends for years. We talk at least once every day. I *knew* why I was having trouble telling her about my illness — I didn't want to hurt her. Or to burden her with my problems. I loved her so much.

As the M.E.'s van bumped down the mountain road, I asked if she had been able to pick up anything at the murder scene.

"There was definitely sexual activity going on before they were killed," she replied confidently. "I could see labial distension around the vagina. Secretions on her thighs.

"This is guesswork — I only had a few minutes — but I think the husband was shot first, Lindsay. The one clean wound to the head suggests he was dispatched without resistance. Head on. Wounds on Rebecca indicate something else. She was shot from the rear. Through the shoulder blades, the neck. From a distance, I would estimate, of no more than three to five feet. If the semen matches up and they were in the act when it took place, it suggests that she was on top. That would mean someone had to get in fairly close, unobserved, while they were at it. Come up at them from behind her. Since you said they didn't use their own car that night, they were obviously on their way somewhere. I think it's consistent with your theory that they were in some kind of vehicle when this took place. The killer in the front seat. So why not a limousine?"

"That's all?" I shook my head and smiled at Claire.

"Like I said, I only had a few minutes. Anyway, it was your theory. If it ends up proving out, all I did was connect the dots."

We drove on a bit. I was still fumbling for the right words.

Claire asked, "So how's the new partner?"

I gave her an affirming nod. "Turns out he's okay. He's backed me up with Roth and Mercer."

"And you were so sure he was only a watchdog from the mayor's office."

"So I was wrong."

"Wouldn't be the first time you ended up wrong about a guy," Claire said.

I wrinkled my face in pretended offense and ignored her grin.

"Anyway, watchdog or not," Claire continued, "he's a damn sight better to look at than Jacobi."

"Smarter, too. When we drove up to Napa yesterday, I flipped on the stereo in his Explorer. A tape of *The Shipping News* came on."

"So," Claire went on, with a look of inquisitiveness, "anything going on?"

"You mean other than four innocent people being killed?"

"I mean with Chris Raleigh, Lindsay. He's working out of the mayor's office, he's a hunk, and your social calendar isn't exactly Gwyneth Paltrow's. You can't tell me he's not your type."

"We've been wrapped up in the case, Claire."

"Yeah." She chortled. "He's not married, right?"

"C'mon, Claire," I pleaded. "I'm just not ready."

As Claire winked, I found myself imagining something going on with Raleigh. If I had driven back with *him* from Napa, instead of Cindy. If I had asked him up, it being nothing but a lonely Sunday, thrown together something out of the fridge. Shared a beer on the terrace as the sun melted into the bay. In my mind, I caught him checking me over again. *You look nice, Boxer.* He had noticed. Truth was, I had noticed things about him, too. *Patient, sensitive eyes.* Even finished *The Shipping News.* It wouldn't be so hard.

Even as I sat there pretending I could fall in love with someone, the daydream crashed. Life was slowly leaking out of me.

Something with Raleigh, or anyone, just wasn't a possibility now.

I glanced over at Claire, who was pulling the car onto 101. I took a deep breath.

"You ever hear of something called Negli's aplastic anemia?" I asked.

# Chapter 40

It came out of the blue — so unexpect-
edly — that it didn't really dawn on Claire
what I had just said.

She answered as if she were fielding a
medical question in her lab. "Blood disorder. Pretty rare, serious. The body stops
producing erythrocytes."

"Red blood cells," I said.

Claire glanced at me. "Why? It's not
Cat?" referring to my sister.

I shook my head. I sat rigid and stared
straight ahead. My eyes were glassy.

It was probably the long pause that
caused it to slowly sink in.

Claire whispered, "Not you?"

An awful stillness took hold in the car.

"Oh, Lindsay." Claire's jaw dropped.

She pulled the Bronco onto the shoulder of the road and immediately reached out and hugged me. "What has your doctor told you?"

"That it's *serious.* That it can be fatal."

I saw the gravity of that wash over her face. The hurt, the pain. Claire was a doctor, a pathologist. She had taken in what was at stake before I even met her eyes.

I told her that I was already undergoing packed–red cell transfusions twice a week.

"That's why you wanted to get together the other day?" she declared. "Oh, Lindsay. Why couldn't you just tell me?"

None of my past reasoning seemed clear now. "I wanted to so much. I was afraid. Maybe even more to admit it to myself. Then I allowed myself to get wrapped up in the case."

"Does anyone know? Jacobi? Roth?"

I shook my head.

"Raleigh?"

I took a breath. "Still think I'm ready for Mr. Right?"

"You poor baby," Claire said softly. "Oh, Lindsay, Lindsay, Lindsay."

Her body was shaking. I could feel it. I *had* hurt her.

Suddenly, I let it all go — fear and shame and uncertainty rushing through me.

I held on to Claire, and I realized she was all that kept me from hurtling out of control. I started to cry, and then we both did. It felt good, though. I wasn't alone anymore.

"I'm here for you, sweetheart," Claire whispered. "I love you, girl."

# Chapter 41

The murder in Napa changed everything.

There were blistering attacks on the way the SFPD was trying to solve the case. We took heat from everywhere.

Sensational headlines announced the handiwork of a sadistic, deranged, completely new kind of killer. Out-of-town news crews buzzed around the Hall. Tragic wedding pictures and wrenching family scenes were the lead on every TV newscast.

The task force that I was heading was meeting twice a day. Two other inspectors from SCU and a forensic psychologist were added on. We had to provide our files for the FBI. The investigation was no longer confined to some embittered figure lurking in David or Melanie Brandt's past. It had grown larger, deeper, more tragic and foreboding.

Canvassing area wine shops, Jacobi's team had unearthed a few names, nothing more.

The bloody jacket was leading us nowhere, too. The problem was, the tux style was from four or five years ago. Of the fifteen Bay Area stores, not one maintained records of manufacturers' styles, so it was virtually impossible to trace. We had to go over their records invoice by invoice.

Mercer *tripled* our investigators.

The killer was choosing his victims with careful precision. Both murders had taken place within a day of the victims' marriages; both reflected specific knowledge of the victims, their lodgings, their itineraries. Both couples still had most of their valuables: watches, wallets, jewelry. The only things missing were the wedding rings.

He had dumped the DeGeorges in a seemingly isolated place, but one where they were sure to be found.

He had left other blockbuster clues for us to follow up. It didn't make sense.

*The killer knows exactly what he's doing, Lindsay.*

*He knows what you're doing.*

*Link the crimes.*

I had to find the common denominator. How he knew his victims. How he knew so much about them.

Raleigh and I divided up the possibilities. He took whoever had booked the Brandts' and the DeGeorges' itineraries: travel agencies, limo services, hotels. I took planners. Ultimately, we would find some link between the crimes.

"If we don't make progress soon," Raleigh grumbled, "there'll be a lot of priests and rabbis in this town with a shit-load of dead time. What's this maniac after?"

I didn't say, but I thought I knew. He was after happiness, dreams, expectations. He was trying to destroy the one thing that kept all of us going: hope.

# Chapter 42

That night, Claire Washburn took a cup of tea into her bedroom, quietly closed the door, and started to cry again. *"Goddamn it, Lindsay,"* she muttered. "You could have trusted me."

She needed to be alone. All evening long, she had been moody and distracted. And it wasn't like her. On Mondays, a night off for the symphony, Edmund always cooked. It was one of their rituals, a family night, Dad in the kitchen, boys cleaning. Tonight he had cooked their favorite meal, chicken in capers and vinegar. But nothing had gone right, and it was her fault.

One thought was pounding in her. She was a doctor, a doctor who dealt only in death. Never once had she saved a life. She was a doctor who did not heal.

She went into her closet, put on flannel pajamas, went into the bathroom, and carefully cleansed her smooth brown face. She looked at herself.

She was not beautiful, at least not in the way society taught us to admire. She was large and soft and round, her shapeless waist merging with her hips. Even her hands — her well-trained, efficient hands that controlled delicate instruments all day — were pudgy and full.

The only thing light about her, her husband always said, was when she was on the dance floor.

Yet in her own eyes she had always felt blessed and radiant. Because she had made it up from a tough, mostly black neighborhood in San Francisco to become a doctor. Because she was loved. Because she was taught to give love. Because she had everything in her life that she ever wanted.

It didn't seem fair. Lindsay was the one who attacked life, and now it was seeping out of her. She couldn't even think of it in a professional way, as a doctor viewing the inevitability of disease with a clinical detachment. It pained her as a friend.

*The doctor who could not heal.*

After he and the boys had finished the dishes, Edmund came in. He sat on the bed beside her.

"You're sick, kitty cat," he said, a hand kneading her shoulder. "Whenever you curl up before nine o'clock, I know you're getting sick."

She shook her head. "I'm not sick, Edmund."

"Then what is it? This grotesque case?"

Claire raised a hand. "It's Lindsay. I rode back from Napa with her yesterday. She told me the most awful news. She's very sick. She's got a rare blood disorder, a form of anemia. It's called Negli's aplastic."

"It's severe, this Negli's anemia?"

Claire nodded, her eyes dim. "Damned severe."

"Oh, God," Edmund murmured. "Poor Lindsay." He took her hand, and they sat there for a moment in stunned silence.

Claire finally spoke. "I'm a doctor. I see death every day. I know the causes and symptoms, the science inside out. But *I can't heal.*"

"You heal us all the time," Edmund said. "You heal me every day of my life. But there are times when even all your love and even your amazing intelligence can't change things."

She nestled her body in his strong arms and smiled. "You're pretty smart for a guy who plays the drums. So what the hell *can* we do?"

"Just this," he said, wrapping his arms around her.

He held Claire tight for a long time, and she knew he thought she was the most beautiful woman in the whole world. That helped.

# Chapter 43

The following afternoon, I got my first glimpse of the killer's face.

Chris Raleigh was talking to the people who had handled the victims' travel arrangements. I was checking into who had planned their weddings.

Two different companies. For the DeGeorges, White Lace. For the Brandts, a fancy consultant, Miriam Campbell. That wasn't the link.

I was at my desk when the duty clerk put through a call.

It was Claire. She had just returned from

examining the bodies of the victims with the county coroner in Napa.

She sounded excited.

"Get over here," she said. "Hurry."

"You found a link. Becky DeGeorge was sexually disturbed?"

"Lindsay, we're dealing with one sick dude."

"They were *definitely* in the act when they were killed," Claire told me minutes later when I met her in the lab. "Semen traces found in Rebecca DeGeorge matched those I scraped off her husband. And the angle of the wounds confirmed what I suspected. She was shot from behind. Rebecca's blood was all over her husband's clothes. She was straddling him. . . . But that's not why I asked you here."

She fixed her large, wide eyes on me, and I could tell it was something important.

"I thought it best to keep this quiet," she said. "Only the local M.E. and I know."

"Know what, Claire? Tell me, for God's sake."

In the lab, I spotted a microscope on a counter and one of those airtight petri dishes I remembered from high school biology.

"As with the first victims," she said excitedly, "there was additional sexual disturbance of the corpse. Only this time, it wasn't so obvious. The labia was normal, what you would assume postintercourse, and there were no internal abrasions like with the first bride. Toll missed it . . . but I was *looking* for signs of additional abuse. And there it was, inside the vagina, sort of shouting, 'Come and get me, Claire.'"

She picked up the petri dish and a tweezer, and gently removed the top. Her eyes lit up with importance.

Out of the clear dish she lifted out a single, half-inch red hair.

"It's not the husband's?"

Claire shook her head. "Look for yourself."

She flicked on the microscope. I leaned in, and against the brilliant white background of the lens, I saw two hairs: one thin, shiny, black brown; the other short, curly, sickle shaped.

"You're looking at two sections from Michael DeGeorge," she explained. "The long one's from his head. The other is genital."

Then she placed the hair from the petri

dish on another slide and inserted it in the microscope lens bay, side by side with the others. My pulse was starting to race. I thought I knew where she was going with this.

The new hair was reddish brown in hue and twice the thickness of either of DeGeorge's. It had tiny filaments twisted around the cortex. It clearly belonged to someone else.

"It's neither cranial nor pubic. *It's from a beard,*" Claire announced, leaning over me.

I pulled back from the scope and looked at her, shocked.

The killer's facial hair had turned up in Becky DeGeorge's vagina.

"*Postmortem,*" she said, to drive it home.

# Chapter 44

As Claire said, we were piecing our killer together, step by step. His height, his face, his
fetishes. The way he murdered.

Now I had to figure out how he was tracking his victims.

Raleigh and I were going full force on the
travel and wedding-planner thing. We had
fifteen detectives out there following up
leads. Now that we had a facial characteristic, we went back to the guests, combing
them for a guy in a beard who might have
been seen trolling around.

I felt confident that some aspect of this
widening search would yield results. One of

the guests would have noticed someone. We would discover a travel agent in common, a leak somewhere. Or one of Jacobi's searches would come up with a match.

The following morning, Hartwig called in. "Sparrow Ridge Vineyards . . . it's owned by a group here known as Black Hawk Partners. A local guy, Ed Lester, an attorney, puts together real-estate partnerships."

"You know where he was over the weekend?"

"Yeah, I checked. Portland. He ran in a marathon there. I caught up with him when he got back to the office. He was definitely in Portland."

I still felt certain that whoever had dumped the bodies there hadn't stumbled on the remote vineyard by accident. It meant something to the killer. "He owns this place outright?"

"Uh-uh. Black Hawk puts together deals. They bring in outside money from well-heeled guys down your way. People who want to break into the wine game. Lester acts as the managing partner."

"So who's he partnered with on this one?"

"I don't know. Investors."

I sucked in my breath, trying to remain patient. "Which investors?"

"Generally, investors who want to remain private. Listen, Inspector, I know where you're heading, but this guy only deals with pretty established people. Believe me, anyone could've found that dump site. Real-estate agents, someone who'd checked it out, anyone local. I have to deal with these people long after you're gone."

I cradled the phone in my neck and spun around in my seat toward the window. "This is a multiple-murder investigation, Lieutenant, the worst I've ever seen. The dump site is three miles up a deserted dirt road. Anyone riding around in the dark with two bodies could've safely dumped them anytime before. Whoever did this had to know the vineyard was there. And I don't think it's a local. I don't think he would draw attention so close to where he lives.

"Come back to me when you know who Lester's partners are." I hung up on Hartwig.

Some of my optimism began to unravel.

Raleigh turned up nothing on the travel agents. The Brandts had booked through Travel Ventures, a society agent that catered to a high-end crowd. The

DeGeorges had used Journeytime, out of Los Altos.

We had people scour through the personnel records of both firms. There was no connection between the two: no cooperative arrangements, not a single travel agent who had worked for both of them. It was possible someone had tapped into their systems, said the manager of Journeytime. But finding such a person was next to impossible.

My end was equally disappointing. I had the files from both wedding planners. Engravers, bands, photographers, caterers, florists. Nothing matched up. The Brandts and the DeGeorges had lived in two separate worlds. However the killer was identifying the victims, I hadn't found a clue.

# Chapter 45

I called Claire and Cindy together for a second meeting of the girls. This time, the mood was decidedly different. There was no laughter or high fives. No festive margaritas. Two more people were dead. We had no suspects, only a widening case. Clues that were rapidly leading nowhere. Intense pressure coming down on all of us.

Claire was first to arrive. She hugged me and asked how I was feeling.

"I don't know," I admitted. I had gone through three treatments.

Sometimes I felt strong. At other times, especially in the afternoon, I felt like a ghost of myself. "Medved said he'd review my red cell count next week."

Cindy arrived next. She was wearing a halter top under a man's plaid shirt, a pair of embroidered jeans. She was very pretty, and city cool. I hadn't spoken to her since Monday, when I had let her run with the story of the second killings. Even holding her story back for a day, she had still scooped the city.

"I guess I'm buying," she announced. She tossed us a new business card with the bright red logo of the *Chronicle* on it. I read the card, *Cindy Thomas, Reporter, Metro Crime Desk.*

We toasted her with warm congratulations, then we roasted her a little, just to keep her ego in check. What else were friends for?

I told them that the travel agents and wedding planners had led nowhere. "A couple of things really bother me," I said. "*The gun.* . . . Sexual killers don't usually change methods. The methods are part of the sexual thrill."

"It's a strange combination," agreed Claire. "He's so in control when he plans his strikes. He seems to know everything.

Where they're married, room numbers, what their honeymoon itinerary is. How to get away. Yet, when he kills, he's close to rage. It's not enough to merely kill them. He has to *defile.*"

I nodded. "That's the key. He's striking at weddings, something about them is intolerable to him. But I think his obsession's with the brides. Both of the grooms were dispatched quickly. It's as if they didn't even matter to him. But the brides . . . that's his real fascination.

"So where would this guy go," I asked aloud, "to scout potential victims? If you wanted to kill brides, where would you check them out?"

"They had to choose a *ring,*" suggested Claire. "A jeweler."

"Or City Hall," said Cindy. "They'd need a license."

I looked at her and chuckled. "It would sure fit if a government employee was behind this."

"Postal employee." Claire and Cindy spoke simultaneously.

"Photographers," said Claire.

I could see a twisted bastard hiding behind the lens. They were all good possibilities. It only required time and manpower to check them out before the killer struck again.

"This bride business isn't exactly my expertise," I said to Claire. "That's why you're here."

"What happened to all that *three sharp cookies* crap?" She laughed. "And the part about my being a top-notch M.E.?"

There was a ripple of frustrated laughter around the table. We all took another sip of beer. *The Women's Murder Club. This was good. No men allowed.*

"Where's the goddamn link?" I asked. "He *wants* us to find it. That's why he's leaving clues. He wants us to uncover the link."

Everyone was silent, lost in thought.

"I can feel it," I went on. "In the ceremony, the celebration, he finds something that drives him into psychopathic rage. Something he needs to stamp out. Hope, innocence? The husbands he kills right away. But the brides? How does he find the brides?"

"If he's living in this twisted dream world," said Cindy, thinking aloud, "he would go to where the fantasy was the strongest, the most vivid. He might want to build up his anger by observing them in an unsuspecting state."

Then Claire looked at us with a spark in her eye. "I was thinking, I'd go where they bought their wedding dresses. That's where I would pick the victims out."

# Chapter 46

When I got to work the following morning, there was a fax from Hartwig listing the partners at Sparrow Ridge. I gave them to Jacobi to check. Then I called my contacts at both wedding planners, White Lace and Miriam Campbell.

I wasn't expecting much. So far, everything had come back empty. To my shock, both planners confirmed it.

Melanie Brandt and Becky DeGeorge *had* bought their dresses at the same place.

The Bridal Boutique at Saks.

It was the first tangible link between the two cases. It could lead to nothing, but I felt in my bones it had the real, promising sensation of something good.

I was at Saks by the time the store opened at ten. The Bridal Boutique was on the third floor, tucked away in a corner next to Gifts and Fine China.

I caught Maryanne Perkins as she was arriving for the day, a cup of steaming coffee in her hand. The department manager was a stylish, affable woman of about fifty, just the type who would work with brides for twenty years. She had someone cover for her and sat down with me in a cluttered back room filled with magazine photos of brides.

"I was devastated when I heard it," she said. She shook her head, ashen faced. "Melanie was just here, two weeks ago." She stared at me glassily. "She was so beautiful. . . . My brides are like my children, Inspector. I feel as if I've lost one of my own."

"One?" I fixed on her eyes. "You haven't heard?"

"Heard what?"

I told Maryanne Perkins about Becky DeGeorge.

Shock and horror swept over her face. Her green eyes bulged, welled with a rush of tears. She stared through me as if she were looking into the wall. "Oh, my God. . . ." She took in a heart-jolting breath. "My husband and I were at our cabin in Modesto for a few days. She was just in. . . . Oh, my God. . . . What's going on here, Inspector?"

An immediate flood of questions tumbled out. Who would know about their customers? Other salespeople? Managers? The killer had been pegged as a male. Did any men work in the department?

Each of these questions elicited a disbelieving negative response from Maryanne Perkins. The staff had all been together for a minimum of eight years. No males. *Just like our murder club.*

She leaned back in her chair, scrolling her memory for any details that she could muster. "We were admiring her. Becky . . . she was stunning. It was as if she had never thought of herself in quite that way, but seeing herself in her dress, it suddenly became clear. Her mother had given her this brooch — pearls, diamonds — and I ran back to the office for flowers. That's when I noticed someone. Standing over there." She pointed. "He was staring in Becky's direction. I remember thinking, 'See, even he thinks you're beautiful.' I remember now."

Frantically, I took down a description: late forties, maybe younger. "I didn't get a really good look," the bridal manager said. "He had a beard."

I was sure it was him! It confirmed that Claire was right. Saks had to be where he found his victims, *where he tracked them.*

I pressed her hard. "How would anyone find out details about someone's wedding? Dates? Locations? Where they would honeymoon?"

"We keep that information," Maryanne Perkins said, "when the girls choose a gown. Some of it we need to know to help us, like dates, deadlines. And it just helps us get a feel for the bride. Most of them register with us as well."

*A feel for the bride.*

"Who has access to this information?"

She shook her head. "Just us . . . my assistants. It's a small department. Sometimes we share it with Fine China and Gifts."

I felt I was finally close. My heart was slamming inside my chest. "I need to see a copy of anything you have on Melanie Brandt and Becky DeGeorge, and every customer you're currently working with." *He was spotting his potential victims here, wasn't he*? There was a good chance he would come back. Someone on the store's list could be next in line.

I saw Ms. Perkins's jaw drop. She appeared to be focusing on a horrible sight. "There's something else you'll want to know."

*"What?"*

"About a month ago, after inventory, we noticed that our folder on the brides was missing."

# Chapter 47

As soon as I got back to the Hall, I did two things: I called Claire and Cindy and told them what I'd found out at Saks, then I went to find Chris Raleigh.

I shared everything with Chris, and we decided to put a woman detective from the Sex Crimes Unit inside the department store. I sent a sketch artist over to see Maryanne Perkins at Saks.

Then Chris shared something important with me. Roth and Mercer had handed over our case files to the FBI.

I felt a knifing pain deep in my chest. I rushed into the bathroom, closed the door behind me, pressed my back against the cold, chipped tile. *Goddamn, son-of-a-bitch, controlling* men. *Goddamn Roth and Mercer!*

I stared at my face in the mirror. My cheeks were flushed. My skin was burning.

The FBI. This was my case — and Claire's, and Cindy's, and Raleigh's. It meant more to me than any other I'd ever worked on.

Suddenly, my legs felt wobbly. *Negli's?* The doctor had said I'd be feeling fits of nausea or light-headedness. I had my fourth transfusion scheduled at Moffett, the hematology unit, at five-thirty.

An overwhelming emptiness tugged at me, alternating between anger and fear. I was just starting to crack this thing. I didn't need outsiders in dark suits and tiepins buzzing around with a clumsy, ham-handed alternative investigation.

I blinked into the mirror. My cheeks, which had been burning with anger, now looked pallid and lifeless. My eyes were watery and gray. My whole body seemed drained of color.

I stared at myself until a familiar voice

came alive inside me. *Come on. Get your-self together. You win — you always win.*

I splashed cold water on my face. The flashing sweat on my neck began to subside.

*You're allowed* one *of these.* I exhaled with a thin smile. *Just don't do that again.*

Gradually, a familiar glimmer came to life in my eyes and normal color seeped back into my cheeks. It was four-twenty. I had to be at Moffett by five. I'd start on the names from Saks tomorrow.

After applying a few dabs of makeup, I made my way back to my desk.

To my chagrin, Raleigh wandered up. "Now you can manage *their* fallout," I snapped unnecessarily, referring to the FBI.

"I didn't know," he said. "As soon as I did, I told you."

"Yeah." I nodded. "I know."

Raleigh got up, came around, and sat on the edge of my desk, facing me. "Something's wrong, isn't it? Tell me. Please." How did he know? Maybe he was a much better detective than I gave him credit for.

For a moment, I wanted to tell him. *God, I wanted it to come out.*

Then Raleigh did something totally unexpected.

He flashed one of those trusting smiles
that I couldn't help but give myself over to.
He pulled me out of my chair and gave me
a hug.

I was so surprised I didn't even resist. I
was quivering jelly in his arms. It wasn't
quite sexual, but no burst of passion had
ever rippled through me more powerfully.

Raleigh held me until the anxiety had
slowly melted away. Right there, in the fucking squad room. I didn't know what to do,
but I didn't want to pull back. Or have him
let me go.

"I could write you up for this," I finally
mumbled into his shoulder.

He didn't move. "You want a pen?"

Slowly, I pulled myself away. Every nerve
in my body felt as if it had retreated from a
tense state of alert. "Thanks," I muttered
with appreciation.

"You didn't seem yourself," he said gently. "Shift's almost done. Want to talk about
it over coffee? Just coffee, Lindsay, not *a
date.*"

I looked at my watch and suddenly saw

that it was almost five o'clock. I had to be at Moffett.

I gave him a look that I hoped reflected, *Ask me again,* but said, "I can't. Gotta go."

# Chapter 48

The pretty, smiling reservations clerk politely nodded for the next person in line. "Welcome to the Lakefront Hilton, sir."

Phillip Campbell stepped up to the counter. He noticed her name, Kaylin. Bright-eyed, bushy-bushed Kaylin. He smiled back. Flirted subtly. He handed her a confirmation slip.

"First time with us, Mr. Campbell?" the desk clerk asked in a high-pitched chirp.

He smiled, let her know that it was.

As she punched in his reservation, he followed her movements, thoughtfully stroking the rough hairs of his beard.

He wanted her to notice. To remember his face. Maybe something he said.

One day, when some diligent FBI agent came by with a drawing or photograph, he wanted this chirpy little squirrel to think back and recall this moment in a close and chilling way. He wanted her to remember everything.

As he had with the saleswoman in the Bridal Boutique at Saks.

"Here for a visit to the museum, Mr. Campbell?" Kaylin asked, as she typed.

"For the Voskuhl wedding," he volunteered.

"Everyone's saying that." She smiled.

He followed the click of her peach-colored nails against the keys as she typed. "I've got you a deluxe room with a beautiful view," she said, handing him a key. She smiled. "Enjoy the wedding. And have a nice stay."

*"I will,"* Campbell said pleasantly. Before he turned away, he caught her eye and said, "Speaking of weddings — I like your ring."

Upstairs, he pulled the curtains aside and, as promised, before him was a sweeping view.

Of Cleveland, Ohio.

# Chapter 49

*I saw him. . . . That bastard. What was he doing here?*

*In a large, fast-moving crowd, on lower Market. Just a quick movement in the throng fighting its way toward the ferry.*

*My blood froze with the sight of him.*

*He was wearing an open blue shirt, brown corduroy jacket. He looked like some college professor. On any other day, I could have passed him by, never noticed. He was thin, gaunt, totally unremarkable in every way but one.*

*It was the reddish-brown beard.*

His head bobbed in and out of the crowd. I followed, unable to narrow the distance.

"Police!" I shouted over the din.

My cry dissolved into the hurrying, unheeding mass of people. At any moment I might lose him.

I didn't know his name, I only knew his victims. Melanie Brandt. Rebecca DeGeorge.

Suddenly, he stopped. He bucked against the flow, turned right toward me.

His face seemed illuminated, shining against a dark background like one of those medieval Russian icons. Amid the commotion, our eyes met.

There was a moment of captured, enlightened recognition. He knew that it was me. That I was the one after him.

Then, to my horror, he fled; the swarm of people engulfed him, swept him away.

"Stop," I shouted. "I'll shoot!"

A cold sweat broke out on my neck. I drew my gun.

"Get down," I cried, but the rush-hour commuters pushed on, shielding him. I was going to lose him. The killer was getting away.

*I raised the gun, focused on the image of his red beard.*

*He turned — with the sneer of someone who had totally outwitted me.*

*I drew a breath, steadied my aim.*

*As if in slow motion, every face in the crowd turned toward me, too.*

*I stepped back. In horror, I lowered the gun.*

*Every face had the same red beard.*

I had been dreaming. I found myself at my kitchen counter, blinking into swirling circles in my glass of chardonnay. There was a familiar calm in my apartment. No rushing crowds, no fleeing faces. Only Sweet Martha, lounging on her futon.

A pot of boiling water was steaming on the stove. I had my favorite sauce ready to go — ricotta, zucchini, basil. A CD was on, Tori Amos.

Only an hour ago, I had had tubes and IV lines sticking out of me. My heart had kept pace to the metronomelike rhythm of a monitor's steady beep.

Damn it, I wanted my old life back. My old, favorite dreams. I wanted Jacobi's sarcasm, Sam Roth's scorn, jogging on the

Marina Green. I wanted kids — even if it meant I had to get married again.

Suddenly, the downstairs buzzer rang. *Who would be here now?* I shuffled over and said, "Who is it?"

"I thought you had somewhere to go," a static voice replied.

It was Raleigh.

# Chapter 50

"What're you doing here?" I called back in surprise.

I was pleased but suddenly tingling with nerves. My hair was pulled up, I was in an old Berkeley T-shirt that I sometimes slept in, and I felt drained and anxious from my transfusion. My little place was a mess.

"Can I come up?" Raleigh said.

"This business or personal?" I asked. "We don't have to go back to Napa, do we?"

"Not tonight." I heard him laugh. "This time I brought my own."

I didn't quite understand that, but I buzzed him up. I ran back to the kitchen, turned the heat down on the pasta, and in the same breath threw a couple of pillows from the floor onto the couch and transferred a pile of magazines to a chair in the kitchen.

I put some lip gloss on and shook out my hair as the doorbell rang.

Raleigh was in an open shirt and baggy khakis. He was carrying a bottle of wine. Kunde. Very nice. He tossed me an apologetic smile. "I hope you don't mind me barging in."

"Nobody barges in here. I let you in," I said. "What're you doing here?"

He laughed. "I was in the neighborhood."

"The neighborhood, huh? You live across the bay."

He nodded, abandoning his alibi without much resistance. "I just wanted to make sure you were okay. You didn't seem yourself back at the station."

"That's nice, Raleigh," I said, looking into his eyes.

"So? Are you?"

"So. I was just feeling a little overwhelmed. Roth. This FBI thing. I'm fine now. Really."

"I'm glad," he said. "Something smells good."

"I was just throwing something together." I paused, thinking about what I wanted to say next. "You had dinner?"

He shook his head. "No, no. I don't want to intrude."

"That why you came with the wine?"

He flashed one of those irresistible smiles. "If you weren't home, I have a corner on Second and Brannan I always head to."

I smiled back and finally held open the door.

Raleigh came into my apartment. He looked around with sort of an impressed nod, gazing at some of the pottery, a black-and-gold satin baseball jacket from Willie Mays, my terrace with its view of the bay. He held out the bottle.

"There's one already open on the counter," I said. "Pour yourself a glass. I'll check on the food."

I went into the kitchen, reminding myself that I had just come from the outpatient clinic for a serious disease, and we were partners, anyway. With an irrepressible flicker of excitement, I took out an extra place setting.

"Number twenty-four, Giants?" he called to me. "This warm-up jacket is the real thing?"

"Willie Mays. My father gave it to me for my tenth birthday. He wanted a boy. I kept it all these years."

He came into the kitchen, spun a stool around at the counter. While I stirred the penne he poured himself a glass of wine. "You always cook for yourself like this?"

"Old habit," I said. "Growing up, my mother worked late. I had a sister six years younger. Sometimes my mother didn't get home till eight. From the time I can remember, I had to make dinner."

"Where was your dad?"

"Left us," I said, whipping together some mustard, grape seed oil, balsamic vinegar, and lemon into a vinaigrette for the salad. "When I was thirteen."

"So your mother brought you up?"

"You could say. Sometimes I feel like I brought myself up."

"Until you got married."

"Yeah, then I sort of brought him up, too." I smiled. "You're pretty nosy, Raleigh."

"Cops are generally nosy. Didn't you know that?"

"Yeah. Real cops."

Raleigh feigned being hurt. "What can I help you with?" he offered.

"You can grate," I said, and grinned. I pushed a block of Parmesan and a metal grater his way.

We sat there as he grated, waiting for the pasta to cook. Sweet Martha padded into the kitchen and let Raleigh pet her.

"You *didn't* seem yourself this afternoon," he said as he stroked Martha's head. "Usually, you handle Roth's bullshit without even blinking. Seemed like there was something wrong."

"Nothing's wrong," I lied. "At least not now. If you were asking."

I leaned against the counter and looked at him. He was my partner, but even more than that, he was a person I thought I could trust. It had been a long, hard time since I had put my trust in anybody whose gender started with an *M. Maybe, in a different time* . . . I was thinking.

Tori Amos's haunting voice hung in the air.

"You like to dance?" Raleigh suddenly asked.

I looked at him, really surprised. "I don't dance. I cook."

"You don't dance . . . you cook?" Raleigh repeated, scrunching up his brow.

"Yeah. You know what they say about cooking."

He looked around. "What *I'd* say is that it doesn't seem to be working. Maybe you should try dancing."

The music was soft and languorous, and as much as I tried to deny it, part of me just yearned to be held.

Without my even saying yes, my goddamn partner took my hand and pulled me from around the counter. I wanted to hold back, but a soft, surrendering voice inside me said, *Just go with it, Lindsay. He's okay. You know you trust him.*

So I gave in and let Chris Raleigh hold me. I liked being in his arms.

At first we sort of stood there, swaying stiffly. Then I found myself letting my head fall on his shoulder, and feeling like nothing could ail me, at least for a while.

"This isn't a date," I muttered.

I let myself drift to a real nice place, where

I felt love and hope and dreams were still there to reach for.

"To tell the truth," I told Raleigh, "I'm glad you stopped by."

"Me, too."

Then I felt him hold me close. A tingle raced down my spine, one that I almost didn't recognize anymore.

"You've got it, don't you, Raleigh?" I said.

"What's that, Lindsay?"

*Soft hands.*

# Chapter 51

Kathy and James Voskuhl were having their first dance — and to break with tradition, it was a rocker.

The driving beat of "La Bamba" jolted through the brightly lit atrium of the Rock and Roll Hall of Fame in Cleveland.

"Everybody!" the groom shouted. "Rock and roll! Join us!"

Hip young girls with dyed hair and wearing shiny green and red prom dresses — sixties style — swung around on the dance floor, their partners in retro silk shirts, Travolta-like. The bride and groom, having changed into party garb, joined in, butting thighs, whooping, arms in air.

*It almost ruined everything,* Phillip Campbell thought.

He had wanted her in white.

And here she was, sweaty red-streaked hair, cat-eye-shaped glasses, a tight green dress.

*This time, Kathy, you've gone too far.*

Forty tables, each with the likeness of some rock and roll icon as a centerpiece, filled out the Great Hall of the museum. A glittery banner that hung from the glass roof proclaimed: *James and Kathy.*

After a loud crescendo the song ended. A throng of sweaty wedding guests milled back toward their tables, catching their breath, fanning themselves. Waiters in black waistcoats scurried about the room, filling wineglasses.

The bride went over and embraced a happy couple in formal dress. Mom and Dad. Phillip Campbell couldn't take his eyes off her. He saw her father give her a loving look, like, *We've come through a lot, honey, but now everything will be all right. Now you're part of the club, trust funds and Country Day, little peach-haired grand-kids.*

The groom wandered over and whispered something in Kathy's ear. She squeezed his arm, flashing him a smile that was both affectionate and coy. As he walked away, the tips of her fingers lingered, as if she were saying, *I'll be right along.*

With a hitch of his belt, the groom drifted out of the main hall. He glanced back once or twice, and Kathy waved.

Campbell decided to follow, hanging back at a safe distance. He went down a wide, well-lit corridor off the atrium. Halfway down, James Voskuhl glanced back once, cautiously. Then he opened a door and went in. The men's room.

The killer moved forward. No one else was in the hall. He felt an irrepressible urge building with force.

His fingers made their way into his jacket pocket, touched the cold heel of the gun. He flicked the safety off. He could no longer control what was going on inside his head.

*Go in,* a voice dared him. *Do it.*

He entered a filmy, sallow light. No one at

the urinals or sinks. The groom was in a closed stall. A pungent smell filled his nostrils: marijuana.

"That you, love?" the groom's affectionate voice called out.

Every wicklike nerve in Campbell's body stood at attention. He mumbled something barely audible.

"Better get in here, hon," the groom gulped, "if you want the end of this bone."

Phillip Campbell pushed open the door.

The groom looked up, bewildered, the tip of a joint on his lip. "Hey, man, who the hell are you?"

"I'm the one who kills useless worms like you." With that, he fired. Just once.

James Voskuhl's head snapped back. A splatter of red sprayed against the tile. The groom rocked once, then crumpled forward in a heap.

The echo of the gun blast seemed to concuss the entire room. It left an effluvium of cordite that mingled with the pot smoke.

A strange calm took over Phillip Campbell, a fearlessness. He pulled the groom's head back and set him upright.

Then he waited.

The sound of the outer door opening and echoes of the distant party rushing in went right through him.

"That you, Vosk?" a woman's voice called out.

*It was her. The bride.*

"What're you smoking in there, tar?" Kathy giggled. She went over to the sinks, and he heard the sound of running water.

Campbell could see her through a crack in the stall. She was at the sink, thrashing a comb through her hair. A vision came to him. How he would set this up. *What the police would find.*

It took everything he had to control himself — to let her come to him.

"You better save me a hit or two, mister," the bride called out.

He watched her dance over to the stall. *So close now. So unbelievably delicious. What a moment.*

When she opened the door, it was her *look* that meant everything to him.

The sight of James, red drool leaking from his mouth. The startled recognition of the killer's face suddenly clicking in; the gun aimed right at her eyes.

"I like you better in white, Kathy," was all the killer said.

Then he squeezed the trigger — and a blinding white flash exploded through the cat-eye lenses.

# Chapter 52

I was in early Monday morning, feeling a little nervous about my first contact with Raleigh after our dancing-and-dining experience, wondering where all this was going to go, when one of the task force inspectors, Paul Chin, rushed up to me. "Lindsay, there's a woman in Interrogation Room Four I think you should check out."

Ever since a physical description of the assailant had hit the airwaves, people had been calling in with fake sightings and dead-end leads. One of Chin's jobs was to follow them up, no matter how unlikely.

"This one a psychic or a police buff?" I asked with a skeptical smile.

"I think this one's the genuine article," said Chin. "She was at the first wedding."

I almost leaped out of my chair after him. At the front of the squad room, I spotted Raleigh coming in. *Chris.*

For a moment, a tingle of pleasure rushed through me. He'd left about eleven, after we ended up polishing off both bottles of wine. We ate, chewed over our separate stints on the force, and the ups and downs of being married or single.

It had been a sweet evening. Took the heat off from the case. It even got my mind off Negli's.

What scared me a little was the tremor inside that it could be something more. I had caught myself staring at him Friday night, while he helped out with the dishes, thinking, *If times were different . . .*

Raleigh ran into me, carrying coffee and a paper. "Hey." He smiled. "Nice vest."

"Chin's got a live one in four," I said, grabbing his arm. "Claims to have a physical sighting. You want to come along?"

In my haste, I was already by him, not even giving him a second of recognition. He put down his paper on our civilian clerk's desk and caught up on the stairs.

In the cramped interrogation room sat a nicely dressed, attractive woman of about fifty. Chin introduced her to me as Laurie Birnbaum. She seemed tight, nervous.

Chin sat down next to her. "Ms. Birnbaum, why don't you tell Inspector Boxer what you just told me."

She was frightened. "It was the beard that made me remember. I didn't even think of it until now. It was so horrible."

"You were at the Brandts' wedding?" I asked her.

"Yes, as guests of the bride's family," she replied. "My husband works with Chancellor Weil at the university." She took a nervous sip from a cup of coffee. "It was just a brief thing. But he gave me the chills."

Chin pushed down the record button of a portable recorder.

"Please, go ahead," I told her soothingly. Once again, I felt close to *him* — the bastard with the red beard.

"I stood next to him. He had this graying red beard. Like a goatee. The kind they wear in Los Angeles. He looked older, maybe forty-five, fifty, but there was something about him. I'm not saying this right, am I?"

"You spoke to him?" I asked, trying to communicate that even though she didn't do this every day, I did. Even the male detectives admitted that I was the best at Q and A on the floor. They joked that it was "a girl thing."

"I had just come in from the dance floor," she said. "I looked up, and there he was. I said something like, 'Nice affair . . . bride or groom?' For a moment, I thought he looked kind of appealing. Then he just sort of glared at me. I took him for one of those arrogant investment-banker types from the Brandt side."

"What did he say to you?" I said.

She massaged her brow, straining to recall. "He said, in the weirdest way, that they were *lucky.*"

"Who was lucky?"

"Melanie and David. I may have said, 'Aren't they lucky?' Meaning the two of them. They were so stunning. And he replied, 'Oh, they're *lucky.*'"

She looked up with a confused expression on her face. "He called them something else . . . *chosen.*"

"Chosen?"

"Yes. He said, 'Oh, they're lucky. . . . You could even say they were chosen.' "

"You say he had a goatee?"

"That's what was so strange. The beard made him seem older, but the rest of him was young."

"The rest of him? What do you mean?"

"His face. His voice. I know this must sound strange, but it was only for a moment, as I came off the dance floor."

We got as much as we could from her. Height, hair color. What he was wearing. Everything confirmed the sparse details that we already had. The killer was a man with a short, reddish beard. He had been wearing a tux — the tux jacket he had left behind in the Mandarin Suite.

A fire was building inside me. I felt sure that Laurie Birnbaum was credible. *The beard. The tux.* We were piecing together his appearance. "Is there anything more, anything at all that stands out to you? Some physical characteristic? A mannerism?"

She shook her head. "It happened so quickly. It was only when I saw the drawing of him in the *Chronicle . . .*"

I looked at Chin, conveying that it was

time to call down an artist to firm up the details. I thanked her, made my way back to my desk. We'd get a sketch from her to use along with the one from Maryanne Perkins at Saks.

The murder investigation had entered a new phase. It was very hot. We had a stakeout operational outside the Bridal Boutique at Saks. One by one, we were contacting the names on the store's list, anyone who had ordered a wedding dress in the past several months.

My heart was pounding. The face I had imagined, my dream of the red-bearded man, was starting to fill in. I felt we had him contained.

My phone rang. "Boxer," I answered, still shuffling through the names in the Saks wedding folder.

"My name's McBride," a deep, urgent voice said. "I'm a homicide detective. In Cleveland."

# Chapter 53

"I got a homicide here that fits the pattern of what you've been dealing with," McBride explained.

"GSWs," McBride continued, "both of them. Gunshot wounds right between the eyes." He described the quick but grotesque deaths of Kathy and James Voskuhl, killed at their wedding at the Rock and Roll Hall of Fame. This time the killer hadn't even waited for the wedding to end.

"What kind of weapon your guy use in Napa?" McBride asked.

"Nine millimeter," I told him.

"Same."

I was reeling a little bit. *Cleveland?*

A voice pounded inside me. *What the hell was Red Beard doing in Ohio?* We had just made the breakthrough, found out where he was casing his victims. Did he know that? If so — *how?*

Cleveland was either a copycat killing, which was entirely possible, or this case had just broken wide open and could lead anywhere.

"You have crime-scene photos there, McBride?" I asked.

McBride grunted, "Yeah. Got them right in front of me. Nasty. Sexually explicit."

"Can you get me a close-up of their hands?"

"Okay, but why the hands?

"What were they wearing, McBride?"

I heard him shuffling through photos. "You mean rings?"

"Good guess, Detective. Yeah."

I was praying that it wasn't our guy. *Cleveland . . .* it would shatter everything that made me feel we were close to him. Was Red Beard taking his killing act across the country?

A minute later, McBride confirmed exactly

the thing I didn't want to hear. "There are no wedding bands."

*The bastard was on the move.* We had a stakeout going where we thought he might show up, and he was two thousand miles away. He'd just murdered a couple at their reception in Ohio. Shit, shit, shit.

"You said the bodies were found in a sexually explicit position?" I asked McBride with dismay.

The Cleveland cop hesitated. He finally said, "The groom was shot sitting on the john. We found him there. Sitting up, legs open. The bride was shot in the stall, too, as she was coming in. There was enough of her brains on the inside of the door to confirm it. But when we found her, she was facedown. Uh, her face was stuffed between his legs."

I was silent, forming the image in my mind, hating this cruel, inhuman bastard more every day.

"You know . . . fellatio style," McBride finally managed. "There's a few things my investigators want to ask you."

"Ask me yourself. I'm gonna be there tomorrow."

# Chapter 54

Six-thirty the next morning, Raleigh and I were on our way to Cleveland, of all places. McBride met us at the plane. He wasn't how I had imagined him. He wasn't flabby, middle-aged, Irish Catholic. He was intense, sharp boned, maybe thirty-eight, and black.

"You're younger than I thought." He smiled at me.

I smiled back. "And you're definitely less Irish."

On the way into town, he brought us up to speed. "Groom's from Seattle. Had something to do with the music business. Worked with rock bands. Producer . . . marketing guy. Bride grew up here in Ohio. Shaker Heights. Father's a corporate attorney. Girl was cute, redhead, freckles, glasses."

He pulled a manila envelope off the dashboard and tossed it over to me in the passenger seat. Inside were a series of glossy eight-by-elevens of the crime scene: stark, graphic, somewhat resembling old photos of gangland rubouts. The groom was sitting in the stall with a surprised expression and the top of his head blown off. The bride was slumped over his lap, curled in a pool of blood, hers and his.

The sight of the couple filled me with a cold dread. As long as the killer was in northern California, I felt we had him contained. Now he was on the loose.

We grilled McBride about the venue — how the victims might have ended up in the men's room and what security was like at the Hall of Fame.

Each answer I heard convinced me even more that it was our guy. *What the hell was he doing here?*

We pulled off the highway at Lake Shore

Boulevard. A modern skyline rose all around us. "There she is," McBride announced.

From a distance, I saw the Rock and Roll Hall of Fame glinting up ahead like a jaggedly cut jewel. A twisted killer had struck in the city's most celebrated venue. By now, he might already be back in San Francisco. Or Chicago? New York? Topeka? Planning another gruesome double murder. Or maybe he was in a hotel room across the square, watching us arrive.

Red Beard could be anywhere.

# Chapter 55

It was the third time in two weeks I had to go over a harrowing double-murder scene.

McBride walked us up to the second floor and through an eerie, empty atrium devoid of pedestrian traffic to a men's room blocked off by crisscrossing yellow crime tape and cops.

"Public bathroom," Raleigh said to me. "He's getting nastier each time."

This time there were no bodies, no horrifying discoveries. The victims had long been transferred to the morgue. In their place were grim outlines of tape and chalk;

gut-wrenching black-and-white crime photos were taped to the walls.

I could see what had happened. How the
groom had been killed first, his blood
smeared on the wall behind the toilet. How
Red Beard had waited, surprised the bride
as she came in, then moved Kathy Voskuhl
into the provocative position between her
husband's legs. *Defiled her.*

"How did they both end up here in the
middle of their wedding?" Raleigh asked.

McBride pointed to a crime-scene photo
on the wall. "We found a smoked-down joint
next to James Voskuhl. Figured he came
here to cop a buzz. My guess is the bride
came in to join him."

"No one saw anything, though? They
didn't leave the reception with anyone?"

McBride shook his head.

I felt the same smoldering anger I had felt
twice before. I hated this killer. This savager
of dreams. With each act I hated him more.
The bastard was taunting us. Each murder
scene was a statement. Each one more de-
grading.

"What was security like that night?" I
asked.

McBride shrugged. "All exits except the

main one were closed down. There was a guard at the front desk. Everyone from the wedding arrived at the same time. A couple of half-assed guards floating, but generally at these affairs they like to keep a low profile."

"I saw cameras all around," Raleigh pressed. "They must have some film."

"That's what I'm hoping," said McBride. "I'll introduce you to Sharp, head of security. We can go over that now."

Andrew Sharp was a trim, wiry man with a square chin and narrow, colorless lips. He looked scared. A day ago he had a fairly cushy job, but now the police and the FBI were all over him.

Having to explain things to two outside cops from San Francisco didn't help matters. He brought us into his office, popped a Marlboro Light out of a pack, and looked at Raleigh.

"I got a meeting with the executive director in about eight minutes."

We didn't even bother to sit down. I asked, "Did your guards notice anyone unusual?"

"Three hundred guests, madam detective. Everyone congregated in the entrance atrium. My staff doesn't usually get involved in a whole lot except to make sure no one with too much to drink gets too close to the exhibits."

"What about how he got out, then?"

Sharp wheeled around in his chair, pointing to a blowup of the museum layout. "Either the main entrance, here, where you came in, or one we left open off the back verandah. It leads down to the Lake Walk. There's a café there during the summer. Mostly it's blocked off, but the families wanted it open."

"Two shots fired," I said. "No one heard anything?"

"It was supposed to be a high-class crowd. You think they want my guards milling around? We keep two, three guys to make sure overzealous guests don't wander into restricted areas. I should have guards patrolling the corridors down by the rest rooms? What ya gonna take, toilet paper?"

"Security cameras?" Raleigh asked.

Sharp sighed. "We've got the exhibition halls covered, of course. The main exits . . . a remote sweep of the Main Hall. But nothing on the corridor where the shooting took place. Nothing in the crapper. Anyway, the police are scanning tape with members of each family as we speak. It would make it a helluva lot easier if we knew who the hell we're looking for."

I reached into my briefcase and took out a copy of a bare-bones artist's sketch. It showed a thin face with a jutting chin, hair combed back, and a lightly shaded goatee.

"Why don't we start with him."

# Chapter 56

McBride had to be back in the office for a press briefing on the investigation. I needed to figure out why the killer had come to Cleveland, and what, if any, connections there were to our murders back in San Francisco. The next step was to talk to the parents of the bride.

Shaker Heights was a posh, upper-end suburb in the height of midsummer bloom. On every street, green lawns led up to graceful, tree-sheltered homes. One of McBride's men drove me out while Raleigh went back to the Lakefront Hilton to meet with the family of the groom.

The Koguts' home was a warm redbrick Normandy under a canopy of tall oaks. I was met at the door by the older sister of the bride, who introduced herself as Hillary Bloom. She sat me down in a comfy, picture-filled den: books, large-screen TV, pictures of the two of them as kids, weddings. "Kathy was always the rebellious one," Hillary explained. "A free spirit. It took her a while to find herself, but she was just settling down. She had a good job — a publicist for a firm in Seattle. Where she met James. She was just coming around."

"Coming around from what?" I asked.

"Like I said — she was a free spirit. That was Kathy."

Her parents, Hugh and Christine Kogut, came into the room. I witnessed the glazed, bewildered shock of people whose lives had been shattered.

"She was always in and out of relationships," her mother eventually admitted. "But she also had a passion for life."

"She was just young," her father said. "Maybe we spoiled her too much. She always had an urge to experience things."

In her pictures — the wispy red hair and dare-me eyes — I could see the same joy for life the killer had obviously seen in his first two victims. It made me feel sad, weary.

"Do you know why I'm here?" I finally asked.

The father nodded. "To determine if there was any connection to those other horrible crimes out west."

"So, can you tell me, did Kathy have any connection to San Francisco?"

I could see a cast of grim recognition creep its way onto their faces.

"After college, for a few years, she did live there," her mother said.

"She went to UCLA," her father said. "For a year or so she stayed in Los Angeles. Tried to catch on with one of the studios. She started out with a temp job at Fox. Then she got this publicity job in San Francisco, covering music. It was a very fast life. Parties, promotions, no doubt a lot worse. We weren't happy, but for Kathy, she thought it was her big break."

*She lived in San Francisco.* I asked if they had ever heard of Melanie Weil or Rebecca Passeneau.

They shook their heads.

"What about any relationships that

might've ended badly? Someone, who out of jealousy or obsession, might've wanted to do her harm?"

"Recklessness always seemed like a basis for Kathy's relationships," Hillary said with an edge.

"I did warn her." Her mother shook her head. "She always wanted to do things on her terms."

"Did she ever mention anyone special from the time she lived in San Francisco?"

Everyone looked at Hillary. "No. No one special."

"No one stands out? She lived there for a while. She didn't keep up with anyone after she left?"

"I seem to remember her saying she still went down there every once in a while," her father said. "On business."

"Old habits are hard to crack." Hillary smirked, with a tightening of her lips.

There had to be some connection. Some contact from the years she had spent there. *Someone* came all the way here to see her dead.

"What about anyone from San Francisco invited to the wedding?" I asked.

"There was one girlfriend," her father said.

*"Merrill,"* said her mother. "Merrill Cole. Shortley, now. I think she's at the Hilton, if she's still here."

I pulled out the artist's sketch we had of the killer's possible appearance. "I know it's rough, but do you know this man? Some-one who knew Kathy? Did you see anyone like this at the wedding?"

One by one, the Koguts shook their heads.

I got up to go. I told them if anything came to mind, regardless of how small or insignificant, to get in touch with me. Hillary walked me to the door.

"There is one more thing," I said. I knew it was a long shot. "By any chance, did Kathy buy her wedding dress in San Francisco?"

Hillary looked at me blankly and shook her head. "No, from a vintage shop. In Seattle."

At first, the answer deflated me. But then, in a flash, I saw that this was really a con-nection I was looking for. The first two mur-ders had been committed by someone stalking his victims from afar. That's why he found them in the way he did. Tracked them.

But this one, Kathy, she had been chosen in a different way.

I was certain that whoever had done this had known her.

# Chapter 57

I drove straight to the Hilton on Lake Shore Boulevard and was able to catch Merrill Shortley just as she was about to depart for the airport. She turned out to be stylish, maybe twenty-seven, with shoulder-length, chestnut brown hair tied back in a bun.

"A group of us were up all night," she said, apologizing for the swollen lines around her face. "I'd like to stay on, but who knows when they'll finally release the body. I have a one-year-old."

"The Koguts told me you live in San Francisco."

She sat on the edge of the bed across

from me. "Los Altos. I moved down two years ago, when I got married."

"I need to know about Kathy Kogut in San Francisco," I explained. "Lovers. Breakups. Someone who might have a cause to do this."

"You think she *knew* this madman?" Her face was clenched.

"Maybe, Merrill. You can help us decide. Will you help?"

"Kathy hooked up with guys," Merrill said after a pause. "She was always free about things in that way."

"Are you saying she was promiscuous?"

"If you want to see it that way. Men liked her. There was a lot of energy going on back then. Music, film. Alternative stuff. Whatever made her feel alive."

I was getting the picture. "Does that include drugs?"

"Like I said, whatever made her feel alive. *Yes,* Kathy did recreational drugs."

Merrill, though pretty, had the hard-edged face of a street survivor who had remade herself as a soccer mom.

"Anyone come to mind who might've wanted to hurt her? Someone who was overly fascinated? Maybe jealous when she moved on?"

Merrill thought a bit, shook her head. "I don't think so."

"You two were close?"

She nodded. At the same time, her eyes hooded.

"Why did she move away?"

"She landed a great job. Must've seemed like she was finally climbing the ladder. Her father and mother always wanted that. The Shaker Heights thing. Look, I really have to catch a plane."

"What are the chances Kathy was running away from something?"

"You live the way we lived, you're always running from something." Merrill Shortley shrugged and looked bored.

There was an attitude, a coldness about Merrill I didn't like. She still surrounded herself with the cynical aura of a dissolute past. And I had the suspicion she was withholding something. "So what'd *you* do, Merrill? Marry the dime-bag mambo king of Silicon Valley?"

She shook her head. Finally, she smiled thinly. "Fund manager."

I leaned forward. "So you don't remember

anyone special? Someone she might've kept up with? Been scared of?"

"Those years," Merrill Shortley said, "I have a hard time remembering anyone special at all."

"This was *your friend*," I said, my voice rising. "You want me to show you what she looks like now?"

Merrill stood up, stepped over to the dresser, and began to pack a leather bag with toiletries and makeup. At some point, she stopped and caught a glimpse of herself in the mirror. Then she looked over her shoulder and caught my eye. "Maybe there was this one guy Kathy was into. Big shot. Older. She said I'd know who he was — but she wouldn't give me a name. I think she met him through the job. As I remember, he was married. I don't know how it ended. Or who ended it. *Or if it ever did.*"

My adrenaline began to flow. "Who is he, Merrill? He might have killed your friend."

She shook her head.

"You ever see this man?"

She shook her head again.

I pushed on.

"You're the one friend from back then she

invites to her wedding and you never met him once? You don't even know a name?"

She gave me a cool smile. "She was protective. She didn't tell me everything. Scout's honor, Inspector. I assume he was a public figure."

"You see her much in the past couple of years?"

Merrill shook her head again. She was being a real bitch. New money in Silicon Valley.

"Her father told me she still used to come to town. On business."

Merrill shrugged. "I don't know. I have to go."

I yanked open my bag and removed one of the crime-scene photos McBride had given me, the one of Kathy, wide-eyed, slumped in a bloody heap in front of her husband.

"Someone she *knew* did this. You want to be met at the plane and thrown in a holding cell as a material witness? You can call in your husband's lawyer, but it'll still take him two days to get you out. How would the tech-fund crowd react to that news? I'm sure I could get it in the *Chronicle*."

Merrill turned away from me, her chin

quivering. "I don't *know* who it was. Just that he was older, married, some big-time SOB. Kinky, and not nice about it. Kathy said he played sex games on her. But whoever he was, she was always quiet about it, protective. The rest you'll have to do on your own."

"She still continued to see this guy, didn't she?" I was starting to put it together. "Even after she moved to Seattle. Even after she met her husband."

She gave me the slightest smile. "Good guess, Inspector. Right up to the end."

"How close to the end?"

Merrill Shortley picked up the phone. "This is four-oh-two. Checking out. I'm in a rush."

She stood up, slung a Prada bag over her shoulder, an expensive-looking raincoat over her arm. Then she looked at me and said dryly, "To the very end."

# Chapter 58

"No wonder the bride didn't wear white," Raleigh frowned and said as I told him about my interview with Merrill Shortley.

McBride had set us up for dinner at Nonni's, an Italian place on the lake, a short walk from our hotel.

Raleigh's interview with the groom's parents had yielded nothing eventful. James Voskuhl had been an aspiring musician who had floated on the edge of the music scene in Seattle, finally hooking his way into representing a couple of upcoming bands. He had no known connection to San Francisco.

"The killer knew Kathy," I said. "How else

would he find her here? They had a relationship."

"Right up to the end?" he mused.

"To the *very* end," I answered. "Meaning
maybe here, in Cleveland. These weren't
choirgirls. Merrill said this guy was older,
married, kinky, predatory. It fits the pattern
of the murders. Someone she knew in San
Francisco must have seen Red Beard.
*Somebody knows.* Merrill claims that Kathy
was protecting her lover, possibly because
he was a celebrity."

"You think this Merrill Shortley has more
to add?"

"Maybe. Or the family. I got the feeling
they were holding something back."

He had ordered a '97 Chianti and when it
came he tilted his glass. "Here's to David
and Melanie, Michael and Becky, James
and Kathy."

"Let's toast them when we catch this pathetic bastard," I said.

It was the first time we'd been alone in
Cleveland, and suddenly I was nervous. We
had an entire evening to fill, and no matter
how we kept steering back to the case or
joking how "this wasn't a date," there was
this pull, this bass chord twanging inside

me, telling me that this was no time to start anything with anyone, not even handsome and charming Chris Raleigh.

Then why had I changed into a baby blue sweater and nice slacks instead of staying with the chambray shirt and khakis I'd worn all day?

We ordered. I had osso bucco, spinach, a salad; Raleigh, a veal paillard.

"Maybe it was someone on her job?" Raleigh said. "Or connected with her job?"

"I told Jacobi to check out her firm in Seattle. Her father said she still came down to San Francisco on business. I want to see if that's the case."

"And if it isn't?"

"Then either she was hiding something or they are."

He took a sip of wine. "Why would she go through with a wedding if she was still involved with this guy?"

I shrugged. "They all said Kathy was finally settling down. I'd like to see what she was like back then, if this is what they meant by settling down."

I was thinking that I wanted another crack at the sister, Hillary. I remembered something she had said. *Old habits are hard to crack.* I had thought she was talking about drugs, parties. *Did she mean Red Beard?*

"McBride tells me tomorrow morning we should be able to review some film at the museum."

"The guy was *there,* Raleigh," I said with certainty. "He was there that night. Kathy knew her killer. We just have to find out who he is."

Raleigh poured a little more wine into my glass. "We're partners now, aren't we, Lindsay?"

"Sure," I said, a little surprised by the question. "Can't you tell I trust you?"

"I mean, we've been through three double murders, we're committed to seeing it through, I backed you up with Mercer. I even helped clean up after dinner at your place."

"Yeah, so?" I smiled. But his face had a cast of seriousness to it. I was trying to figure out where he was going.

"What do you say, maybe it's about time you started calling me Chris."

# Chapter 59

After dinner, Chris and I walked down by the tree-lined lakefront toward our hotel. A cool, misty breeze lapped at my face.

We didn't say much. That same nervous apprehension was tingling on the surface of my skin.

Occasionally, our arms brushed. He had his jacket off, and there was a solid outline to his shoulders and arms. Not that I was noticing superficial things like that.

"It's still early," he said.

"Five-thirty, our time," I replied. "I could

still catch Roth. Maybe I should bring him up to date."

Raleigh grinned. "You already called Jacobi. I bet he was probably in Roth's office before he hung up the phone."

As we walked, it was as if this unbearable force were pulling me close, then pushing me away. "Anyway," I said, "for once I don't feel like calling in."

"What do you feel like?" Raleigh asked.

"Why don't we just walk."

"The Indians are playing. You want to sneak our way in? It must be the fifth inning."

"We're cops, Raleigh."

"Yeah, that would be bad. You want to dance, then?"

*"No,"* I said, even firmer. "I don't want to dance." Every word seemed charged with a hidden, electric message. "What I'm starting to feel like" — I turned to him — "is that I'm having a hard time remembering to call you Chris."

"And what I'm starting to feel like," he answered, facing me, "is I'm having a hard time trying to pretend that nothing's going on."

"I know," I murmured breathlessly. "But I just can't."

It sounded really stupid, but as much as I wanted him, there was a greater hesitation inside holding me back.

"I know . . . but I just can't. What does that mean?"

"It means I'm feeling things, too. And that part of me wants to go with those feelings. But right now, I just don't know if I can. It's complicated, Chris."

Every nerve in my body was on alert.

We found ourselves walking again, the breeze from the lake suddenly cooling the sweat that had broken out on my neck.

"You mean it's complicated because we're working together?"

"That," I lied. I'd dated guys on the force once or twice.

"*That* . . . and what else?" Raleigh said.

A thousand desires inside me were screaming to give in. What was going through my mind was crazy. I wanted him to touch me; and I didn't. We were alone on the waterfront. At that moment, if he held me, if he bent and kissed me, I didn't know what I would do.

"I *do* want to," I said, my fingers reaching for his hand, staring into his deep blue eyes.

"You're not telling me everything," he said.

It took everything I had to hold off confessing. I don't know why I didn't. A deep part of me wanted him to want me, and to keep thinking I was strong. I could feel the heat from his body, and I thought he could feel the wavering resolve in mine. "I just can't right now," I said softly.

"You know, I won't always be your partner, Lindsay."

"I know that. And maybe I won't always be able to say no."

I don't know if I was disappointed or relieved to see our hotel up ahead. Part of me wanted to run to my room, throw open the windows, and just breathe in the night air.

I was sort of happy I wouldn't have to make that decision, when Raleigh took me by surprise.

He leaned over without warning and pressed his lips on mine. The kiss was so soft, as if he were gently asking, *Is this okay?*

I let the kiss linger warmly. *Soft hands . . . soft lips.*

It wasn't as if I hadn't imagined this happening. It was just as I had imagined. I wanted to be in control, but here it was, out of the blue, and I was giving in. But just as I was starting to give him myself, the fear caught up to me — the fear of the inescapable truth.

I dropped my head, slowly pulled away.

"That was nice. For me, anyway," Raleigh said, resting his forehead against mine.

I nodded but said, "I can't, Chris."

"Why are you always holding back, Lindsay?" he asked.

I wanted to say, *Because I am deceiving you.* Tell him everything that was going on.

But I was content to deceive, though I did it with the greatest yearning I had felt in years. "I just want to nail Red Beard," I answered.

# Chapter 60

The next morning, Detective McBride left a message for us to meet him in Sharp's office at the Hall of Fame.

*Something had come back on the film.*

In a sparsely decorated conference room, the museum's security chief, McBride, and several members of the CPD Homicide staff sat facing a wide-screen video monitor on a walnut cabinet.

"At first," Sharp began self-importantly, "we were just randomly going through the tape with members of the families, stopping on anyone who didn't look familiar. Your sketch," he turned to me, "helped narrow it down."

He flicked a handheld controller toward the screen. "The first clips you're gonna see are the main entrance."

The screen lit up, standard black-and-white surveillance footage. It was so weird and strange. Several gaudily dressed guests seemed to be arriving at once, many of them outfitted as famous rockers. One was Elton John. His date had teased hair dyed in various light and dark shades, Cyndi Lauper–style. I recognized a Chuck Berry, a Michael Jackson, a couple of Madonnas, Elvis, Elvis Costellos.

Sharp fast-forwarded, the film advancing like individual, edited stills. An older couple arrived dressed in traditional evening wear. Behind them, almost tucked into their backs, came a man who was clearly shying from the camera, averting his face.

*"There!"* Sharp said.

I saw him! My heart pumped madly in my chest. Goddamn Red Beard!

It was a horrible, grainy likeness. The man, sensing the direction of the camera, quickly hurried by. Maybe he had come there earlier, scouting for security cameras.

Maybe he was just smart enough to avoid a direct shot. Whatever it was, he sneaked into the crowd and disappeared.

A ball of anger knotted in my chest. "Can you back up, home in?" I said to Sharp. "I need to see his face."

He leveled his remote, and the image channeled in to a higher magnification.

I stood up. I was staring at a partially obscured shot of the killer's face.

No eyes, no clear feature. Only a shadowy profile. A jutting chin. And the outline of a goatee.

There was no doubt in my mind that this was the killer. I didn't know his name. I could barely see his face. But the fuzzy image I had first sketched together in my mind with Claire was now in front of me.

"Is that the best you can do?" Raleigh pressed.

A member of the museum tech staff replied, "Might be able to get it technologically enhanced. On this rough footage, this is what we have."

"We pick him up again later on," Sharp said.

He quickly fast-forwarded and stopped at a wide-angle view of the Main Hall, the wedding reception. They were able to zoom in on the same tuxedoed man standing at the edge of the crowd, observing. When the image was magnified, though, it became grainy and lost its resolution.

"He's purposely avoiding looking at the camera," I whispered to Raleigh. "He knows where they are."

"We ran these shots by both families," Sharp said. "No one places him. No one can identify who he is. I mean, there's a chance it's not him. But considering your sketch . . ."

"It's *him,*" I said firmly. My eyes burned on the grainy screen. I was also sure we were looking at Kathy Voskuhl's mysterious lover.

# Chapter 61

Hillary knew. I was almost sure of it. But why she would conceal such a thing related to her sister's death, I couldn't imagine. *Old habits are hard to crack,* she had said.

I wanted another shot at her, and I reached her by phone at the family house in Shaker Heights.

"I had a chance to speak to Merrill Shortley," I told her. "I just need a few details cleared up."

"You realize this is a very stressful time for my family, Inspector," Hillary replied. "We told you what we knew."

I didn't want to come on too strong. She

had lost her sister in a horrible way. Her parents' home was filled with mourners and grief. And she was under no obligation to talk to me at all.

"Merrill told me a few things about Kathy. Her lifestyle . . ."

"*We* told you all that," she replied defensively. "But we also told you that after meeting James she had begun to settle down."

"That's what I want to talk to you about. Merrill recalled there *was* someone she was seeing in San Francisco."

"I thought we told you Kathy dated lots of men."

"This one went on for a long time. He was older. Married. Some kind of big shot. Possibly famous."

"I wasn't my sister's keeper," Hillary complained.

"I need a name, Ms. Bloom. This man could be her killer."

"I'm afraid I don't understand. I already told you what I know. My sister didn't exactly confide in me. We lived very different lives. I'm sure you've put two and two together already — there was a lot I didn't approve of."

"You said something to me the first time

we talked. *Old habits are hard to crack.* What sort of habits were you referring to?"

"I'm afraid I don't know what you mean. The Cleveland police are handling this, Inspector. Can't we just let them do their job?"

"I'm trying to help you, Ms. Bloom. Why did Kathy move away from San Francisco? I think you know. Was someone abusing her? Was Kathy in trouble?"

Hillary sounded frightened. "I appreciate what you're trying to do, but I'm going to hang up now, Inspector."

"It's going to come out, Hillary. It always does. An address book. Her phone bill. It's not just Kathy. There are four others, back in California. They were just as hopeful about the rest of their lives as your sister. Just as deserving."

There was a tiny sob in her voice. "I have no idea what you're talking about."

I felt I had one last chance. "Here's the really ugly truth about murder. If I've learned one thing as a homicide detective, it's that the lines don't stay fixed. Yesterday you were an innocent victim, but now you're in this, too. This killer will strike again, and you will regret whatever you didn't tell me for the rest of your life."

There was a heavy silence on the line. I knew what it meant. It was the struggle inside Hillary Bloom's conscience.

I heard a click. She had hung up the phone.

# Chapter 62

Our flight back to San Francisco left at 4:00 P.M. I hated, *hated* to leave without a name. Especially when I felt we were so close.

*Somebody famous.*

*Kinky.*

*Why were they protecting him?*

Anyway, we had accomplished a lot in just two days. It was clear to me that all three murders were committed by the same person. We had a strong lead tying him to San Francisco, a possible identity, a confirmed description. The trail was warm here, and would grow ever hotter when we got home.

Both investigations would proceed locally. Cleveland would contact the Seattle police force to do a search of the bride's home. Maybe something in her personal effects, an address book, an e-mail in her computer, would divulge who her San Francisco lover was.

Waiting to board our plane out of Cleveland, I called my voice mail for messages. One each from Cindy and Claire inquiring about my trip, *our case.* Reporters pushing for my comments on the Cleveland crime.

Then I heard the throaty voice of Merrill Shortley. She had left her California number.

I punched the number as fast as I could. A housekeeper answered, and I could hear the wail of a baby crying.

When Merrill got on, I could tell that some of her cool veneer had cracked. "I was thinking," she began, "there was something I didn't mention yesterday."

"Yes? That's good to hear."

"This guy I told you about? The one Kathy was hooked up with in San Francisco? I was telling you the truth. I never knew his name."

"Okay, I hear you."

"But there were some things . . . I said he didn't treat her well. He was into intense sex games. Props, scenarios. Maybe even a little filming. Problem was, *Kathy liked the games.*"

There was a long pause before Merrill went on. "Well . . . I think he pushed her, forced her, to do more than she was comfortable with. I remember marks on her face, bruises on her legs. Mostly it was her spirit that was broken. None of us were exactly bringing home Tom Cruise then, but there was a time when Kathy was real scared. She was in his control."

I began to see where this was heading. "It's why she moved away, isn't it?" I said.

I could hear Merrill Shortley sigh on the other end. "Yes, it was."

"Then why did she continue to see him from Seattle? You said she was involved with him right up to the end."

"I never said," Merrill Shortley replied, "that Kathy knew what was good for her."

Now I saw Kathy Kogut's life take on the shape of tragic inevitability. I was sure she had fled San Francisco, tried to break away from the grip of this man. But she couldn't break free.

*Was that true of the other murdered brides?*

"I need a name, Ms. Shortley. Whoever this was, he might've killed your friend. There are four others. The longer he's out there, the greater the chance he'll do it again."

"I told you, I *don't know his name,* Inspector."

I raised my voice above the din in the terminal. "Merrill, *someone* must know. You knew her for years, partied together."

Merrill hesitated. "In her own way, Kathy was loyal. She said his name was well known. Some kind of celebrity. Someone I would know. She was protecting him. Or maybe protecting herself."

My mind raced to the film and music businesses. *She was into a bad scene.* She was in over her head, and like many people who feel trapped, she ran. She just couldn't get far enough away.

"She must've told you something," I pressed. "What he did? Where he lived? Where they would meet? You guys were like sisters." *Wicked sisters?*

"I swear, Inspector. I've been racking my brain."

"Then someone must know. Who? Tell me."

I heard Merrill Shortley let out a mirthless laugh. "Ask her sister."

Before we boarded, I beeped McBride and left a detailed message on his voice mail. Kathy's lover was probably someone famous. It was why she had moved away from San Francisco. The profile fit the pattern of our killer. Her sister, Hillary, might know the killer's name.

On board, all I could think about was that we were getting close. Raleigh was there beside me. As the plane rose, I leaned into his arm, surrendering to total exhaustion.

All my physical troubles seemed a million miles away. I remembered something I'd said to Claire. I had told her that finding this bastard gave me the resolve to go on. The red-bearded man in my dream who had gotten away.

"We're going to get him," I said to Raleigh. "We can't let him kill another bride and groom."

# Chapter 63

Eight the next morning, I was at my desk.

There were several ways I could go with this investigation. Hillary Bloom was the most direct, assuming, as Merrill had implied, that she was able to give us a name. It was clear that in a twisted way she was trying to save her family the added pain of having Kathy publicly branded as some kind of pathetic sexual victim, cheating on her husband-to-be right up until their vows.

Sooner or later a name would emerge. From her, or from Seattle.

Before I did anything else, I called Medved's office and rescheduled the blood

treatment I had canceled for five o'clock today. After a brief wait, the receptionist said
the doctor would see me himself.

Maybe it was good news. Truth was, I
*was* feeling a little stronger. Maybe the treatments were beginning to do their work.

It was hard picking up where I had left off
in San Francisco. The best leads were now
in Cleveland. I read some reports on the
evidence Jacobi was tracking down, held a
meeting of the task force at ten.

Actually, the most promising leads — the
hair and the Bridal Boutique at Saks — had
come from my meetings with Claire and
Cindy. I couldn't resist calling Claire a little
before noon.

"Bring me up to date," she said excitedly.
"I thought we were partners."

"I will," I replied. "Get Cindy. Meet me for
lunch."

# Chapter 64

The three of us leaned against a stone wall in City Hall Park, picking at salad sandwiches we had bought at a nearby grocer's. *The murder club meets again.*

"You were right," I said to Claire. I passed her a copy of the security photo showing Red Beard sneaking into the Cleveland wedding.

She stared at it, her eyes focusing intensely. Claire looked up only when the confirmation of her first physical supposition brought out a curious half smile. "I only read whatever that bastard left behind."

"Maybe," I said, tossing her a wink. "But I bet Righetti would've missed it."

"This is true," she allowed with a satisfied beam.

It was a bright, breezy late-June day; the air was fragrant from a crisp Pacific breeze. Office folk worked on their tans; secretaries gabbed in groups.

I recounted what I had found in Cleveland. I never mentioned what had taken place by the lake between Chris Raleigh and me.

When I finished with Merrill Shortley's shocking revelation, Cindy said, "Maybe you should've stayed out there, Lindsay."

I shook my head. "It's not my case. I was only there on a consult. Now I'm running point between three jurisdictions."

"You think Merrill Shortley has more to tell?" asked Claire.

"I don't think so. If she knew, I think she would have told me."

"The bride must have had other friends here," said Cindy. "She was in publicity. If this guy was famous, maybe she met him through her job."

I nodded. "I have someone checking that

out. We also have the Seattle PD combing through her apartment."

"Where'd she work when she lived here?" Claire asked.

"An outfit called Bright Star Media. Apparently, she was connected into the local music scene."

Cindy took a sip of iced tea. "Why not let me have a go at it?"

"You mean like you did at the Hyatt?" I said.

She grinned. "No, more like Napa. C'mon . . . I'm a reporter. I sit all day with people trained to find the dirt on anybody."

I bit into my sandwich. "Okay," I finally said, "be my guest."

"In the meantime," Cindy inquired, "can I run with what we have so far?"

Much of it was classified. If it came out, it would point back to me. "You can run with the similar pattern of murder in Cleveland. How we found the bodies. The bride's background here. Absolutely *no mention* of Merrill Shortley." In that way, I hoped the killer would sense that we were closing in on him. It might cause him to think twice about killing again.

Cindy went over to a nearby ice cream

cart to buy a gelato. Claire took the moment to ask, "So how are you feeling? You okay?"

I blew out a long breath and shrugged. "Queasy. Light-headed. I was told to expect it. I'm having a blood treatment this afternoon. Medved said he'd be there." I saw Cindy on her way back.

"Here," Cindy announced brightly. She was carrying three gelatos.

Claire clutched her chest and pretended she was going into cardiac arrest. "I need gelato about as much as Texas needs a warm breeze in August."

"Me, too." I laughed. But it was mango, and with the infection attacking me inside, it seemed like wasted caution to refuse.

Claire ended up taking hers, too. "So what you specifically *haven't* told us," she said with a slow roll of her tongue, "is what went on between you and Mr. Chris Raleigh in Oh-hi-oh."

" 'Cause there was nothing to tell," I said and shrugged.

"One thing about cops" — Cindy laughed — "is you would think they would learn how to lie."

"You writing for the gossip page now?" I asked.

Against my will, I felt my face blush. Claire and Cindy's greedy eyes bore down on me, driving home that it was pointless to resist.

I pulled a knee up on the edge of the wall and sat yoga style. Then I took them through where things stood: the long, slow dance in my apartment, eliciting *"You don't dance, girl,"* from Claire. *"You cook."* I described the anticipation of sitting next to him on the plane; the nervous walk down by the lake; my own doubts, hesitation; the inner conflicts holding me back.

"Basically, it took every bit of self-control not to rip his clothes off right there on Lakefront Walk." I laughed at how it must have sounded.

"Girl, why didn't you?" Claire said, wide-eyed. "Might've done you some good."

"I don't know," I said, shaking my head.

But I did know. And though she tried to smile through it, Claire knew, too. She squeezed my hand. Cindy looked on, not knowing what was going on.

Claire joked, "I'd give up losing twenty pounds to see Cheery's expression if the two of you got picked up for going at it in the woods."

"Two San Francisco cops," announced

Cindy in a newscaster tone, *"in Cleveland* in pursuit of the bride and groom killer, were discovered *au naturel* in the bushes by the Cleveland waterfront."

The three of us choked with laughter, and it felt *so good.*

Cindy shrugged. "That, Lindsay, I would've had to print."

"From now on" — Claire giggled — "I can see things growing pretty humid in that squad car."

"I don't think that's Chris's style," I defended him. "You forget, the man's into *The Shipping News.*"

"Oh . . . it's *Chris* now, huh?" mooned Claire. "And don't be so sure about that. Edmund plays three instruments, knows everything from Bartok to Keith Jarrett, but he's risen to the occasion in some very unexpected places."

"Like where?" I laughed, the surprise caught in my throat.

She coyly shook her head. "I just don't want you thinking that 'cause a man keeps himself with a certain dignity there's any dignity when it comes to that."

"C'mon," I exhorted, "you put it in play. Let's hear."

"Let's just say that a few John Does aren't the only thing that have been stiff on our examining tables."

I almost fumbled my gelato onto the ground. "You've got to be kidding. You? And Edmund?"

Claire's shoulders jiggled in delight. "As long as I've gone this far . . . Once we did it in a parterre box at the symphony. After a rehearsal, of course."

"Whatta you guys do? Just go around leaving your mark like poodles?" I exclaimed.

Claire's round face broadened with delight. "You know, it was a long time ago. But as I think of it, that time in my office at the coroner's Christmas party — that *wasn't* so long ago."

"As long as we're baring our souls," injected Cindy, "when I first got to the *Chronicle* I had this fling with one of the senior guys from Datebook. We used to meet down in the library. In the far reaches of the Real Estate section. Nobody ever went there."

Cindy scrunched her face, abashed, but Claire cackled with approval.

I was amazed. I was learning the hidden,

suppressed side of a person I had known for ten years. But there was a little shame building in me as well. *I didn't have a story.*

"So," Claire said, looking at me. "What's Inspector Boxer got to share from her closet?"

I tried to recall a single moment when I'd done something totally crazy. I mean, when it came to sex I didn't think of myself as someone who held back. But somehow, no matter how hard I searched my memory, my passion always ended up between the sheets.

I shrugged, empty-handed.

"Well, you better get started," Claire said with a wag of her finger. "When I'm drawing my last breath, I won't be thinking about all those fancy degrees or conferences I spoke at. You only have a few times in your life to really cut loose, so you might as well take them when they come."

A little tremor of remorse knifed through me. At that moment, I didn't know what I wanted more: my place on the list — or a goddamn name for Red Beard. I suppose I wanted both.

## Chapter 65

A couple of hours later, I sat in my hospital smock in the hematology clinic at Moffett.

"Dr. Medved would like a word with you before we start," said Sara, my transfusion nurse.

I felt nervous as she unpacked an IV setup for my treatment. Truth was, I had been feeling okay. Not much pain or nausea other than the incident in the ladies' room last week.

Dr. Medved walked in with a manila folder under his arm. His face was friendly but un-confiding.

I smiled weakly. "Only good news?"

He sat across from me on the ledge of a counter. "How are you feeling, Lindsay?"

"I wasn't feeling so bad when I saw you before."

"Fatigued?"

"Only a little. End-of-day kind of thing."

"Sudden nausea? Queasiness?"

I admitted I *had* vomited suddenly once or twice.

He made a quick notation on a chart.

He paged through some medical charts in the folder. "I see we've undergone four packed–red cell transfusions so far. . . ."

My heart was racing the longer he took. Finally, he put down the folder and he looked squarely at my face.

"I'm afraid your erythrocyte count has continued to decline, Lindsay. You can see the trend line here."

Medved passed me a sheet.

Leaning forward, he took a Cross pen out of his breast pocket. The paper had a computer graph on it.

He traced the pattern with his pen. The line went steadily down. *Shit.*

I felt the air rush out of my lungs with disappointment. "I'm getting worse," I said.

"To be frank," the doctor acknowledged, "it's not the trend we were hoping for."

I had ignored the possibility that this might happen, burying myself in the case, sure that the numbers would improve. I had built this view on a natural trust that I was too young and energetic to be truly sick. I had work to do, important work, a life to live.

*I was dying, wasn't I? Oh, God.*

"What happens now?" I managed to say. My voice came out as a whisper.

"I want to continue with the treatments," Medved replied. "In fact, increase them. Sometimes these things take a while to kick in."

"Super hi-test," I joked glumly.

He nodded. "From this point on, I'd like you to come in three times a week. And I'm going to increase the dosage by thirty percent." He shifted his weight off the counter. "In and of itself, there's no immediate cause for alarm," he declared in a marginally uplifting tone. "You can continue to work — that is, if you feel up to it."

"I *have* to work," I told Medved.

# Chapter 66

I drove home in a daze. One moment I was battling to unravel this damned case, and the next I was fighting for my life.

*I wanted a name.* I wanted it now more than ever. And I wanted my life back. I wanted a shot at the whole deal — happiness, success, someone to share it with, a child. And now that I had met Raleigh, I knew there was a chance that I could have these things. If I could hold out. If I could will good cells into my body.

I went into my apartment. Sweet Martha was all over me, so I took her for a short walk. But then I moped around, alternating between resolve to fight through this mess and sadness that I couldn't. I even contemplated making a meal. I thought it would calm me.

I took out an onion and cut two desultory slices. Then I realized how crazy it all was.

I needed to talk to someone. I wanted to shout, *I don't fucking deserve this,* and this time I wanted someone to hear it.

I thought of Chris, his comforting arms around me. His eyes, his smile. I wished I could tell him. He would come in an instant. I could rest my head on his shoulder.

I called Claire. She could tell from my first tremulous sound. She realized something was terribly wrong.

"I'm scared," was all I said.

We talked for an hour on the phone. *I* talked.

I went back and forth with Claire in a numbed state — panicked by the impending nearness of Negli's next stage. I told Claire that nailing this bastard gave me the will to fight on. It separated me from being just another person who was sick. I had a special purpose.

"Has that changed for you, Lindsay?" she asked softly.

"No, I want to get him more than ever."

"Then that's what we're going to do. You, me, little Cindy. We're here to help you fight. We're your support, Lindsay. Just this one time, don't try to do it yourself."

In an hour, she had calmed me enough so we could say good-night.

I curled up on the couch. Martha and I snuggled under a blanket and watched the movie *Dave.* One of my favorites. When Sigourney Weaver visits Kevin Kline in his new campaign office at the end, it always makes me cry.

I fell asleep, hoping for a happy ending in my own life.

# Chapter 67

The next morning I went at it stronger than ever. I still believed we were close, maybe just hours from a name for Red Beard.

I checked in with Roth's contact, Jim Heekin, on the Seattle police force. Heekin said they were sorting through the bride's possessions as we spoke. If something came up he would let me know immediately.

We got a reply back from Infortech, where Kathy Voskuhl had worked in Seattle. In the three years she had held her job, there was no record of any reimbursements for business trips to San Francisco. Her job was to work with developing clients in Seattle. A junior account manager. If she repeatedly went down there, she was on her own.

Finally, I called McBride. The Koguts were still claiming that they knew nothing more. But yesterday he'd met with the father, who seemed ready to give in. It was wrenching that some desperate attempt to hold together their daughter's virtue was clouding their judgment.

Since I was a woman, McBride suggested, maybe one more try from me would push them over the edge. I placed a call to Christine Kogut, the bride's mother.

When she came on, her voice was different: remote but freer, as if she were in a less tormented state. Maybe, I just hoped, she was.

"Your daughter's killer is running free," I said. I could no longer hold back. "Two other couples' families are suffering. I think you *know* who was hurting Kathy. Please, help me put him away."

I heard her take in a long breath. When she spoke, grief and the release of shame trembled in her voice. "You raise a child, Inspector, you think she is always part of you.

You love her so much and you think there is always that part that will never go away."

"I know," I said. I could feel she was teetering. *She knew his name, didn't she?*

"She was this beautiful thing . . . she could make anyone love her. A free spirit. One day, we thought, another free spirit would shape her into the kind of person she was meant to be. We cultivated it with our children. My husband insists we always favored Kathy. Maybe we helped bring it all on."

I didn't say a word. I knew what it was like to finally give up what you were holding inside you. I wanted to let her reach that point on her own.

"Do you have children, Inspector?"

"Not yet," I told her.

"It's so hard to believe, *your baby,* the cause of so much pain. We begged her to break free. We even got her the new job. Moved her ourselves. We thought, If she could only get away from him."

I was silent, letting her go at her own pace.

"She was sick, like an addict is sick, Inspector. She couldn't stop herself. But what I don't understand is *why* he would hurt her so badly. He took away all that was pure about her. Why did he need to hurt Kathy?"

*Give me the name. Who is he?*

"She was mesmerized by who he was. It was as if she had no self-control when it came to this man. She shamed us right up until the end. But even now" — her voice lowered — "I still wonder how someone who loved my daughter could possibly kill her. I'm afraid that I don't believe it. That's partly why I wouldn't tell you."

"Tell me now," I said.

"I think she met him at the opening of one of his films. He told her he had a face like hers in mind when he dreamed up one of his characters. His *heroine.*"

It was then that Mrs. Kogut told me.

My body went numb.

I knew the name. Recognized it. He *was* famous, Red Beard.

# Chapter 68

I sat there, ratcheting the possible connections through my mind. Things were starting
to piece together. He was one of the minor-
ity partners at Sparrow Ridge Vineyards,
where the *second* couple had been
dumped. He had known Kathy Kogut for
years in San Francisco. Preyed on her. He
was older. Married.

*Famous.*

By itself, the suspect's name proved
nothing. He had merely known the last
bride. He had a circumstantial connection
to the crime scene of the second killings.

But based on the descriptions of Merrill

Shortley and Christine Kogut, he had the brutal temperament, and maybe the motive, to commit these vicious murders. The conviction built up inside me that this was Red Beard.

I grabbed Raleigh. "What's going on?" he asked. "Where's the fire?"

"I'm going to start one in here. Watch."

I dragged him into Roth's office.

"I have a name," I announced, as I threw my fist in the air.

They looked at me in wide-eyed surprise. *"Nicholas Jenks."*

"The writer?" Raleigh gaped.

I nodded. "He was Kathy Kogut's lover here in San Francisco. Her mother finally gave it up." I walked them through the not-so-random connections he had with at least three of the victims.

"This guy's . . . *famous*," blurted Roth. "He made those movies, blockbusters."

"That's exactly the point. Merrill Shortley said it was someone Kathy was trying to conceal. The guy's got two connections, Sam."

"He's got connections, all right," Roth cried. "Jenks and his wife are invited to all the big affairs. I've seen his picture with the mayor. Wasn't he part of the bid to keep the Giants here?"

The air in Cheery's office became heavy with the weight of dangerous possibilities and risk.

"You should have heard how the Koguts described him, Sam," I said. "Like some kind of animal. A predator. I think we're going to find he had something going with *all three girls.*"

"I think Lindsay's right, Sam," Chris said.

We watched Roth slowly clicking the facts in his head. Nicholas Jenks was famous. A national figure. Untouchable. The lieutenant's face twisted as if he had swallowed a bad clam.

"You've got nothing right now," he came back. "All of it. It's *beyond* circumstantial."

"His name has popped up in connection with four dead people. We could get face to face, like I would with anyone else. We could talk to the district attorney."

Roth held up a hand. Nicholas Jenks was one of San Francisco's most prominent citizens. Implicating him on a murder charge was dangerous. *We'd better be right.* I didn't know what Cheery was thinking. Finally, there was the slightest relaxation in his neck, only a tight swallow, but in Roth-speak it was a go-ahead. "You could talk to the D.A.," he agreed. "Call Jill Bernhardt."

He turned to Raleigh. "This *can't* get out until we have something really firm."

Unfortunately, Assistant District Attorney Jill Bernhardt was stuck in court. Her secretary said she wouldn't be out until the end of the day. Too bad. I knew Jill a little, liked her. She was tough, with dazzling smarts. She even had a conscience.

Raleigh and I got a cup of coffee, going over what we should do next. Roth was right. As far as a warrant was concerned, we had nothing. A direct confrontation could be dangerous. A guy like this, you had to be sure. He would fight back.

Warren Jacobi shuffled in, a self-satisfied smirk puffing up his face. "Must be raining champagne today," he muttered.

I took it as another sardonic zinger aimed at Raleigh and me.

"For weeks, I can't even get a bite on this shit." He sat down and cocked his head toward Raleigh. *"Bite . . . champagne . . .* that works, Captain, doesn't it?"

"Works for me," Raleigh said.

Jacobi continued, "So yesterday Jennings comes back with three places that had sold a few cases of the bubbly in question. One of the buyers is this accountant in San Mateo. Funny thing is, his name's on file. Ends up he did two years up in Lampoc for securities fraud. Kind of a reach, isn't it? Serial killing, securities fraud . . ."

"Maybe the guy's got a thing against people who file joint returns," I said, and smiled at Jacobi.

He puckered up his face. "The second is some woman manager at 3Com who's stocking up for a fortieth-birthday bash. This Clos du Mesnil is a real collectible. It's French, I'm told."

I glanced up, waiting for him to get to the point.

"Now the third one, that's what I mean by *raining* . . . big auction house, Butterfield and Butterfield. Three years back sold two cases of the eighty-nine. Went for twenty-five hundred per case, plus commish. Private collector. At first they wouldn't give out the name. But we squeezed. Turns out he's a big shot. My wife, she happens to be a fan. Read every one of his books."

Raleigh and I froze. "Whose, Warren?" I pressed.

"I figure, I check it out, I can be a hero, bring home a signed copy. You ever read *Lion's Share* by Nicholas Jenks?"

# Chapter 69

Jacobi's statement felt like an elbow to my solar plexus. At the same time it removed all doubt for me.

Kathy Kogut, Sparrow Ridge, the Clos du Mesnil champagne. Jenks was now tied in to all three murders.

He was Red Beard.

I wanted to run and confront Jenks, but I knew I couldn't. I wanted to get up close, glare in his smug eyes, let him know I knew.

At the same time, a suffocating tightness swept up into my chest. I didn't know if it was a flash of nausea, Negli's, or the release of my bottled-up rage.

Whatever it was, I knew I had to get out. "I'm leaving," I said to Raleigh. I was scared.

He looked stunned and confused as I rushed out.

"Hey, I say something wrong?" I heard Jacobi say.

I grabbed my jacket and purse and ran down the steps to the street. My blood was rioting inside me like an angry demon. A cold sweat had broken out all over me.

I ran out into the cool day, started to walk fast down the street.

I had no idea where I was going. I felt like a foreign tourist wandering in the city for the first time. Soon, there were crowds, stores, people rushing by who knew nothing about me. I wanted to lose myself for a few minutes. *Starbucks, Kinko's, Empress Travel.* Familiar names flashed by.

I felt drawn by a single, irrepressible urge. *I wanted to look in his eyes.*

On Post, I found myself standing in front of a Borders bookshop. I went inside.

It was large and open, bright with merchandised stands and shelves of all the current books. I didn't ask. I just looked. On a table in front of me, I spotted what I was searching for.

*Lion's Share.* Maybe fifty copies, thick, bright blue, some stacked, some propped up.

*Lion's Share.* By Nicholas Jenks.

My chest was exploding. I felt in the grip of unspeakable but undeniable right. A mission, a purpose. This was why I was an investigator. *This very moment.*

I took a copy of Jenks's book and looked at the back cover.

I was staring at the killer of the brides and grooms. I was sure of it.

It was the cut of Nicholas Jenks's face, sharp as a stone's edge, that told me. The gray eyes, cold and sterile, controlling.

And one more thing.

*The red beard, flecked with gray.*

## Book Three

# RED BEARD

# Chapter 70

Jill Bernhardt, the tough, savvy assistant district attorney assigned to the bride and groom case, kicked off her Ferragamos and curled her leg up on the leather chair behind her desk. She fixed her sharp blue eyes directly on my face.

"Let me get this straight. You think the bride and groom killer is Nick Jenks?" she asked.

"I'm sure of it," I said.

Jill was dark, disarmingly attractive. Curly jet-black hair framed a narrow, oval face. She was an achiever, thirty-four, a rising star in Bennett Sinclair's office.

All you needed to know about Jill was that as a third-year prosecutor, it was she who had tried the La Frade case, when the mayor's old law partner was indicted on a RICO charge for influence peddling. No one, including the D.A. himself, wanted to submarine his or her career by taking on the powerful fund-raiser. Jill nailed him, sent him away for twenty years. Got herself promoted to the office next to Big Ben himself.

One by one, Raleigh and I laid out Nicholas Jenks's connections to the three double murders: the champagne found at the first scene; his involvement in Sparrow Ridge Vineyards; his volatile relationship with the third bride, Kathy Voskuhl.

Jill threw back her head and laughed. "You want to bust this guy for messing up someone's life, be my guest. Go try the *Examiner.* Here, I'm afraid, they make us do it with facts."

I said, "We have him tied to three double murders, Jill."

Her lips parted into a skeptical smile that read, *Sorry, some other time.* "The champagne connection might fly, *if* you had him nailed down. Which you *don't.* The real-estate partnership's a nonstarter. None of it pins him directly to any of the crimes. A guy like Nicholas Jenks — public, connected — you don't go around making unsubstantiated accusations."

With a sigh, she shifted a tower of briefs aside. "You want to take on the big fish, guys? Go back, get yourself a stronger rod."

My mouth dropped at her hard-edged reaction to our case. "This isn't exactly my first homicide, Jill."

Her strong chin was set.

"And this isn't exactly my first page-one case." Then she smiled, softened. "Sorry," she said. "It's one of Bennett's favorite expressions. I must be spending too much time around the sharks."

"We're talking about a multiple killer, " Raleigh said, the frustration mounting in his eyes.

Jill had that implacable, prove-it-to-me resistance. I had worked with her on murder cases twice before, knew how tireless and prepared she was when she got to court. Once, she had invited me to go "spinning" with her during a trial I was a witness at. I gave up in a sweat after thirty grueling minutes, but Jill, pumping without pause, went on at a mad pace for the full forty-five. Two years out of Stanford Law, she had married a rising young partner at one of the city's top venture firms. Leapfrogged a squadron of career prosecutors to the D.A.'s right hand. In a city of high achievers, Jill was the kind of girl for whom everything clicked.

I passed her the security photo from the Hall of Fame, then Nicholas Jenks's photograph.

She studied them, shrugged. "You know what an adversarial expert witness would do with these? It's pupshit. If the cops in Cleveland feel they can convict with this, be my guest."

"I don't want to lose him to Cleveland," I said.

"So come back to me with something I can take to Big Ben."

"How about a search and seizure," Raleigh suggested. "Maybe we can match up the champagne bottle from the first crime scene to the lot he purchased."

"I could run it by a judge," Jill mused. "There must be someone out there on the bench who thinks Jenks has done enough to bring down the structure of literary form to the point where they'd go for it. But I think you'd be making a mistake."

"Why?"

"Some two-time crack whore, *her* you can bring in on suspicion. You bring in Nicholas Jenks, you better arraign. You alert him that you're onto him — you'll spend more time fending off his lawyers and the press than making your case. If he's it, you're gonna have one shot and one shot only to dig up what you need to convict. Right now, you need more."

"Claire has a hair in her lab from the second killing, the DeGeorges," I said. "We can make Jenks give us a sample of his beard."

She shook her head. "With what you have, his compliance would be totally voluntary. Not to mention, if you're wrong, what you might lose."

"You mean by narrowing the search?"

"I was talking politically. You know the game rules, Lindsay."

She riveted those intense blue eyes directly at me. I could envision the headlines, turning the case back against us. Like the screwups with O. J. Simpson and Jon

Benet Ramsey. In both cases it seemed the cops were as much on trial as any possible defendants.

Jill got up, smoothed her navy skirt, then leaned on her desk. "Look, if the guy's guilty, I'd like to tear him apart as much as you. But all you're bringing me is an unlucky preference in champagne and an eyewitness on her third vodka and tonic. Cleveland's at least got a prior relationship with one of the victims, bringing up a possible motive, but right now none of the jurisdictions have enough to go on."

"I've got two of the biggest headline grabbers in the city looking over my every move," Jill finally admitted. "You think the district attorney and the mayor want to pass this thing on?" Then she fixed unflappably on me. "What's the litmus test here? You're sure it's him, Lindsay?"

He was linked to all three cases. The desperate voice of Christine Kogut was clear in my mind. I gave Jill my most convincing nod. "He's the killer."

She got up and made her way around the desk. With a half-smile, she said, "I'm gonna make you pay if this blows any chance of getting my memoirs in print by forty."

Through the sarcasm, I saw a look flare up in Jill Bernhardt's eyes, the same resolute look I had seen when she was spinning. It hit me like a spray of Mace.

"Okay, Lindsay, let's make this case."

I didn't know what made Jill tick. Power? An urge to do right? Some manic drive to outperform? Whatever it was, I didn't think it was far from what had always burned through me.

But listening to her cogently mapping out what we needed to indict, a tantalizing thought took hold of me.

*I thought about getting her together with Claire and Cindy.*

# Chapter 71

At an old-fashioned steel desk in the dingy halls of the *Chronicle*'s basement library, Cindy Thomas scrolled through four-year-old articles on microfiche. It was late. After eight. Working alone in the underbelly of the building, she felt as if she were some isolated Egyptologist scraping the dust off of long-buried hieroglyphic tablets. She now knew why it was referred to as "the Tombs."

But she felt she was onto something. The dust was coming off secrets, and something worthwhile would soon be clear to her.

*February . . . March, 1996.* The film shot by with indistinguishable speed.

*Someone famous,* the Cleveland bride's friend had said. Cindy pushed the film onward. This was how stories were earned. Late nights and elbow grease.

Earlier, she had called the public relations firm Kathy Kogut had worked for in San Francisco, Bright Star Media. News of their former staffer's death had reached them only that day. Cindy inquired about any feature films Bright Star might have had an association with. She was disappointed when she was told the firm didn't handle films. *The Capitol,* she was told. The concert palace. That was Kathy's account.

Undeterred, Cindy plugged Bright Star's name into the *Chronicle*'s data bank. Any subjects of articles, names, companies, reviews written in the past ten years were recorded there. To her mild delight, the search came back with several live responses.

It was assiduous work, and discouraging. The articles covered a period of more than five years. That would tie in with the time Kathy was in San Francisco. Each article was on a different microfiche cassette.

It required going back into the files. Requisitioning. Three items at a time. After four sets, the night librarian handed her the clipboard, saying, "Here, Thomas. It's all yours. Knock yourself out."

It was quarter past ten — she hadn't heard a peep from anyone in over two hours — when she finally came upon something interesting.

It was dated February 10, 1995. Arts Today section. "For Local Band Sierra, New Film Taps into a Hit."

Cindy's eyes shot down the text, fast-forwarding to anything that stuck out: plans for their album, an eight-city tour. Quotes from the lead singer.

*"Sierra will perform the song at tomorrow night's bash at the Capitol to kick off release of the film* Crossed Wire.*"*

Her heart stood still. She zoomed ahead to the following day's Arts section.

She consumed the article almost in a single suspended breath: *". . . took over the Capitol. Chris Wilcox, the star, was there."* A photo, with a dishy actress. *"Bright Star . . . other recording stars in attendance."*

Her eyes traveled over the three accompanying news photos. In tiny print, under-

neath each shot, she noticed the photo-
grapher's name: "Photography by Sal
Esposito. *Property of the Chronicle.*"

*Photography* . . . Cindy jumped out of her
seat at the microfiche desk and hurried
back through the musty, ten-foot-high
stacks of bundled, yellowing editions. On
the other side of the Tombs was the *Chronicle's* photography morgue. Rows and rows
of unused shots.

She had never even been in here . . .
didn't know how it was laid out.

Creepy, creepy place, especially this late
at night.

In a flash, she recognized that the aisles
were chronological. She followed the signs
at the end of each aisle until she found February 1995. She ran her eyes along the outside of the stacked plastic bins dated the
tenth.

When she spotted it, it was on the high-
est shelf. Where else? She stepped up on
the lower shelf, on her tiptoes, and wiggled
the bin down.

On the dusty floor, Cindy frantically leafed
through folders bunched up in elastic. As if
in a dream, she came upon a folder marked

in large black letters: "*Crossed Wire* Opening — *Esposito*." This was it. . . .

Inside were four contact sheets, several black-and-white glossies. Someone, probably the reporter, had written the names of each person, in pen, at the bottom of each shot.

Her eyes froze as she came upon the photo she was hoping for. Four people toasting the camera, with arms locked.

She recognized Kathy Kogut's face from the photos Lindsay had come back with. Red hair, curly. Trendy inlaid glasses.

And next to her, smiling into the camera, was another face Cindy knew. It took her breath away. Her fingers trembled with the realization that she had deciphered the hieroglyphics at last.

It was the trimmed, reddish-colored beard. The narrow, complicit smile — as if he knew where all this might one day lead.

Next to Kathy Kogut was the novelist Nicholas Jenks.

# Chapter 72

I was totally surprised when Cindy appeared at my door at half past eleven. With a look of wide-eyed elation and pride, she blurted, "I know who Kathy Kogut's lover was."

"Nicholas Jenks," I replied. "C'mon in, Cindy. *Down,* Martha." She was tugging at my Giants nightshirt.

"Oh, God," she groaned, loudly. "I was so pumped up. I thought I had found it."

She *had* found it. She had beaten McBride *and* Seattle. Two squads of trained investigators as well as the FBI. I looked at her with genuine admiration. *"How?"*

Too restless to sit, Cindy stalked around my living room as she took me through the steps of her amazing discovery. She unfolded a copy of the news photo showing Jenks and Kathy Kogut at the movie opening. I watched her circle the couch, trying to keep up with herself: *Bright Star . . . Sierra . . . Crossed Wire . . .* She was hyper. "I'm a good reporter, Lindsay," she said.

"I know you are." I smiled at her. "You just can't *write* about it."

Cindy stopped — the sudden realization of what she had overlooked hitting her like a pie in the face.

"Oh, God," she moaned. "That's like being in a shower with Brad Pitt, but you can't touch." She looked at me, half smiling, half like nails were being driven into her heart.

"Cindy" — I reached out and held her — "you wouldn't have even known to look for him if I hadn't clued you in on Cleveland."

I went to the kitchen. "You want some tea?" I called out.

She collapsed on the couch and let out another wail. "I want a beer. No, not beer. *Bourbon.*"

I pointed to my small bar near the terrace. In a few moments, we sat down. Me with my Nocturnal Seasonings, Cindy with a stiff glass of Wild Turkey, Martha comfortable at our feet.

"I'm proud of you, Cindy," I told her. "You did crack the name. You scooped two police forces. When this is over, I'm gonna make sure you get a special mention in the press."

"I am the press," Cindy exclaimed, forcing herself to smile. "And what do you mean, 'When this is over'? You have him."

"Not quite." I shook my head. I explained that everything we had, even stuff she didn't know — the vineyard, the champagne — was circumstantial. We couldn't even force him to submit a hair.

"So what do we need to do?"

"Tie Nicholas Jenks solidly in to the first crime."

Suddenly, she began pleading, "I have to run with it, Lindsay."

"No," I insisted. "No one knows. Only Roth and Raleigh. And one more. . . ."

"Who?" Cindy blinked.

"Jill Bernhardt."

"The assistant district attorney? That office is like a colander trying to sail across the Pacific. It's nothing but leaks."

"Not Jill," I promised. "She won't leak this."

"How can you be so sure?"

"Because Jill Bernhardt wants to nail this guy as much as we do," I said with conviction.

"That's all?" groaned Cindy.

I sipped a soothing mouthful of tea, met her eyes. "*And* because I invited her into our group."

# Chapter 73

The following day we met after work for a drink at Susie's; it was Jill's introduction to our group.

All day, I couldn't fix on anything other than the thought of confronting Jenks with what we knew and bringing him in. I wanted to accelerate everything — a face-to-face confrontation. I wanted to let him know we had him. *Goddamn Red Beard.*

As we waited for drinks, I threw out a couple of new developments. A search of Kathy Kogut's home in Seattle had uncovered Jenks's name and phone number in the dead bride's phone book. A trace by

Northwest Bell had turned up three calls to him in the past month — including one three days before the Cleveland wedding. It confirmed what Merrill Shortley had told us.

*"Right up to the very end,"* said Claire. "Creepy. Both of them, actually."

We had run Jenks's photo by Maryanne Perkins of Saks as part of a photo spread with five others. We desperately needed something that pinned him to the first crime. She paused over his likeness for a few seconds. "It's him," she declared. Then she paused. "But then, it's hard to tell. It was so quick. And far away."

The thought of a defense attorney cross-examining her didn't sit well with me. It didn't surprise me that Jill agreed.

It took no longer than a single margarita for her to make a seamless entry into our group.

Claire had met her a few times when she testified at trials. They had developed a mutual respect for each other's rise through their male-dominated departments.

We asked Jill about herself, and she told us she was Stanford Law and her father was a corporate attorney back in Dallas. No interest in the corporate thing. That was for her husband, Steve, who was running a venture fund for Bank America.

They lived in Burlingame — affluent, exclusive — took rock-climbing treks in the desert at Moab. No kids. "It just doesn't fit right now," she said.

Jill seemed to live the epitome of the fast, successful life. At the same time, there seemed to be something missing. Maybe she was tired from the grind, the pace of her accomplishments.

When our drinks arrived, Claire and I toasted Cindy's ingenuity in coming up with Jenks's name in such short time. And beating two police departments to the punch.

Claire raised a glass to her. "You're pretty good for a rookie, of course. But you're still not the king." She smiled at me.

"So I'm thinking," Jill said, looking around the table. "I know I can hold my own at dinner parties and all . . . but that's not why you asked me in, is it? Seems like we have all the angles covered here: the press, the force, medical examiner. Just what kind of a group is this?"

I answered, since it was I who had invited

her in. "Women. Climbing the ladder in their careers. Law enforcement."

"Yeah, with soft, pushover types for bosses," put in Cindy.

"Well, I qualify there," said Jill. "And it doesn't hurt that each of you seems to have *some connection* with the bride and groom case."

I held my breath. Jill could blow this whole thing if she wanted to, but she was here. "We have been sort of working together," I admitted. "Outside the investigation."

Over margaritas, I explained how we had originally gotten together. How we had come upon this case, trying to solve it, sharing what we knew, freelance. How it had become a sort of bond. How things had just gotten a bit deeper.

Jill arched her eyebrows. "I assume you're sharing all this with the investigation?"

"Of course," I insisted. "Well, sort of." I told her how we were giving Cindy only what the department was about to release to the press at large. How there was a thrill in cutting through the departments, advancing the case.

"I know it's a different game when everything starts to get legal," I said. "If any of this makes you uncomfortable . . ."

We were all sort of hanging there, awaiting her response. Loretta came, and we ordered another round. *We were still hanging — waiting on Jill.*

"How about I let you know when things start to get uncomfortable," Jill said. She widened her blue eyes. "In the meantime, you're gonna need a lot stronger corroboration if we want to take this thing to court."

The three of us breathed a sigh of relief. We tilted our near-empty glasses toward our new member.

"So, this outfit have a name?" Jill inquired.

We looked around, shrugged, shook our heads. "We're sort of a murder club," I said.

"Lindsay's deputized us." Claire grinned.

"The Margarita Posse," Jill threw out. "That has possibilities."

"Bad-ass Bitches." Claire giggled.

"One day, we're all gonna be running things," Cindy said. "Homicide Chicks," she came back with a satisfied grin. "That's who we are. That's what we do."

"Just shut me up if I start to roar," said Jill.

We looked around the table. We were bright, attractive, take-no-shit women. We were going to run things — some day.

The waitress brought our drinks. We raised four glasses toward one another. "To us."

# Chapter 74

I was driving home, really pleased at having brought Jill into the group, but it didn't take long for the thought to worm its way in that I was still *withholding* from my friends.

My beeper sounded.

"What're you doin'?" Raleigh asked when I buzzed him back.

"I was headed home. *Beat.*"

"You up for talking just a little? I'm at Mahoney's." Mahoney's was a dark, crowded bar near the Hall that was usually thick with off-duty cops.

"Already ate," I told him.

"Meet me anyway," Raleigh said. "It's about the case."

I was only a few minutes away. Mahoney's was on Brannan. To get to Potrero, I had to go right by it.

I found myself a little nervous again. I was scared we were no longer playing things by the book. The book was, partners didn't get involved. Nor people with their lives ebbing away. I knew that if I let things go, anything could happen. This wasn't some casual fling we could go at for a night and try to rationalize away the next day. As much as I wanted him, I was holding back. Scared to let it all come out. Of letting myself go. Of dragging him in.

I was relieved when I saw Raleigh waiting for me outside the bar. He came up to my car. I couldn't help noticing that he looked good, as usual.

"Thanks for not making me go in," I said.

He leaned on the edge of my open window. "I looked into Nicholas Jenks," he said.

"And?"

"The guy's forty-eight. Went to law school but never finished. Started writing novels his first year. Wrote two books that didn't go anywhere. Then this twisted thriller, *Crossed Wire,* hit.

"There's something you should know. Maybe seven years ago, give or take a few, cops were called out to his home in a domestic dispute."

"Who made the call?"

"His wife. His first wife." Raleigh leaned in closer. "I pulled up the report. First-on-the-scene described her as pretty beat-up. Bruises up and down her arms. Large bruise on her face."

A thought flashed in my head — Merrill Shortley, on Kathy's boyfriend: *He was into intense sex games.*

"Did the wife file?" I asked.

Chris shook his head. "That's as far as it went. Never pressed charges. Since then, he's cashed in big-time. Six huge bestsellers. Movies, screenplays. New wife, too."

"That means there's an old one out there who might be willing to talk."

He had a satisfied expression on his face. "So, can I buy you a meal, Lindsay?"

A hot bead of sweat burned a slow path down my neck. I didn't know whether to get

out or stay in. I thought, *If I got out . . .*
"Chris, I already ate. Had a commitment."

"Jacobi." He grinned. He could always get me with that smile of his.

"Sort of a women's thing, a group of us. We meet once a month. Go over our lives. You know, nanny problems, personal trainers, country homes. Affairs, things like that."

"Anyone I know?" Raleigh raised his eyebrows.

"Maybe one day I'll introduce you."

We sort of hung there, my blood slowly throbbing in my chest. The hair on Raleigh's forearm gently grazed against mine. This was driving me insane. I had to say something. "Why'd you call me out here, Chris?"

"Jenks," he replied. "I didn't tell you everything. We ran a firearms check on him with Sacramento." He looked at me with a glint in his eye. "He's got several registered. A Browning twenty-two-caliber hunting rifle, a Renfield thirty-thirty. A Remington forty-point-five."

He was leading me on. I knew he had struck pay dirt.

"There's also a Glock Special, Lindsay. Nineteen-ninety issue. *Nine millimeter.*"

A rush of validation shot through my veins.

Chris frowned. "He has the weapon of choice, Lindsay. We've got to find that gun."

I made a fist and brought it down against Raleigh's in triumph. My mind was racing. Sparrow Ridge, the phone calls, now a Glock Special. It was all still circumstantial, but it was falling into place.

"What're you doing tomorrow, Raleigh?" I asked with a smile.

"Wide open. Why?"

"I think it's time we talked to this guy face-to-face."

# Chapter 75

High on the cliffs above the Golden Gate Bridge, 20 El Camino del Mar was a stucco, Spanish-style home with an iron gate guarding the terra-cotta driveway.

Red Beard lived here — Nicholas Jenks.

Jenks's home was low, stately, surrounded by decoratively trimmed hedges and bright, blossoming azaleas. In the driveway's circle, there was a large iron sculpture, Botero's *Madonna and Child.*

"Fiction must be good." Raleigh let out a whistle, as we stepped up to the front door. We had made an appointment through Jenks's personal assistant to meet him at noon. I had been warned by Sam Roth not to come on too hard.

A pleasant housekeeper greeted us at the door and took us back to a spacious sun-room, informing us that Mr. Jenks would be down in a short while. The lavish room seemed straight out of some designer magazine — with rich jacquard wallpaper, Oriental chairs, a mahogany coffee table, shelves of mementos and photographs. It opened onto a fieldstone patio overlooking the Pacific.

I had lived in San Francisco all my life but never knew you could come home every night to this kind of spectacular view.

While we waited, I examined photos arranged on a side table. Jenks with a series of well-known faces: Michael Douglas, the top guy from Disney, Bill Walsh from the 49ers. Others were with an attractive woman I took to be his new wife — sunny, smiling, strawberry-blond hair — in various exotic locations: beaches, skiing, a Mediterranean isle.

In a silver frame, there was a four-by-six of the two of them in the center of an enormous lit-up rotunda. The dome of the Palace of Fine Arts. It was a wedding photo.

It was then that Nicholas Jenks walked in. I recognized him immediately from his photographs.

He was slighter than I had imagined. Trim, well-built, no more than five-ten, wearing an open white dress shirt over well-worn jeans. My eyes were drawn immediately to the reddish, gray-flecked beard.

*Red Beard, it's good to meet you, finally.*

"Sorry to put you off, inspectors," he said with an easy smile, "but I'm afraid I get cranky if I can't get my morning pages in." He held out his hand, noticing the photograph I was still holding. "A bit like the set of *Marriage of Figaro,* wasn't it? Myself, I would've gone for a small civil ceremony, but Chessy said if she could snare me in a tux, she'd never, ever doubt my commitment to her."

I wasn't interested in being charmed by this man, but he was handsome and immediately in control. I could see what some women found attractive about him. He motioned us to the couch.

"We were hoping," I said, "to ask you a few questions."

"About the bride and groom killings . . . My assistant advised me. Crazy . . . terrible.

But these acts, so incredibly desperate, cry out for at least a small measure of sympathy."

"For the victims," I said, placing his wedding photograph back on the table.

"Everyone always goes to the plight of the victims," Jenks said. "But it's what's inside the killer's head that puts cash in the account. Most people figure these acts are simply about revenge. The *sickest* kind of revenge . . . Or even subjugation, like most rapes. But I'm not so sure."

"What's your theory, Mr. Jenks?" Chris asked. He made it sound as if he were a fan.

Jenks held out a pitcher of iced tea. "Something to drink? I know it's a hot one, though I've been holed up in the study since eight."

We shook our heads. I took a manila folder out of my bag and placed it on my lap. I remembered Cheery's admonition: *"Keep it light. Jenks is a VIP. You're not."*

Nicholas Jenks poured himself a tall glass of tea and went on. "From what I've read, these killings appear to be a form of rape, rape of innocence. The killer is acting in a way that *no one can forgive.* In the most sacred setting of our society. To me, these killings are the ultimate act of purification."

"Unfortunately, Mr. Jenks," I said, ignoring his bullshit, "we didn't come up here seeking your professional advice. I have some questions related to these killings we'd like to run by you."

Jenks sat back in his chair. He looked surprised. "You make that sound awfully official."

"That's entirely up to you," I said. I took out a portable cassette tape player from my bag. "You mind if I turn this on?"

He stared at me, his eyes shifting suspiciously, then he waved his hand as if it were of no concern.

"So where I'd like to start, Mr. Jenks, is, these killings . . . Do you have any specific knowledge of any of the crimes other than what you've read in the papers?"

"Knowledge?" Jenks took a breath, nominally reflecting. Then he shook his head. "No. None at all."

"You read there was a third killing? Last week. In Cleveland."

"I did see that. I read five or six papers every day."

"And did you also read who the victims were?"

"From Seattle, weren't they? One of them, I remember, was some kind of concert promoter."

"The groom." I nodded. "James Voskuhl. The bride actually lived for a while in town, here. Her maiden name was Kathy Kogut. Do either of those names mean anything to you?"

"No. Should they?"

"So you never met either of them? Any interest you had in this case was just like anyone's . . . morbid curiosity?"

He fixed his eyes on me. "That's right. Morbid curiosity's my business."

I opened my manila folder and took out the top photo. He was playing us, just as he had been playing us by leaving dead-ending clues along the way.

I slid the photo across the table. "This might sharpen your memory," I said. "That's Kathy Kogut, the bride who was murdered the other night. The man next to her, I believe, is *you*."

# Chapter 76

Slowly, Red Beard picked up the photo and stared at it. "It *is* me," he declared. "But the lady, though quite beautiful, I don't recognize. If I can ask, where's this picture from?"

"The San Francisco opening of *Crossed Wire.*"

"Ah," he sighed, as if that classified something for him.

I watched the gears in his brain start to shift for the right response. He was definitely smart, and a pretty good actor.

"I meet a lot of people at these events. It's

why I try to avoid them. You say this was
that girl who was killed in Cleveland?"

"We were hoping this was someone you
might've remembered," I replied.

Jenks shook his head. "Too many fans,
not much appetite to meet them, even the
really pretty ones, Inspector."

"The price of fame, I imagine . . ." I took
the photo back, thumbed it for a moment,
then slid it back in front of him.

"Nevertheless, I have to come back to
this particular fan. I'm curious why she
doesn't stick out for you. From *all those
other fans.*" I withdrew a copy of a Northwest Bell phone bill from my folder and
handed it to him. On it were several high-
lighted calls. "This is your private number?"

Jenks held the copy of the bill. His eyes
dimmed. "It is."

"She called you, Mr. Jenks. Three times in
just the past few weeks. Once . . . *here,* I
circled it for you, for twelve minutes only
last week. Three days before she was married, then killed."

Jenks blinked. Then he picked up the
photo again. This time he was different:
somber, apologetic. "Truth is, Inspector," he
took a breath and said, "I was *so, so* sorry

to hear what had taken place. She seemed, in the last month, so full of anticipation, hope. I was wrong to mislead you. It was foolish. I *did* know Kathy. I met her the night of the photo there. Sometimes, my fans are rather impressionable. And attractive. At times I, to my detriment, can be an impressionable man."

I wanted to lunge across the table and rip Nicholas Jenks's impressionable face off. I was certain he was responsible for six vicious murders. Now he was mocking us, and the victims. Goddamn him.

"So you're admitting," Raleigh interjected, "that you *did* have a relationship with this woman."

"Not in the way you're insinuating," Jenks replied. "Kathy was a woman who hoped to satisfy her own vague artistic aspirations through an association with someone engaged in the act of creating. She wanted to write herself. It's not exactly brain surgery, but I guess if it was so damn easy we'd all have a book on the bestseller list, right?"

Neither of us responded.

"We spoke, maybe met, a few times over a few years. It never went beyond that. That's the truth."

"Sort of mentoring?" Raleigh suggested.

"Yes, that's right. Good choice of words."

"By any chance" — I leaned forward, no longer able to control my tone — "were you *mentoring* Kathy in Cleveland last Saturday, the night she was killed?"

Jenks's face turned granitelike. "That's ridiculous. What an inappropriate thing to say."

I reached into the folder one more time, this time taking out a copy of the security photo of the killer arriving at the Hall of Fame. "This is a security photo from the night she was killed. Is that you, Mr. Jenks?"

Jenks didn't even blink. "It might be, Inspector, *if* I had been there. Which I categorically was not."

"Where were you last Saturday night?"

"Just so I understand," he said, stonily, "are you suggesting *I'm* a suspect in these crimes?"

"Kathy Kogut talked, Mr. Jenks." I glared at him. "To her sister. To her friends. We know how you treated her. We know she left the Bay Area to try to get away from your domination. We know things were going on between you right up to the wedding night."

I wouldn't take my eyes off Jenks. There was nothing in the room but him and me.

"I *wasn't* in Cleveland," he said. "I was right here that night."

I ran the whole body of evidence by him. From the bottle of Clos du Mesnil left behind at the Hyatt, to his involvement in the real-estate trust that owned Sparrow Ridge Vineyards, to the fact that two of the murders had been committed with nine-millimeter guns and according to the state, he owned one.

He laughed at me. "This is not what you're basing your assumptions on, I hope.

"I got that champagne ages ago." He shrugged. "I don't even recall where it is."

"You *can* locate it, I assume?" Raleigh asked, then explained that it was a sign of respect that we were asking him to turn it over voluntarily.

"Would you mind supplying us with a hair sample from your beard?" I asked.

*"What!"* His eyes met mine with a churlish defiance. I imagined the look Melanie Brandt might have seen as he attacked her. What Kathy Kogut saw as he raised his gun to her head.

"I think," Nicholas Jenks finally answered,

"that this fascinating interview has come to an end." He held out his wrists. "Unless you're intent on taking me away, my lunch is waiting."

I nodded. "We'll need to follow up. On your whereabouts. And on the gun."

"Of course," Jenks said, standing up. "And should you need any further cooperation — feel free to request it through my attorney."

I assembled the photographs and put them back into the folder. Raleigh and I got up.

At that moment, the attractive strawberry blonde from the photographs walked into the room.

She was undeniably pretty, with gentle, aquamarine eyes, a pale complexion, long, free-flowing hair. She had a tall dancer's body, and was dressed in thigh-length leggings and a Nike T-shirt.

"Chessy!" Jenks exclaimed. "These are officers from the San Francisco Police Department. My wife, inspectors."

"Sorry, Nicky," Chessy Jenks apologized. "Susan's coming over. I didn't know you had guests."

"They were just leaving."

We nodded stiffly, moved toward the door. "If you could locate what we talked about," I said to him, "we'll send someone by to pick it up."

He gazed right through me.

I hated to leave without taking him in, and to have treated him with kid gloves. But we were still a few steps away from an arrest.

"So," Chessy Jenks smiled and said, "has my husband finally gone homicidal?" She went up to Jenks, clasped his arm in a teasing way. "I always told him, with those creepy-crawler characters he writes about, it was inevitable."

*Could she know?* I wondered. She lived with him, slept with him. How could she not be aware of what was going on inside his head?

"I truly hope not, Ms. Jenks," was all I said.

# Chapter 77

"What did she mean by that?" Chessy Jenks asked her husband, confused, after the police inspectors left the house.

Jenks brushed her away. He paced over to the large French doors leading out to the Pacific.

"Idiots," he muttered. "Amateurs. Who the hell do they think they're dealing with?"

He felt a prickly, stabbing heat racing over his shoulders and back. *They were stupid, tiny-minded. Beetles. That's why they were cops. If they had any brains, they'd be doing what he was doing. Living high over the Pacific.*

"That's why they dig landfills," he replied distractedly. "A place for cops to feel at home."

Chessy picked up the wedding photo from the coffee table and set it back in its rightful spot. "What did you do now, Nick?"

*Why did she always drive him to this? Why did she always need to know?*

She came over, looked at him with those lucid, patient eyes.

As always, his anger leaped up in a flash.

He didn't even realize he had hit her.

It was just that suddenly his hand hurt and Chessy was sprawled on the floor — and the bamboo table on which the pictures were had toppled over — and she was holding her mouth.

He shouted, "Don't you know when to keep away from me? What do you need, a road map?"

"Uh-uh, Nick," Chessy said. "Not here . . . not now."

"Not here what?" he was shouting. He knew he was shouting, losing control. That the staff might hear.

"Please, Nick," Chessy said, pulling herself off the floor. "Susan will be here soon. We're going to lunch."

It was the notion that Chessy thought she could just sit there and judge him that really set him off. Didn't she see who she really was? Just some blonde with freckles he had picked out of a cattle call and turned into God's gift to Martha Stewart.

He grabbed her by the arm and put his face inches from her beautiful, terrified eyes. "Say it!"

The arm he held was trembling. A tiny stream of mucus ran out of her nose. "Jesus, Nick . . ."

That's what he liked, her fear of him, even though she never showed it in public.

"I said say it, Chessy." He twisted her arm behind her back.

She was breathing heavily now, sweat forming under her T-shirt. Her little tits poked through. When she glared back at him with her paltry defiance, he twisted harder, digging his fingers into her arm. He shoved her toward the bedroom, her bare feet stumbling along.

In the bedroom he kicked the door shut.

*Who did the lead cop think she was? Coming in here . . . accusing him like that. In her cheap Gap ensemble. What a fucking insolent bitch.*

He dragged Chessy into the clothes closet. *Hers.* It was dark in there. Only the dark and her sobs and the pervasive smell of her perfume. He pushed her forward against the wall, rubbed himself against her buttocks.

He pulled Chessy's gym shorts down, her panties along with them. "Please," she cried. "Nicky?"

He found the familiar place where her small cheeks parted. He was very hard, and he pushed himself in deep.

He was driving himself inside Chessy. "Say it," he gasped. "You know how to make it stop. Say it."

"Ruff . . . ," she finally murmured in a tiny whisper.

Now she was loving it, as she always did. It wasn't bad — it was good. They all ended up wanting and loving it. He always picked them so well.

"Ruff," she whimpered. "Ruff, ruff. Is that what you want, Nick?"

*Yes, that was part of what he needed. It was all he expected from Chessy.*

"You love it, Chessy," he whispered back. "That's why you're here."

# Chapter 78

We kept a close watch on Jenks's movements with a surveillance team of three
cars. If he made a move to dump the gun,
we'd know. If he moved to kill again, we
hoped we could stop him. No matter how
clever he was, I didn't see how he could ex-
ecute another murder right now.

I wanted to speak with someone who
knew him, who might be willing to talk.
Raleigh had mentioned an ex-wife, a history
of violence between them. I needed to talk
with her.

It wasn't hard to track down Joanna

Jenks, now Joanna Wade. A search through the police files had her maiden name listed as part of the domestic complaint she had filed against her husband years before. A Joanna Wade was currently residing at 1115 Filbert Street on Russian Hill.

It was an attractive limestone town house on the steepest part of the hill. I buzzed, identified myself to the housekeeper who answered. She informed me that Ms. Wade was not at home. *"Ehersizing,"* she said. "Gold's Gym. On Union."

I found the gym around the corner between a Starbucks and an Alfredson's market. At reception, a buffed, ponytailed staffer informed me that Joanna was in Exercise Room C. When I asked what Joanna Wade looked like, the staffer laughed. "Think blond. And kick-ass fit."

I wandered in, and through a large observation window, spotted a Tae-Bo class in Exercise Room C. About eight women sweating in Lycra and jog bras were kicking their legs out karate style to loud music. I knew that Tae-Bo was the latest exercise craze, the biggest burn. Any one of these women looked as if she could take a resisting suspect up against a wall, then beat the patrol car back to the precinct with breath to spare.

The only blonde was in front. Trim, sculpted, pushing herself hard and barely breaking a sweat. It was her class.

I hung around until she finished up and most of the class had rushed out. She toweled the sweat off her face.

"Great workout," I said, as she headed my way.

"The best in the Bay Area. Looking to sign up?"

"Maybe. First I thought I could ask you a couple of questions."

"Try Diane up front. She can tell you the whole deal."

"I wasn't talking Tae-Bo." I flashed her my badge. "I'm talking Nicholas Jenks."

Joanna stared at me, flapping her blond ponytail off her shoulders to cool her neck. She smirked. "What'd he do, get caught shoplifting one of his books out of Stacey's downtown?"

"Can we talk?" I asked.

She shrugged and led me over to a changing area that was unoccupied. "So what could I tell you about Nick that you couldn't find out from one of his jacket flaps?"

"I know it was several years ago," I said, "but you once filed a domestic complaint against him."

"Listen, in case the paperwork didn't catch up, I dropped the charge back then."

I could see the terror of the moment exploding all over again for her. "Look," I said genuinely, "no one's trying to dig up old wounds, Ms. Wade. I'd just like a read on your ex-husband."

"Up to his old tricks again?"

I could see her sizing me up. Was I an ally or a foe? Then she let out a capitulating breath and looked right at me.

"If you're here about Chessy, I could've warned her. If he hadn't been such a creep about how he dumped me. How did he put it, *I write through her, Jo. She inspires me.* You ever read his books, Inspector?" she asked. "She didn't have to inspire him by holding a job down while he went off and found himself, did she? She didn't have to read his drafts, deal with his rages when he got rejected, tell him every night how much she believed in him. You know where he met her? In the makeup room at *Entertainment Tonight*."

"What I'm asking, Ms. Wade," I said, "is how violent is Nicholas Jenks?"

She paused, looked away. When she turned back, her eyes had filled up as if she were about to cry.

"You know, you come in here after all this time and make me go through this again. What do you want me to say? That his mother didn't love him? That he's a screwed-up, dangerous man? Life with Nick . . . it's so hard. He's holding something in and God only knows when it's going to come out. I would ask myself, *Why? What had I done?* I was just a kid." Her eyes glistened.

"I'm sorry." I truly felt for her. For both Mrs. Jenkses. I couldn't even imagine what it was like to wake up and find myself married to someone like him.

"I need to ask," I said. "What are the chances things with your ex-husband have intensified? Become more serious."

She looked stunned. "Is Chessy all right, Inspector?"

"*Chessy's* all right." I nodded, making it clear I felt there were others who might not be.

She waited for me to blink. When I didn't, she gave me a mirthless laugh. "So I guess we're talking a lot deeper than pilfering a book from Stacey's bookstore?"

I nodded again. Woman to woman now, I said, "I need to ask you a crucial question, Ms. Wade."

# Chapter 79

What I asked Joanna Wade was *whether Nicholas Jenks was capable of murder.*

I couldn't tell her the reason, but it didn't matter. Joanna was a quick study. I saw the shock in her eyes. After she calmed, I watched her go through a thoughtful evaluation.

Finally, she looked at me and asked again, "Have you ever read his books, Inspector?"

"One, *Fatal Charm.* Tough book."

"He lives with those characters, Inspector. Sometimes I think he forgets it's only what he does for a living."

I saw the self-judging look in her eyes. I leaned in closer. "I don't mean to hurt you. But I have to know."

"Could he kill? Is he capable of murder? I know he's capable of completely debasing another human being. That's murder, isn't it? He's what they call a sexual sadist. His father used to beat his mother in their bedroom closet as an aphrodisiac. He preys on weakness. Yes, the famous Nicholas Jenks humiliated me. . . . But let me tell you the worst thing, the very worst. He left me, Inspector. I didn't leave him."

Joanna leaned back and gave me sort of a compassionate smile. "I've seen Chessy around a few times. Luncheons, benefits. We've even spoken a bit. He hasn't changed. She knows I know exactly what she's going through. But it's something we can't share. I see the fear. I know how it is. When she looks in the mirror, she no longer recognizes the person she once was."

My blood was at the boiling point. Through the tough veneer, I saw a glimpse of the woman Joanna Wade had been — young, needing, confused.

I reached out and touched her hand. *I had*

*my answer.* I closed my pad, ready to get up, when Joanna surprised me.

"I thought it was him. Not really. But I thought of Nick when I heard about those terrible crimes. I thought about his book, and I said, *It could be him.*"

I stopped Joanna. "What book?"

"That first thing he wrote. *Always a Bridesmaid.* I figured that's what brought you here, what connected him to the murders."

I stared at her, confused. "Just what are you talking about?"

"I barely remember it. He wrote it before we met. I was lucky enough to come in for the second unpublished one, which, I'm told, he recently sold for two million. But this book I'd totally forgotten about until recently. It was about a student in law school who discovers his wife with his best friend. He kills them both. Ends up going on a rampage."

"What kind of rampage?" I asked. What she said next made me gasp.

"He goes around killing brides and grooms. A lot like what happened."

# Chapter 80

That was the piece of the puzzle I needed. If Jenks had premeditated these crimes, mapped them out in some early book, it would constitute unimpeachable knowledge. No longer circumstantial. With everything else we had, I could definitely bring him in.

"Where can I find this book?" I asked.

"It wasn't very good," Joanna Wade replied. "Never published."

Every nerve in my body was standing on end. "Do you have a copy?"

"Trust me, if I did I would have burned it years ago. Nick had this agent in town, Greg

Marks. He dumped him when he got successful. If anyone would have it, it might be him."

I called Greg Marks from the car. I was really humming now. I loved this.

The operator connected me and after four rings, an answering tape came on: *"You've reached Greg Marks Associates ..."* I cringed with disappointment. *Damn, damn, damn.*

Reluctantly, I left him my pager number. "A matter of great urgency," I said. I was about to tell him why I was calling when a voice cut in on the tape — "This is Greg Marks."

I explained I needed to see him immediately. His office wasn't too far; I could be there in ten minutes. "I have an engagement at One Market at six-fifteen," the agent replied curtly. "But if you can get here ..."

"You just stay right there," I told him. "This is police business and it's important. If you leave, I'll arrest you!"

Greg Marks worked out of his brownstone, a third-floor loft in Pacific Heights with a partial view of the bridge. He answered the door with a suspicious reserve.

He was short, balding, smartly dressed, a jacquard shirt buttoned to the top.

"I'm afraid you haven't picked a popular topic with me, Inspector. Nicholas Jenks hasn't been a client for over six years. He left me the day *Crossed Wire* hit the *Chronicle*'s bestseller list."

"Are you still in touch?" I wanted to make sure anything I asked him wouldn't get back to Jenks.

"Why? To remind him how I baby-sat him through the years when he could barely use a noun with an adjective, how I took his obsessed midnight calls, stroked that gigantic ego?"

"I'm here about something Jenks wrote early on," I interrupted. "Before any big deals. I spoke to his ex-wife."

"Joanna?" Marks exclaimed with surprise.

"She said he had written a book that never got published. She thought it was called *Always a Bridesmaid.*"

The agent nodded. "It was an uneven first effort. No real narrative power. Truth is, I never even sent it out."

"Do you have a copy?"

"Packed it back to him as soon as I

turned the final page. I would think Jenks must, though. He thought the book was a suspense masterpiece."

"I was hoping I wouldn't have to go through him," I said, without conveying the basis of my interest.

I leaned forward. "How do I get my hands on a copy of that novel, without going to Jenks directly?"

"Joanna didn't save it?" Marks rubbed a finger across his temple. "Jenks was always paranoid about people ripping him off. Maybe he had it copyrighted. Why don't you check into that?"

I needed to run this by someone.

I needed to run it by the girls.

"Do you want to hear something really scary about Jenks?" the agent said then.

"Please, go ahead."

"Here's the idea for a book he always wanted to write. It's about a novelist who is obsessed — the kind of thing Stephen King does so well. In order to write a better book, a *great* book, he actually murders people to see what it's like. Welcome to the horrible mind of Nicholas Jenks."

# Chapter 81

This was why I had become a homicide detective. I rushed back to the office, my head whirling with how to get my hands on this lost book, when the next bombshell hit.

It was McBride.

"Are you sitting?" he asked, as if he were about to deliver the coup de grace. "Nicholas Jenks was here in Cleveland. The night of the Hall of Fame murders. The son of a bitch was here."

*Jenks had lied right to my face. He hadn't even blinked.*

It was now clear; the unidentifiable man

at the Hall of Fame had been him after all. He had no alibi.

McBride explained how his men had scoured the local hotels. Finally, they uncovered that Jenks had been at the Westin, and amazingly, he had registered under his own name. A desk clerk working there that night remembered him. She knew it the minute she saw Jenks — she was a fan.

My mind raced with the ramifications. This was all McBride needed. They had a prior relationship with the victim, a possible sighting at the scene. Now Jenks was placed in his town. He had even lied under questioning.

"Tomorrow, I'm going to the district attorney for an indictment," McBride announced. "As soon as we have it, I want you to pick Nicholas Jenks up."

The truth hit me like a sledgehammer. We could lose him to Cleveland. All the evidence, all those right hunches, wouldn't help us. Now we might only be able to tag on a concurrent life sentence at a second trial. The Brandts and the Weils, the DeGeorges and the Passeneaus would be crushed. *Mercer would go ballistic.*

I was left with an absolutely demoralizing

choice: Either pick Jenks up and hold him for McBride, or make our move now with less than an airtight case.

*I should run this up the ladder,* the voice sounded in my head.

But the voice in my heart said run it by the girls.

# Chapter 82

I got them together on an hour's notice.

"Cleveland's ready to indict," I told them. Then I dropped the bombshell about the book *Always a Bridesmaid.*

"You've got to find it," Jill declared. "It's the one link we can tie in to all three crimes. Given that it was unpublished, it's as good as exclusive knowledge of the killings. It might even parallel the actual crimes. You find that book, Lindsay, we put Jenks behind bars. Forever!"

"How? Joanna Wade mentioned a prior agent, and I went to see him. *Nada.* He said check out the office of copyrights. Where is that?"

Cindy shook her head. "Washington, I think."

"That'll take days, or more. We don't have days." I turned to Jill. "Maybe it's time for a search warrant. Blow in on Jenks. We need the gun and the book. And we need them now."

"We do that," Jill said nervously, "we might bungle this whole investigation."

"Jill, you want to lose him?"

"Anyone know about this yet?" she asked.

I shook my head. "Just the first team — you guys. But when Mercer finds out, he'll want to jump in with everything he has. Cameras, microphones, the FBI waiting in the wings."

"If we're wrong, Jenks'll sue our ass," Jill said. "I don't even want to think about it."

"And Cleveland'll be waiting," said Claire. "Make us look like a bunch of fools."

Finally, Jill sighed. "All right . . . I'm with you, Lindsay. If you can't think of another way."

I looked at all three of them to make certain we were unanimous. Suddenly, Cindy burst in. "Can you give me another twenty-four hours?"

I looked at her. "I don't know. Why?"

"Just until tomorrow. And I need Jenks's Social Security number."

I shook my head. "You heard what I said about McBride. Anyway, for what?"

She had that same look as the other night, when she burst into my apartment — holding the photo of Jenks and Kathy Kogut, the third bride. "Just give me until tomorrow morning."

Then she got up and left.

# Chapter 83

The following morning, Cindy sheepishly pushed open the glass doors leading to the office of the San Francisco Writers Guild. This felt a lot like the day at the Grand Hyatt. At the reception desk, a middle-aged woman with the punctilious look of a librarian looked up at her. "May I help you?"

Cindy took in a deep breath. "I need to find a manuscript. It was written quite a while ago."

The word *copyright* had set her off. She had written short stories in college. They were barely good enough to get into the school's literary journal, but her mother had insisted, *Get them copyrighted.* When she investigated, it turned out it took months and was way too costly. But a friend who had published told her about another way she could register documents locally. He told her, *All the writers do.* If Nicholas Jenks had wanted to protect himself in his salad days, he might've gone the same route.

"It's sort of a family thing," Cindy told the woman. "My brother wrote this history. Going back three generations. We don't have a copy."

The woman shook her head. "This isn't the library, hon. I'm afraid that whatever we have here is restricted. If you want to find it, you'll have to have your brother come in."

"I can't," Cindy said solemnly. "Nick is dead."

The woman softened, looked at her slightly less officiously. "I'm sorry."

"His wife said she can't locate a copy. I'd like to give it to our dad, a sixtieth-birthday present." She felt guilty, foolish, lying through her teeth like this, but everything was riding on getting this book.

"There's a *process* for all of this," the woman replied sanctimoniously. "Death certificate. Proof of next of kin. The family lawyer should be able to help you. I just can't go letting you in here."

Cindy's mind raced. This wasn't exactly Microsoft here. If she had found her way to the crime scene at the Grand Hyatt, tracked Lindsay to the second crime, she ought to be able to handle this. Everyone was counting on her.

"There must be a way you can let me take a look. Please?"

"I'm afraid not, dear. Not without some documentation. What makes you even think it's registered with us?"

"My sister-in-law is sure it is."

"Well, I can't just go giving out registered documents on someone's hunch," she said with finality.

"Maybe you can at least look it up," Cindy proposed. "To see if it's even here."

The dachshund-nosed defender of the free press finally relaxed. "I guess I can do that. You say it was several years ago?"

Cindy felt an adrenaline surge. "Yes."

"And the name?"

"I think it was called *Always a Bridesmaid.*" She felt a chill just saying the words.

"I meant the name of the author, please."

"Jenks," Cindy said, holding her breath. "Nicholas Jenks."

The woman peered at her. "The mystery writer?"

Cindy shook her head, faked a smile. "The insurance salesman," she said as calmly as she could.

The woman gave her a strange look but continued to punch in the name. "You have proof of relationship?"

Cindy handed her a piece of paper with Jenks's Social Security number on it. "This should be on his registration."

"That won't do," the woman said.

Cindy fumbled through a zipper in her knapsack. She felt the moment slipping away. "At least tell me if it's here. I'll come back later with whatever you want."

"Jenks," the woman muttered skeptically. "Looks like your brother was a bit more prolific than you thought. He's got *three* manuscripts registered here."

Cindy wanted to let out a shout. "The only one I'm looking for is called *Always a Bridesmaid.*"

It took what seemed like several minutes, but the stony resistance on the woman's face finally weakened. "I don't know why

I'm doing this, but if you can verify your story, there seems to be a record of that manuscript's being here."

Cindy felt a surge of validation. The manuscript was the final piece they needed to crack a murder case and put away Jenks.

Now she just had to get it out.

## Chapter 84

"I found it!" exclaimed Cindy, her voice breathless on the phone. *"Always a Bridesmaid!"*

I pounded my desk in elation. *This meant we could definitely make our move.* "So what does it say, Cindy?"

"I *found* it," Cindy clarified. "I just don't actually *have* it."

She told me about the Writers Guild. The book was there, but it would take a little coaxing to actually get it into our hands.

It took barely two hours — starting with a frantic call to Jill. She had a judge pulled out of chambers, and we had our court order mandating the release of Jenks's manuscript *Always a Bridesmaid.*

Then Jill and I ran down to meet Cindy. On the way, I made one more call. To Claire. It seemed fitting that *all* of us should be there.

Twenty minutes later, Jill and I met Cindy and Claire in front of a drab building on Geary where the Writers Guild maintained its offices. Together, we rode to the eighth floor.

"I'm back," announced Cindy to a surprised woman behind the reception desk. "And I brought my documentation."

She eyed us suspiciously. "Who are these, cousins?"

I flashed the clerk my badge and also presented the officially stamped search warrant.

"What's going on with this book?" the woman gasped. Clearly out of her authority, she went inside and came back with a supervisor, who read over the court order.

"We usually only hold them for up to eight years," he said with some uncertainty. Then he disappeared for what seemed a lifetime.

We all sat there in the stark reception area

like pacing relatives waiting for a baby to be born. *What if it had been thrown out?*

Finally, the supervisor came out with a dusty bundle wrapped in brown paper. "In the back of the bins," he announced with a self-satisfied smile.

There was a coffee shop right down the street. We took a table in back and crowded around with anticipation. I plopped the manuscript down on the table, peeled off the brown-paper wrapping.

I read the cover. *Always a Bridesmaid.* A novel by Nicholas Jenks.

Nervously, I opened it and read the first page.

The narrator was reflecting on his crimes from jail. His name was Phillip Campbell.

"What is the worst thing," the novel began, "anyone has ever done?"

# Chapter 85

We split up the book into four sections. We each paged silently, searching for some scene or detail that would parallel the real-life crimes.

Mine was about this guy's life, Phillip Campbell. His picture-perfect wife, catching her with another man. He killed them both — and his life changed forever.

"Bingo!" Jill spoke up suddenly. She read out loud, bending back the sheaf of paper like a deck of cards.

She described a scene with Phillip Campbell — "breath pounding inside, voices ringing in his head" — stealing through the halls of a hotel. The Grand Hyatt. A bride and groom in a suite. Campbell breaks in on them — he kills them without a second thought.

" 'In a single act," Jill read from the manuscript, "he had washed away the stench of betrayal and replaced it with a fresh, heretofore unimagined desire. He liked to kill.' "

Our eyes locked. This was beyond creepy. Jenks was crazy — but was he also crafty?

Claire was next. It was another wedding. This time outside a church. The bride and groom coming down the steps, rice being thrown, shouts of congratulations, applause. The same man, Phillip Campbell, at the wheel of the limo that will take them away.

We looked at one another, stunned. It was how the second murders were committed.

Jill murmured, "Holy shit."

Claire just shook her head. She looked sad and shocked. I guess we all were.

A long-suppressed cry of satisfaction built up in my chest. We had done it.

We had solved the bride and groom murders.

"I wonder how it ends?" Cindy mused, fanning to the end of the book.

"How else?" said Jill. *"With an arrest."*

# Chapter 86

I rode up to Jenks's house with Chris Raleigh. We barely spoke, both of us brimming with anticipation. Outside, we were met by Charlie Clapper and his CSU team. They would grid-search the house and grounds as soon as we took Jenks in.

We rang the bell. Each second I waited, my heart pounded harder. Every reason I became a cop was grinding in my chest. This was it.

The door opened, and the same housekeeper answered. This time, her eyes went wide as she took in the convergence of blue-and-whites outside.

I flashed my badge. "We need to see Mr. Jenks."

We made our way back toward the sitting room where we had met Jenks only the day before. A startled Chessy Jenks met us in the hall. "Inspector," she gasped, recognizing me. "What's going on? What are all those police cars doing out front?"

"I'm sorry," I said, meeting her eyes. I *was* sorry for her. "Is your husband at home?"

"Nick!" she cried, realizing in a panic why we had come. Then she ran along with us, trying to block me, shouting, "You can't just come in here like this. This is our home."

"Please, Mrs. Jenks," Raleigh implored.

I was too wound up to stop. I wanted Nicholas Jenks so bad it hurt. A second later he appeared, coming in from the back lawn overlooking the Pacific. He was holding a golf club.

"I thought I told you," he said, looking perfectly unruffled in his white shirt and linen shorts, "the next time you need something from me you should contact my lawyer."

"You can tell him yourself," I said. My heart was racing. "Nicholas Jenks, you are under arrest for the murders of David and

Melanie Brandt, Michael and Rebecca DeGeorge, James and Kathleen Voskuhl."

I wanted him to hear every name, to bring to mind every one of them he'd killed. I wanted to see the callous indifference crack in his eyes.

"This is insane." Jenks glared at me. His gray eyes burned with intensity.

"Nick?" cried his wife. "What are they talking about? Why are they here in our house?"

"Do you know what you're doing?" he asked, the veins bulging on his neck. "I asked you, *do you have any idea what you're doing?*"

I didn't answer, just recited the Miranda warning.

"What you're doing," he raged, "is engaging in the biggest mistake of your little life."

"What are they saying?" His wife was pale. "Nick, please tell me. What is going on?"

"Shut up," Jenks spat out at her. Suddenly, he spun back toward me with a vicious fire in his eyes. He lunged forward with his fist. He swung at me.

I cut his feet out from under him. Jenks fell across an end table to the floor, photos falling everywhere, glass shattering. The writer moaned loudly in pain.

Chessy Jenks screamed, stood there in a paralyzed state. Chris Raleigh cuffed her husband and dragged him to his feet.

"Call Sherman," Jenks shouted at his wife. "Tell him where I am, what's happened."

Raleigh and I pushed Jenks out to our car. He continued to struggle, and I saw no reason to be gentle.

"What's your theory on the murders now?" I asked him.

# Chapter 87

After the last news conference had ended, after the last flashbulb had dimmed, after I had rehashed for what seemed the hundredth time how we had narrowed in on Jenks, after a beaming Chief Mercer had been chauffeured away, I hugged Claire, Cindy, and Jill. I then passed on a celebratory beer and wandered back to the Hall of Justice.

It was well past eight, and only the prattle of the night shift interrupted my being alone.

I sat at my desk, in the well-earned silence of the squad room, and tried to re-member the last time I felt this *good.*

Tomorrow we would begin meticulously compiling the case against Nicholas Jenks: interrogating him, accumulating more evidence, filling out report after report. But we had done it. We had caught him just as I had hoped we eventually would. I had fulfilled the promise I made to Melanie Brandt that horrible night in the Mandarin Suite at the Grand Hyatt.

I felt proud of myself. Whatever happened with Negli's, even if I never made lieutenant, no one could take this away.

I got up, stepped over to the freestanding blackboard that listed the cases we were working on.

Under "Open Cases," somewhere near the top, was her name: Melanie Brandt. I took the eraser and rubbed her name, then her husband's, until they disappeared, until the blue smear of chalk was no more.

"I bet you that feels good," Raleigh's voice sounded behind me.

I turned. He was there, looking smug.

"What are you doing here?" I asked. "So late."

"Thought I'd straighten up Roth's desk,

steal a few brownie points," he said. "What do you think, Lindsay? I came to find you."

We were in a corner of the squad room, and there was no one around. He never had to move. I went to him. Nothing in the way. No reason to deny this.

I kissed him. Not like before. Not just to let Chris know I was interested. I kissed him the way I had wanted him to kiss me that night in Cleveland. I wanted to steal the breath right out of him. I wanted to say, *I wanted to do this from the first time I saw you.*

When we finally pulled apart, he repeated with a smile, "Like I said, I bet that feels good."

It *did* feel good. Right now, it *all* felt good. It also felt unavoidable.

"What're your plans?" I smiled at him.

"How loosely are we talking?"

"Specifically, right now. Tonight. The next several hours, at least."

"I thought I would come back, straighten Cheery's desk, and see if you wanted me to take you home."

"Let me get my purse."

# Chapter 88

I don't know how we got all the way to my apartment in the Potrero. I don't know how Chris and I talked and drove and ignored what was tearing at us inside.

Once we got through my door, there was no stopping it. I was all over Chris; he was all over me. We only got as far as the rug in the foyer, kissing, touching, fumbling for buttons and zippers, breathing loudly.

I had forgotten how good it was to be held, to be desired by somebody I wanted, too. Once we touched, we knew enough to take our time. We both wanted it to last.

Chris had what I needed more than anything else, *soft hands.*

I loved kissing him, loved his touch, his gentleness, then his roughness, the simple fact that he was concerned about my pleasure as much as his own. You never know until you try it out — but I loved being with Chris. I absolutely loved it.

I know it's a cliché, but that night I made love as if it might never happen again. I felt Chris's current, warming me, electrifying — from my womb to my thighs to the tips of my fingers and my toes. His grasp was all that held me together, kept me from breaking apart. I felt a trust for him that was unquestioning.

I held nothing back. I gave myself to Chris in a way I never had to anyone before. Not only with my body and my heart; these were things I could pull back. I gave him my hope that I could still live.

When I cried out, tremors exploding inside me, my fingers and toes stiff with joy, a voice inside me whispered what I knew was true.

*I gave him everything. He gave it back.*

Finally, Chris pulled off me. We were both tingling, still on fire.

"What?" I gasped for breath. "Now what?"

He looked at me and smiled. "I want to see the bedroom."

# Chapter 89

A cool breeze was blowing in my face. *Oh, God, what a night. What a day. What a roller coaster.*

I sat wrapped in a quilt out on my terrace, overlooking the south end of the bay. Nothing moving, only the lights of San Leandro in the distance. It was quarter of two.

In the bedroom, Chris lay asleep. He'd earned some rest.

I couldn't sleep. My body was too alive, tingling, like a distant shore with a thousand flickering lights.

I couldn't help but smile at the thought: It *had* been a great day. *"June twenty-sev-*

enth," I said aloud, *"I'm gonna remember you."* First we find the book. Then we arrest Jenks. I never imagined it could go any further.

But it had. It went *way* further. Chris and I had made love that night twice more, the last three hours a sweet dance of touching, panting, loving.

I didn't want to feel Chris's hands ever leave me. I didn't ever want to *miss* the heat of his body. It was a new, electrifying sensation. For once, I had held nothing back, and that was very, very good.

But here, in the dark of the night, an accusing voice needled me. *I was lying.* I hadn't given it all. There was the one inescapable truth that I was hiding.

I hadn't told him about Negli's. I didn't know how to. Just as we had felt such life, how could I tell him I might be dying. That my body, which a moment ago was so alive with passion, was infected. In a single day, it seemed that everything in my life was transformed. I wanted to soar. I deserved it. I deserved to be happy.

But he deserved to know.

I heard a rustling behind me. It was Chris. "What are you doing out here?" he asked.

He came up behind me, placed his hands on my neck and shoulders.

I was hugging my knees, the quilt barely covering my breasts. "It's gonna be hard," I said, leaning my head on him, "to go back to the way things were."

"Who said anything about going back?"

"I mean, like partners. Watching you across the room. Tomorrow we have to interrogate Jenks. Big day for both of us."

His fingers teased my breasts, then the back of my neck. He was driving me crazy. "You don't have to worry," he said. "Once the case is made, I'm going back. I'll stick around for the interrogation."

"Chris," I said, as a chill shot through me. I had gotten used to him.

"I told you we weren't going to be partners forever." He bent down, inhaling the smell of my hair. "At least not *that* kind of partners."

"What kind does that leave?" I murmured. My neck was on fire where his hands caressed me. *Oh, let this go somewhere, I begged inside. Let this go all the way to the moon.*

Could I just tell him? It was no longer that

I couldn't find a way. It was just, now that we were here, I didn't want it to end.

I let him take me into the bedroom.

"This keeps getting better and better," I whispered.

"Doesn't it? I can't wait to see what happens next."

## Chapter 90

I had just gotten to my desk the following morning. I was flipping the *Chronicle* to the continuation of Cindy's article on Jenks's arrest when my phone rang.

It was Charlie Clapper. His crime scene team had spent most of the night meticulously going over everything in Jenks's house.

"You make a case for me, Charlie?" I was hoping for a murder weapon, maybe even the missing rings. Something solid that would melt Jenks's sneering defiance.

The CSU leader let out a weary breath. "I think you should come down here and see."

I grabbed my purse and the keys to our

work car. In the hallway, I ran into Jacobi. "Rumors say," he grunted, "I'm no longer the man of your dreams."

"You know you should never believe what you read in the *Star,*" I quipped.

"Right, or hear from the night shift."

I pulled myself to a stop. Someone had spotted Chris and me last night. My mind flashed through the red-hot copy that was probably running through the office rumor mill. Behind my anger, I knew that I was blushing.

"Relax," Jacobi said. "You know what can happen when you get caught up in a good collar. And it *was* a good collar."

"Thank you, Warren," I said. It was one of those rare moments when neither of us had anything to hide. I winked and hit the stairs.

"Just remember," he called after me, "it was the champagne match that got you on your way."

"I remember. I'm grateful. Thank you, Warren."

I drove down Sixth to Taylor and California to Jenks's home in Sea Cliff. When I arrived, two police cars were blocking the street, keeping a circle of media vans at bay. I found Clapper — looking weary and unshaven — catching a brief rest at the dining room table.

"You find me a murder gun?" I asked.

"Just these." He pointed to a pile of guns in plastic bags on the floor.

There were hunting rifles, a showcase Minelli shotgun, a Colt automatic .45 pistol. No nine millimeter. I didn't make a move to examine them.

"We went through his office," Clapper wheezed. "Nothing on any of the victims. No clippings, no trophies."

"I was hoping you might've come across the missing rings."

"You want rings?" Clapper said. He wearily pushed himself up. "His wife's got rings. Plenty of them. I'll let you go through them. But what we did find was this. Follow me."

On the floor of the kitchen, with a yellow "Evidence" marker on it, was a crate of wine, champagne. *Krug. Clos du Mesnil.*

"That we already knew," I said.

He kept looking at me, as if I had somehow insulted him with the obvious. Then he lifted a bottle out of the open case.

"Check the numbers, Lindsay. Each bottle's registered with a number. Look here, four-two-three-five-five-nine. Must make it go down all the more smoothly." He took out a folded-up green copy of a "Police Property" voucher from his chest pocket. "The one from the Hyatt. Same lot. Same number." Charlie smiled.

The bottles *were* the same. It was solid evidence that tied Jenks to where David and Melanie Brandt were killed. It wasn't a weapon, but it was damning, no longer circumstantial. A rush of excitement shot through me. I high-fived the pale, heavy-set CSU man.

"Anyway," Charlie said, almost apologetically, "I wouldn't have brought you all the way out here for just *that.*"

Clapper led me through the finely furnished interior of the house to the master bedroom. It had a vast picture window looking out on the Golden Gate Bridge. He took me into a spacious closet. *Jenks's.*

"You remember the bloody jacket we found at the hotel?" In the rear of the closet, Charlie squatted over a large shoe rack. "Well, now it's a set."

Clapper reached behind the shoe rack

and pulled out a crumpled Nordstrom's shopping bag. "I wanted you to see how we found it."

Out of the bag, he pulled balled-up black tuxedo trousers.

"I already checked. It's the other half of the jacket at the Hyatt. Same maker. Look inside; same style number."

I might as well have been staring at a million dollars in cash, or a ton of stolen cocaine. I couldn't take my eyes off the pants, imagining how Nicholas Jenks would squirm now. Claire had been right. She'd been right from the start. The jacket hadn't come off the victim. It had always belonged to Jenks.

"So whaddaya think, Inspector?" Charlie Clapper grinned. "Can you close your case or what? Oh, yeah," the CSU man exclaimed, almost absentmindedly. "Where'd I put it?"

He patted his pockets, searched around in his jacket. He finally found a small plastic bag.

"Straight out of the sucker's electric razor," Charlie announced.

In the bag were several short red hairs.

# Chapter 91

Claire said, "I've been expecting you, honey." She took my arm and led me back into the lab to a small room lined with chemicals. Two microscopes were set up side by side on a granite-block counter.

"Charlie told me what he came up with," she said. "The champagne. Matching pantalones. You got him, Lindsay."

"Match these" — I held out the plastic bag — "we put him in the gas chamber."

"Okay, let's see," she said, smiling. She opened a yellow envelope marked "Priority, Evidence," and took out a petri dish identical to the one I had seen after the second murders. It had *Subject: Rebecca DeGeorge, #62340* written on the front in bold marker.

With a tweezer, she placed the single hair that had come from the second bride onto a clear slide. Then she inserted it under the scope. She leaned over it, adjusting the focus, then caught me by surprise, asking, "So how're you feeling, woman?"

"You mean Negli's?"

"What else would I mean?" she said, peering into the scope.

In the rush of apprehending Jenks, it was the first time in the past few days that I had really thought about it. "I saw Medved late last week. My blood count's still down."

Claire finally looked up. "I'm sorry, Lindsay."

Trying to sound upbeat, I walked her through my regimen. The increased dosage. The higher frequency. I mentioned the possibility of a bone marrow transplant.

She flashed me a big smile. "We're gonna have to find a way to get those red cells of yours shaken up."

Even in the laboratory, I must've started to blush.

"What?" asked Claire. "What're you hiding? Trying unsuccessfully to hide?"

"Nothing."

"*Something's* going on. Between you and Mr. Chris Raleigh, I bet. C'mon, this is *me* you're talking to. You can't pull that blue-wall-of-silence stuff."

I told her. From the first kiss at the precinct to the slow, torturous ride home to the burst of heat right there on the hallway rug.

Claire grasped me by my shoulders. Her eyes were as bright and excited as mine. "So?"

"*So?*" I laughed. "*So* . . . it was awesome. It was . . . *right.*" I felt a chill of doubt come over me. "I just don't know if I'm doing the right thing. Considering what's going on." I hesitated. "I could love him, Claire. Maybe I already do."

We stared at each other. There wasn't much more to say.

"Well." Claire's eyes returned to her microscope. "Let's see what we have here. Hairs from his chinny-chin-chin."

Three hairs from Jenks's razor were set on a cellular slide. She loaded it into a scope. The two scopes were side by side.

Claire looked first, leaned over as she focused the new one in. Then she went back and forth. "Mm-hmm," she uttered.

I held my breath. "What do you think?" I asked.

"You tell me."

I leaned in. Immediately, I recognized the first hair, the one from inside Rebecca De-George's vagina. Thick, reddish, a white filament twisted around its base like the coil of a snake.

Then I looked at the hairs from Jenks's razor. There were three of them, shorter, clipped, but each had that same reddish hue, that same coil of filament around it.

I was no expert. But there was no doubt in my mind.

*The hairs were a perfect match.*

# Chapter 92

Nicholas Jenks was in a holding cell on the tenth floor of the Hall of Justice. He was headed to arraignment later today.

His lawyer, Sherman Leff, was with him, looking as if this were all just a formality and the scales of justice were resting on the shoulders of his English-tailored suit.

Jill Bernhardt accompanied Raleigh and me. Jenks had no idea what was coming his way. We had the champagne, the tuxedo pants, matching hairs from his beard. We had him in the suite with David and Melanie

Brandt. I couldn't wait to tell him all the good news.

I sat down across from Jenks and looked him in the eye. "This is Assistant District Attorney Jill Bernhardt," I said. "She's going to be handling your case. She's going to convict you, too."

He smiled — the same, gracious, confident, and condescending glint — as if he were receiving us in his home. *Why* does he look so confident? I wondered.

"If it's all right," Jill said, "I'd like to begin."

"Your meeting," Sherman Leff said. "I've no objection."

Jill took a breath. "Mr. Jenks, in an hour you are going to be arraigned for the first-degree murder of David and Melanie Brandt at the Grand Hyatt hotel on June fifth. Shortly after, I believe a Cleveland court will do the same for the murders of James and Kathleen Voskuhl. Based on what the medical examiner has just uncovered, I believe you can expect a Napa Valley court to follow through as well. We have overwhelming evidence linking you to all three of these crimes. We're sharing this with you, and with your counsel, in the hope that your response to this evidence might spare the city, the families of the deceased, and your family the further humiliation of a trial."

Sherman Leff finally cut in. "Thank you, Ms. Bernhardt. As long as consideration is the spirit of the day, we'd like to begin by expressing my client's deep regret for his emotional outburst toward Inspector Boxer at the time of his arrest. As you might imagine, the shock and the suddenness of such an accusation, so totally preposterous after he had fully complied with your questioning . . . in his own home . . . I'm certain you can understand how the wrong emotions might take hold."

"I do deeply regret that, Inspector," Jenks spoke up. "I realize how this must look. My being less than forthcoming about my relationship with one of the deceased. And now you seem to have stumbled upon that unfortunate book."

"Which," Leff interjected, "I must advise you, we will be making a motion to suppress. Obtaining it was an unjustified intrusion into my client's private domain."

"The warrant was totally justified," Jill said calmly.

"On what grounds?"

"On the grounds that your client gave

false testimony concerning his whereabouts when Kathy Voskuhl was killed."

Leff hung in midmotion, stunned.

"Your client *was* in Cleveland, Counselor," I sprang on him. Then I said to Jenks, "You were registered at the Westin. You stayed two nights, coinciding with the Voskuhl murders. You said you were at home, Mr. Jenks. But you were *there.* And you were at the Hall of Fame."

Jenks's smile disappeared and his eyes flicked around the room. He swallowed, and I could see the knot sliding down his throat. He was retracing his alibis and lies. He looked at Leff, somewhat apologetically.

"I *was* there," he admitted. "I *did* conceal it. As it happens, I was in town to address a local readers group. You can check. The Argosy Bookstore. I didn't know how to explain it. Coupled with knowing Kathy, it seemed so incriminating. But let me make this clear. You're wrong about the wedding. I was nowhere near it."

My blood rose. I couldn't believe this guy. "You had a reading? *When,* Mr. Jenks?"

"Saturday afternoon. At four. A small group of very loyal fans. The Argosy was very kind to me when I first started out."

"And after that?"

"After that I did what I always do. I stayed at the hotel and wrote. I took a swim, had an early dinner. You can ask my wife. I always spend the evenings alone when I'm on the road. It's been written up in *People* magazine."

I leaned across the table. "So this was all some bizarre coincidence, right? A woman with whom you've denied having a sexual relationship is brutally murdered. You just happen to be in town. You just happen to lie about the relationship and about being there. Your likeness just happens to be caught by a security camera at the scene. Is that how it goes, Mr. Jenks?"

Leff placed a cautionary hand on Jenks's arm.

*"No!"* His client snapped, his self-control clearly chipping away.

Then he became calmer and wiped the sweat off his brow. "I lied . . . for Chessy . . . to preserve my marriage." He straightened himself up in the wooden chair. His alibi was collapsing. "I'm not a perfect man, Inspector. I slip. I deceived you about Kathy. It was wrong. The answer is *yes*. What you assume to be true *is* true. We *were* lovers on and off for five years. It continued . . . well into her relationship with James. It was folly. It was the desperate thrill of a fool. But it was *not* murder. I did not kill Kathy. And I did not kill the others!"

Jenks stood up. For the first time, he looked scared. The reality of what was happening was clearly sinking in.

I leaned forward and said, "A bottle of champagne was left in the suite at the Hyatt where the Brandts were killed. It matched the same lot you purchased at an auction at Butterfield and Butterfield in November nineteen ninety-six."

Leff objected, "We know that. Surely the unfortunate coincidence of my client's taste in champagne doesn't implicate him in this act. He didn't even know the Brandts. That wine could have been purchased anywhere."

"It could've, yes; however, the registration number on the bottle from the Hyatt matched those from the rest of the lot we uncovered at your home last night."

"This is getting absurd," Jenks said angrily. "This sort of bullshit wouldn't even make one of my books."

"Hopefully this will be better, then." From

under the table, I pulled out the Nordstrom's shopping bag holding the balled-up tuxedo pants. I tossed them onto the table in front of everybody. "You recognize these?"

"Pants . . . What kinds of games are we playing now?"

"These were found last night. In this bag. In the back of your bedroom closet."

"So? What're you saying, they're mine? Joseph Abboud. They could be. I don't understand where you're going."

"Where I'm going is that these pants match the tuxedo jacket that was found in the Brandts' suite. They're a suit, Mr. Jenks."

"A suit?"

"It's the pants to the jacket you left in their hotel room. Same brand. Same style number. Same size."

A deepening panic began to sweep over his face.

"And if all this *still* falls short of your usual material," I said, fixing on his eyes, "then how's this. *The hair matched.* The hair you left inside Becky DeGeorge. With hairs taken from your house. It belonged to you, you animal. You convicted yourself."

Jill leaned forward. "You're going away,

Jenks. You're going away until the appeals finally run out and they come to stick a loaded needle in your arm."

"This is insane," he cried. He was leaning over me, veins in his neck swelling, shouting in my face, "You bitch. You're setting me up. You fucking ice bitch. I didn't kill anyone."

Suddenly, I found that I couldn't move. Seeing Jenks unwind was one thing. But there was something else going on. I felt pinned to my chair.

I *knew,* but I couldn't fight it — Negli's.

I finally got up and went to the door, but my head swirled and the room tilted. My legs began to buckle. *Not here,* I begged.

Then I felt Raleigh supporting me. "Lindsay . . . you all right?" He was looking at me, worried, unsuspecting. I saw Jill there, too.

"You all right, Lindsay?"

I leaned against the wall. I willed my legs to work. "I'm okay." I whispered, holding on to Raleigh's arm.

"I just hate that bastard," I said, and walked out of the interrogation room. I was very weak, swaying. I barely made it to the ladies' room.

I felt faint, then nauseated, as if some angry spirit were trying to claw out of my lungs. I closed my eyes, leaned over the sink.

I coughed, a raw, burning stinging in my chest, then I shook and coughed some more.

Gradually, I felt the spell recede. I took a breath, opened my eyes.

I shuddered.

There was blood all over the sink.

# Chapter 93

Four hours later, in District Criminal Court, I felt well enough to watch Nicholas Jenks be arraigned for murder.

A buzzing crowd filled the halls outside the courtroom of Judge Stephen Bowen. Photographers flashed cameras blindly, reporters surged for a glimpse of the sullen, shaken bestselling writer.

Raleigh and I squeezed through, took a seat behind Jill in the front row. My strength having returned, the riot in my chest subsided. *I wanted Jenks to see me there.*

I saw Cindy, sitting in the press section.

And in the back of the courtroom, I spotted Chancellor Weil and his wife.

It was over before it began. Jenks was led in, his eyes as dead and hollow as craters on the moon. The clerk read the docket, the suspect rose. The bastard pleaded Not Guilty. What were they going to argue, that all the evidence was inadmissible?

Leff, the consummate showman, was unusually respectful, even demure before Judge Bowen. He made a pleading case for release on recognizance based on Jenks's stature in the community. For a moment, the killer's accomplishments almost even swayed me.

Jill fought him head-on. She graphically detailed the savagery of the murders. She argued that the suspect had the means and the lack of roots to flee.

I felt a surge of triumph rippling through me when the judge struck his gavel and intoned, "Bail denied."

# Chapter 94

Now we were celebrating.

It was the end of the day, a day I had long waited for, and I met the girls for a drink at Susie's.

We had earned this. Nicholas Jenks had been arraigned. No bail. No consideration of the court. The four of us had pulled it off.

"Here's to the Women's Murder Club," Cindy cheered, with her beer mug in the air.

"Not bad for a collection of gender-impaired public servants," Claire agreed.

"What did Jenks call me?" I shook my head and smiled. "A fucking ice bitch?"

"I can do ice bitch," Jill said, grinning.

"To the ice bitches of the world," Cindy toasted, "and the men who cannot thaw us out."

"Speak for yourself," said Claire. "Edmund thaws me just fine." We all laughed and clinked beers.

"Still," I said, letting out a deep breath, "I'd like to turn up a murder weapon. And I want to nail him to the second crime."

"When I'm through with him," Jill tugged at her beer and said, "you won't have to worry about him serving time for the second crime."

"You see Jill chop down his lawyer's bail request?" Cindy said with admiration. "You see the look on his face?" She made her fingers into a scissors. *"Snip, snip, snip, snip, snip.* Straight for the testicles. That man was left standing there in his suit with a two-inch dick."

We all laughed. Cindy's cherubic nose twisted as she said, *Snip, snip, snip.*

"Still," I said, "without a weapon, his motive still needs work."

"Damn his motive, child!" Claire exclaimed. "Let well enough alone."

Jill agreed. "Why can't his motive simply be that he's a sick bastard? He's had a his-

tory of sexual sadism for years. He's brutal-
ized three women that we know of. I'm sure
more will come out as the trial moves on.

"You saw the bastard, Lindsay," she went
on. "He's crazed. His little perfect world
gets rocked, he goes insane. This morning,
he looked like he was about to plant a death
grip on your throat." She grinned toward the
group. "Lindsay just sort of glares up at him
like, *Get the fuck out of my face.*"

They were about to raise a glass to me —
the tough hero cop who would always carry
the tag that she was the one who nailed
Jenks — when the realization shot through
me that I could never have done it without
them. It wasn't my steel nerves that had
taken over in the interrogation room, but the
grip of my disease squeezing my energy. I
had kept it concealed — never shared —
even with the ones who had become my
closest friends.

"That wasn't about Jenks," I said.

"Sure seemed like it."

"I don't mean the confrontation. I mean
what happened after." I paused. "When I almost collapsed. That wasn't about Jenks."

They were still smiling, except Claire, but

one by one the gravity in my eyes alerted them.

I looked around the table and told them about the Pac Man–like disease that was eating my red blood cells, and that I'd been fighting it for three weeks now. Packed–red cell transfusions. My blood count was deteriorating. I was getting worse.

I started strong, my voice firm, because it'd been part of my life for several weeks now, but when I finished, I was speaking in a hushed, scared tone. I was blinking back tears.

Jill and Cindy just sat there, rocked in disbelieving silence.

Then, there were three hands reaching out for me. Cindy's, Jill's, then last and warmest, Claire's. For a long time no one said anything. They didn't have to.

Finally, I smiled, choking back tears. "Isn't it just like a cop to go and shut down a party just when it's going good."

It broke the tension, cut through the sudden pall.

They never said, *We're with you.* They never told me, *You're gonna be all right.* They didn't have to.

"We're supposed to be celebrating," I said.

Then I heard Jill's voice, out of the blue, solemn, confessing.

"When I was a little girl, I was real sick. I was in a brace and hospitals between the ages of four and seven. It broke my parents, their marriage. They split up as soon as I got better. I guess that's why I always felt I had to be stronger and better than anyone else. Why I always had to win.

"It started in high school," Jill went on.

I wasn't sure what she was referring to.

"I didn't know if I would be good enough. I used to . . ." She unbuttoned the cuffs of her blouse, rolled the sleeves up over her elbows. "I've never showed these to anybody except Steve."

Her arms were marked with scars. I knew what they were — self-inflicted slashes. Jill had been a cutter.

"What I meant to say was, you just have to fight it. You fight it, and fight it, and fight it . . . and every time you feel it getting stronger, you fight it some more."

"I'm trying," I whispered, my voice choking. "I really am trying." Now I knew what propelled her, what was behind that icy gaze. "But how?"

Jill's hands were holding mine. There were tears in both our eyes.

"It's like with Jenks, Lindsay," she said. "You just don't let it win."

# Chapter 95

In the cold, cramped cell, Nicholas Jenks paced anxiously.

He felt as if dynamite were about to explode at the center of his chest. He hadn't done anything. How could they destroy his name, attack him with those wild fictions, disgrace him all over the news?

It was dark and he was freezing. The cot in his jail cell wasn't fit for a monk. He was still in the damp clothes they had brought him in. A cold, unrepentant sweat began to break out on his palms.

He'd make the little inspector-bitch pay.

*One way or another, he'd get her in the end.*
That was a promise.

*What was his fucking poodle of a lawyer doing? When would Leff get him out of there?*

*It was as if all reason had been sucked out of his world.*

*What the hell was going on?*

Or at least, Phillip Campbell thought, that's what Jenks *ought* to be feeling. What he *thought* the bastard would be saying in his mind.

Campbell sat in front of the mirror. *Time for you to go away. Your work is finally done. The last chapter's been written.*

He dabbed a wet cloth in a bowl of warm water.

It was the last time he would ever have to play the part.

*So how does it feel, Nicholas?*

He pulled out the pins that held his hair and let his locks shake out.

*How does it feel to be a victim, a prisoner? To feel the same degradation and shame you cast on others?*

Slowly, he wiped the dark makeup off his eyes, dabbing with the cloth, feeling a sheen begin to return to his face.

*How does it feel to be helpless and alone? To be kept in a dark space? To feel betrayed?*

One by one, Phillip Campbell tugged at the hairs of the reddish beard on his chin, until they came out and a new person was revealed.

*Not able to recognize in the mirror the person you once were?*

Scrubbing the face until it came out clean and smooth. Unbuttoning the shirt, Nicholas's shirt, and soon, from underneath a bodysuit, a well-defined woman's body came to life: the outline of breasts, shapely legs, arms rippling with lean strength.

She sat there, newly revealed, a bright glow in her eyes.

*This is rich.*

*How does it feel, Nicholas, to be royally fucked? The tables turned for once.*

She couldn't restrain the thought that it was fitting and funny that in the end he had been trapped by his own twisted mind. It was more than funny. It was absolutely brilliant.

*Who's laughing now, Nick?*

# Book Four

## THE WHOLE TRUTH

# Chapter 96

The night following Jenks's arraignment, Chief Mercer had gotten the skybox at Pac-Bell from one of his wealthy buddies. He invited several of us, including me, Raleigh, and Cheery, to a Giants game. It was a warm summer evening. They were playing the Cards. My father would have loved it.

I didn't really want to go, didn't want to feel on display as the cop who'd caught Jenks, but Mercer pressed.

And it was Mark McGwire and all, so I put on a windbreaker and went along for the ride.

All evening long, Chris and I kept sneaking looks at each other. There was a special energy in the box, a glowing ring around just him and me.

The game was background noise. In the third, Mighty Mac hit one off Ortiz that went out of sight and almost landed in the bay. The stadium cheered wildly, even for a Card. In the fourth, Barry Bonds tied it with a shot of his own.

Chris and I couldn't stop watching each other. We had our legs up on the same chair, like schoolkids, and every once in a while our calves brushed together. *Jesus, this was better than the ball game.*

Finally, he winked at me. "Want something to drink?" he said.

He went over to the bowl of drinks, which was elevated from the seats, and I followed. The others didn't look back. As soon as we were out of sight, he placed his hands on my thighs and kissed me. I felt on fire. "You want to hang around?"

"Still beer left," I joked.

His hand brushed against the side of my breast, and I felt a tremor. *Soft hands.* My breath quickened. A flicker of sweat broke through on my neck.

Chris kissed me again. He drew me in

close, and I felt the cadence of a heart pounding between us. I didn't know if it was his or mine.

"Can't wait," he said.

"Okay, let's get out of here."

"No." He shook his head. "I meant I *can't* wait."

"Oh, Jesus." I sighed. I couldn't hold back. My whole body was heating up to the boiling point. I glanced down at Cheery and Mercer and the two Mill Valley types. *This is crazy, Lindsay.*

But everything lately was crazy, everything speeding out of control.

It seemed as if every natural force in the universe was driving Chris and me to find a secluded spot. There was a bathroom in the skybox, barely large enough to put on makeup in. We didn't care.

Chris led me into the bathroom while the baseball crowd roared at something. We could barely squeeze in. *Jesus,* I could not believe I was doing this here. He unbuttoned my blouse, I unfastened his belt. Our thighs were pressed tightly together.

Gently, Chris lifted me onto him. I felt as if a shooting star had exploded in my veins. Chris was up against the counter; I was in the palms of his hands; we were squeezed into this tiny space, but we were in a perfect rhythm.

A crowd roar echoed in from outside: Maybe McGwire had hit another, maybe Bonds had robbed him — who cared. We kept rocking, Chris and I. I couldn't breathe. My body was slick with sweat. I couldn't stop. Chris kept it going, I gripped on tight, and in a moment we both gasped.

*Two hero cops,* I thought.

It was the best, the freest, the most excited I had ever felt. Chris rested his forehead on my shoulder. I kissed his cheek, his neck.

Then the strangest thought took hold of me. I began to laugh, a mixture of laughter and exhausted sighs. We were pinned there, spent, a few feet from my boss. I was giggling like a damn fool. I was going to get us caught!

"What's so funny?" Chris whispered.

I was thinking of Claire and Cindy. And what we had just done.

"I think I just made the list," I said.

# Chapter 97

The next day, Jenks asked to meet again. Jill and I went to see him on the tenth floor. We wondered what was up.

This time, there was no cat and mouse, no bullshit at all. Leff was there, but he rose, *humbly,* as soon as we came in.

Jenks looked far less threatening in his gray prison garb. The worried look on his face was a clear message.

"My client wants to make a statement," Leff announced as soon as we sat down.

I was thinking, This is it. He wants to make a deal. He's seen how ridiculous it is to play this game.

But he came out with something unexpected.

"I'm being framed!" Jenks announced angrily.

It took about a half second for Jill's glance to bump into mine.

"I have to hear this again," she said. "What's going on?" She looked at Jenks, then at Leff.

"We've got your client tied to all three crime scenes; we've got him in Cleveland at the time of the last murder; we've got him lying about a prior relationship with Kathy Kogut, one of the last victims; we've got his book detailing an astonishingly similar criminal pattern; we've got his facial hairs matched to one found in another victim's vagina. And you're claiming he's being framed?"

"What I'm claiming," Jenks said, ashen faced, "is that I'm being *set up.*"

"Listen, Mr. Jenks," Jill said, still looking at Leff, "I've been doing this eight years. I've built cases on hundreds of criminals, put over fifty murderers behind bars myself. I've never seen such a preponderance of evidence implicating a suspect. Our case is so airtight it can't breathe."

"I realize that." Jenks sighed. "And that I've given you every reason to find my plea implausible. I've lied about being in Cleveland, my relationship with Kathy. On the others, I can't even account for my whereabouts. But I also know setups. I've mapped out more of them than anybody. I'm a master at this. And I assure you, someone is setting me up."

I shook my head with disbelief. "Who, Mr. Jenks?"

Jenks sucked in a long breath. He actually looked scared. "I don't know."

"Someone hates you enough to set all this up?" Jill couldn't hold back a snicker. "The little I know of you, I might buy that." She turned to Leff. "You looking forward to presenting this case?"

"Just hear him out, Ms. Bernhardt," the lawyer pleaded.

"Look," Jenks said, "I know what you think of me. I'm guilty of many things. Selfishness, cruelty, adultery. I have a temper; sometimes I can't hold it in. And with women . . . you can probably line up a dozen of them who would help put me away for these murders. But clear as that is, I did not kill these people. Any of them. Someone is trying to set me up. That's the truth. Someone has done a brilliant job."

# Chapter 98

"You buy any of that shit?" Jill smirked at me as we waited for the elevator outside Jenks's holding cell.

"I might buy that he somehow believes it," I told her.

"Give me a break. He'd be better off going for insanity. If Nicholas Jenks wants to narrow down a list of people who might want to set him up, he might as well start with anyone he ever fucked."

I laughed, agreeing that the list would be long. Then the elevator door opened and, to my surprise, out walked Chessy Jenks. She was dressed in a long, taupe summer dress. I immediately noticed how pretty she was.

Our eyes met in an awkward, silent moment. I had just arrested her husband. My crime-scene team had ripped apart her house. She would have every reason to look at me with complete disdain — but she didn't.

"I'm here to see my husband," she said in a shaky voice.

I stiffly introduced her to Jill, then I pointed her to the visiting area. At that moment, she seemed about as alone and confused as anyone I had ever seen.

"Sherman tells me there's a lot of evidence," she said.

I nodded politely. I don't know why I felt something for her, other than she seemed a young, vulnerable woman whose fate had been to fall in love with a monster.

"Nick didn't do this, Inspector," Chessy Jenks said.

Her outburst surprised me. "It's only natural for a wife to want to defend her husband," I acknowledged. "If you have some concrete alibi . . ."

She shook her head. "No alibi. Only that I know my husband."

The elevator door had closed, and Jill and I stood there waiting again. As in hospitals, it would take minutes for it to go down and come back up. Chessy Jenks didn't make a move to walk away.

"My husband's not a simple man. He can be very tough. I know he's made enemies. I know how he came at you. From the outside, it must be very hard to believe this, but there are times when he's also capable of tenderness, incredible generosity, and love."

"I don't mean to sound unsympathetic, Ms. Jenks," Jill stepped in, "but under the circumstances you really shouldn't be talking with us."

"I have nothing to hide," she came back. Then she looked downcast. "I already know what you know."

I was dumbfounded. *I already know what you know?*

"I spoke with Joanna," Chessy Jenks continued. "She told me you'd been by. I know what she told you about him. She's bitter. She's got every right to be. But she doesn't know Nick like I do."

"You should review the evidence, Ms. Jenks," I told her.

She shook her head. "Guns . . . maybe, Inspector. If that's all there was. But a knife. That first murder. Slicing that poor couple to bits. Nick can't even fillet a fish."

My first thought was that she was young and deluded. How had Jenks described it? *Impressionable* . . . but something struck me as curious. "You said that you and Joanna talk?"

"We have. A lot more in the past year. I've even had her over. When Nick was away, of course. I know she was bitter after the divorce. I know he hurt her. But it's sort of our own support group."

"Your husband knew about this?" I asked.

She forced a smile. "He didn't even mind. He still likes Joanna. And, Inspector, she's still in love with him."

The elevator returned and we said goodbye. As the door closed, I looked at Jill. Her eyes were wide and her tongue was puffing out her cheek.

"Whole fucking family gives me the creeps," she said with a shudder.

# Chapter 99

I knew it the minute Medved walked in the office. I saw it in his face. He didn't have to say a word.

"I'm afraid I can't be very positive, Lindsay," he said, meeting my eyes. "Your red count continues to decline. The dizzy spells, the fatigue, blood in your chest. The disease is progressing."

"Progressing?"

Medved nodded soberly. "Stage three."

The words thundered in my head, bringing with them the fear of the increased treatments I dreaded. "What's the next step?" I asked weakly.

"We can give it one more month," Medved said. "Your count's twenty-four hundred. If it continues to decline, your strength will start to go. You'll have to be hospitalized."

I could hardly comprehend what he was saying; it was all crashing in my brain so fast. *A month. That's too close. Too fast.* Things were just starting to work out now that Jenks had been arrested. Everything else, everything I wanted to hold on to, was resolving, too.

*A month — four lousy weeks.*

When I got back to the office, a few of the guys were standing around grinning at me. There was a beautiful bouquet of flowers on my desk. Wildflowers.

I smelled them, taking in the sweet, natural scent. I read the card. *There's a hill of these where I have a cabin up at Heavenly. Tomorrow's Friday. Take the day off. Let's go there.*

It was signed *Chris.*

It sounded like what I needed. The mountains. Chris. I would have to tell him, now that the truth would come clear soon.

My phone rang. It was Chris. "So?" No

doubt someone in the office, playing cupid, had alerted him that I was back.

"Haven't opened your card yet." I bit my lip. "Too many others to sort through."

I heard a disappointed sigh, let it linger just a moment. "But on the chance you were asking me away, the answer is, I'd love to. It sounds great. Let's be on the road by eight."

"Late riser," he said. "I was hoping we'd beat the morning rush."

"I was talking *tonight*."

I had a month. I was thinking, *Mountain air, running streams, and wildflowers is a good way to begin.*

# Chapter 100

We spent the next two days as if we were in a beautiful dream.

Chris's cabin was funky and charming, a redwood A-frame ski chalet on Mason Ridge overlooking Heavenly. We hiked in the woods with Sweet Martha, took the tram to the top of the mountain, and walked all the way down. We grilled swordfish on the deck.

In between, we made love in the comfort of his large four-poster bed, on the sheepskin rug in front of the wood-burning stove, in the chilly thrill of the outdoor shower. We laughed and played and touched each other like teenagers, discovering love again.

But I was no starry-eyed adolescent. I knew exactly what was taking place. I felt the steady, undeniable current rising inside me like a river spilling over its banks. I felt helpless.

Saturday, Chris promised me a day I would never forget.

We drove down to Lake Tahoe, to a quaint marina on the California side. He had rented a platform boat, an old puttering wooden barge. We bought sandwiches and a bottle of chardonnay, and went out to the middle of the lake. The water calm and turquoise, the sky cloudless and bright. All around, the rocky tips of snow-capped mountains ringed the lake like a crown.

We moored, and for a while it was our own private world. Chris and I stripped down to our suits. I figured we'd kick back, enjoy the wine in the sun, look at the view, but Chris had sort of an expectant, dare-you look in his eye. He ran his hands through the frigid water.

"No way," I said, shaking my head. "It's got to be fifty degrees."

"Yeah, but it's a dry cold," he teased.

"Right," I chortled. "You go, then. Catch me a coho if you see one swim by."

He came toward me with playful menace in his eyes. "You can catch one yourself."

"Not a chance." I shook my head in defiance. But I was laughing, too. As he stepped forward, I backed to the rear of the craft until I ran out of room.

He put his arms around me. I felt the tingle of his skin on mine. "It's sort of an initiation," he said.

"An initiation for what?"

"Exclusive club. Anyone who wants to be in it has to jump in."

"Then leave me out." I laughed, squirming in his strong arms. With only weak resistance, he yanked me up on the cushion seat in the stern of the boat.

"Shit, Chris," I cried as he took hold of my hand.

"*Geronimo* works better," he said, pulling at me. I screamed, *"You bastard!"* and we toppled in.

The water was freezing, a total, invigorating rush. We hit the surface together, and I screamed in his face, *"Goddamn you!"* Then he kissed me in the water and all at once I felt no chill. I held on to him, at first for warmth, but also because I never wanted to let him go. I felt a trust for him that was so complete it was almost scary. *Fifty degrees,* but I was burning up.

"Check this out," I dared him, kicking free of his grasp. There was an orange boat marker bobbing fifty yards away. "Race you to that buoy." Then I cut out, surprising him with my speed.

Chris tried to keep up with steady, muscular strokes, but I blew him away.

Near the buoy I slowed, waited for him to catch up.

Chris looked totally confounded. "Where'd you learn to swim?"

"South San Francisco YMCA; fourteen-, fifteen-, sixteen-year-old division champ." I laughed. "No one could keep up. Looks like I still have it."

Moments later, we had guided the boat to a private, shady cove near the shore. Chris cut the engine and put up a canvas shade around the cabin that was supposed to protect us from the sun. With bated breath, we crept inside, blocked off from anyone's view.

I let him slowly unfasten my bathing suit, and he licked beads of water off my arms

and breasts. Then I kneeled down and unbuttoned his shorts. We didn't have to
speak. Our bodies were saying everything. I
lay back, pulling Chris onto me.

I had never felt so connected to another
person, or to a place. I arched against him
silently, the lake lapping gently at our sides.
I thought, *If I speak, it will change everything.*

Afterward I just lay there, tremors of
warmth radiating through my body. I never
wanted this to end, but I knew that it had to
end. Reality always gets in the way, doesn't
it?

# Chapter 101

Sometime that evening, I found myself starting to cry.

I had made spaghetti carbonara, and we ate in the moonlight on the deck with a bottle of pinot noir. Chris put a cello concerto by Dvořák on the stereo, but eventually we switched to the Dixie Chicks.

As we ate, Chris asked about where and how I had grown up.

I told him about my mom, and how my dad had left when I was just a kid; how she had worked as a bookkeeper at the Emporium for twenty years. How I had practically raised my sister.

"Mom died of breast cancer when she was only fifty." The irony of this certainly wasn't lost on me.

"What about your father? I want to know everything about you."

I took a sip of wine, then told him how I'd only seen him twice since I was thirteen. At my mother's funeral. And the day I became a cop. "He sat in the back, apart from everybody else." Suddenly, my blood became hot with long-buried feelings. "What was he doing there?" I looked up, my eyes moist. "Why did he spoil it?"

"You ever want to see him?"

I didn't answer. Something was starting to take shape in my head. My mind drifted, struck by the fact that here I was, maybe the happiest I had been, but it was all built on a lie. I was blinking back the impact of what was going through my mind. Not doing real well.

Chris reached over and grasped my hand. "I'm sorry, Lindsay. I had no right to . . ."

"That's not it," I whispered, and squeezed his hand. I knew it was time to really trust him, time to finally give myself over to Chris.

But I was scared, my cheeks trembling, my eyes holding back tears.

"I have something to tell you," I said. "This is a little heavy, Chris."

I looked at him with all the earnestness and trust my worried eyes could manage. "Remember when I almost fainted in the room with Jenks?"

Chris nodded. Now he looked a little worried. His forehead was furrowed with deep lines.

"Everyone thought I was just freaked out, but it wasn't that. I'm sick, Chris. I may have to go into the hospital soon."

I saw the light in his eyes suddenly dim. He started to speak, but I put my finger to his lips.

"Just listen to me for a minute. Okay?"

"Okay. I'm sorry."

I poured out everything about Negli's. I was not responding to treatments. Hope was fading. What Medved had warned only days before. I was in stage three, serious. A bone marrow transplant might be next.

I didn't cry. I told him straight out, like a cop. I wanted to give him hope, to show him

I was fighting, to show him I was the strong person I thought he loved.

When I was done, I clasped his hands and took a monumental breath. "The truth is, I could die soon, Chris."

Our hands were tightly entwined. Our eyes locked. We couldn't have been more in touch.

Then he placed his hand gently on my cheek and rubbed it. He didn't say a word, just took me and held me in the power and softness of his hands and drew me to him.

And that's what made me cry. He was a good person. I might lose him. And I cried for all the things we might never do.

I cried and cried, and with each sob he pressed me harder. He kept whispering, "It's all right, Lindsay. It's all right. It's all right."

"I should've told you," I said.

"I understand why you didn't. How long have you known?"

I told him. "Since the day we met. I feel so ashamed."

"Don't be ashamed," he said. "How could you know you could trust me?"

"I trusted you pretty quickly. I didn't trust myself."

"Well, now you do," Chris whispered.

# Chapter 102

I think we rocked all night. We laughed some, cried some. I don't even remember how I woke up in bed.

The following day, I barely left his touch. With all that was threatening, all that seemed uncertain, I felt so safe and sure in his arms. I never wanted to leave.

But something else happened during that weekend — apart from Negli's, apart from Chris and me. Something gripping, invading my sense of comfort and security.

It was something Jacobi had said that planted the thought.

One of those thrown-out remarks you

didn't pay much attention to but somehow got filed away in your mind. Then it comes back at the oddest time, with more force and logic than before.

It was Sunday night. The weekend was over. Chris had driven me home. Hard as it was to leave him, I needed to be alone for a while, to take inventory of the weekend, to figure out what I would do next.

I unpacked, made some tea, curled up on my couch with Her Sweetness. My mind wandered to the murder case.

Nicholas Jenks was behind me now. Only the countless reports to fill out. Even though he was still ranting about being set up. *It was just more insanity, more lies.*

It was then that Jacobi's words snaked into my brain.

*Good collar,* he'd said, early Tuesday morning.

He had that annoying, persistent look in his eyes. *Just remember,* he'd called after me, *it was the champagne match that got you on your way. . . . Why do you think Jenks left that champagne?*

I was barely paying attention. Jenks was locked away. The case was a slam dunk. I was thinking about the night before, and

Chris. I stopped on the stairs and turned to him. *I don't know, Warren. We've been over this. Heat of the moment, maybe.*

*You're right.* He nodded. *That must be why he didn't ball up the jacket and take it with him, too.*

I looked at him, like, *Why are we going through this now? Jenks needed a clean tux jacket to get out of the hotel undetected.* The DNA match on the hair made it all academic, anyway.

Then he said it. *You ever read the whole book?* he asked.

*Which book?*

*Jenks's book.* Always a Bridesmaid.

*The parts that matter,* I replied. *Why?*

He said, *I don't know, it just sort of stuck with me. Like I said, my wife happens to be a fan. There were some copies of the manuscript around, so I took one home. It was interesting how it all came out in the end.*

I looked at him, trying to figure out where all this was heading.

*It was a setup,* Jacobi said. *This Phillip Campbell guy, he gets off. He pins the whole thing on someone else.*

Days later, Warren's words came creeping

back into my mind. *A setup. He pins the whole thing on someone else.*

It was ridiculous, I told myself, that I was even dignifying this scenario, running through it in my mind. Everything was solid, airtight.

*Setup,* I found myself thinking again.

"I must be an idiot," I said aloud. "Jenks is clinging to any story he can to wiggle his way out of this."

I got up, brought my tea into the bathroom, began to wash my face.

In the morning I would tell Cheery about my disease. I had some time coming. I would face this thing head-on. Now that the case was complete, it was the right time. *Now that the case was complete!*

I went into the bedroom, ripped the tags off a "Little Bit of Heaven," a T-shirt Chris had bought me. I got into bed, and Martha came around for her hug.

Memories of the weekend began to drift in my head. I closed my eyes. I could hardly wait to share it with the girls.

Then a thought from out of the blue hit me. I shot up as if I'd had a nightmare. I stiffened. "Oh, no. Oh, Jesus, no," I whispered.

When Jenks had lunged at me at his house, he had swung *with his left hand.*

When he'd offered me a drink, he'd picked up the pitcher *with his left hand.*

*Impossible,* I thought. This can't be happening.

Claire was certain David Brandt's killer had been *right-handed.*

# Chapter 103

Jill, Claire, and Cindy looked at me as if I were insane.

The words had barely tumbled out of my mouth. "What if Jenks is right? What if someone *is* trying to set him up?"

"That's a crock!" snapped Jill. "Jenks is desperate and only moderately clever. We've got him!"

"I can't believe you're saying this," exclaimed Cindy. "You're the one who found him. *You're* the one who made the case."

"I know. I know it seems crazy. Hopefully, it is crazy. Just hear me out."

I took them through Jacobi's comment

about the novel, then my lightning bolt about Jenks's left-handedness.

"Proves nothing," Jill said.

"I can't get past the science, Lindsay," Claire said with a shake of her head. "We've got his goddamn DNA at the scene."

"Look," I protested, "I want the guy as much as anybody. But now that we have all this evidence — well — it's just so *neat.* The jacket, the champagne. Jenks has set up complicated murders in his books. Why would he leave clues behind?"

"Because he's a sick bastard, Lindsay. Because he's an arrogant prick who's connected to all three crimes."

Jill nodded. "He's a writer. He's an amateur at actually doing anything. He just fucked up."

"You saw his reactions, Jill. They were deeper than simply desperation. I've seen killers on death row still in denial. This was more unsettling. Like *disbelief.*"

Jill stood up, her icy blue eyes spearing down at me. "Why, Lindsay, why the sudden about-face?"

For the first time I felt alone and separated from the people I had most learned to trust. "No one could possibly hate this man more than I do," I declared. "I hunted him. I saw what he did to those women." I turned to Claire. "You said the killer was right-handed."

"*Probably* right-handed," Claire came back.

"What if he simply held the knife in his other hand?" proposed Cindy.

"Cindy, if you were going to *kill* someone," I said, "someone larger and stronger, would you go at him with your opposite hand?"

"Maybe not," injected Jill, "but you're throwing all this up in the face of *facts.* Evidence and reason, Lindsay. All the things we worked to assemble. What you're giving me back is a set of hypotheticals. 'Jenks holds his pitcher with his left hand. Phillip Campbell sets someone up at the end of his book.' Lindsay, we have the guy pinned to three double murders. I need you firm on this." Her jaw was quivering. "I need you to testify."

I didn't know how to defend myself. I had wanted to nail Jenks as eagerly as any one of us. *More.* But now, after being so sure, I couldn't put it away, the sudden doubt.

*Did we have the right man?*

"We still haven't uncovered a weapon," I said to Jill.

"We don't need a weapon, Lindsay. We have his hair *inside* one of the victims!"

Suddenly, we were aware that people from other tables were looking at us. Jill huffed and sat back down. Claire put her arms around my shoulders.

I puffed a deep breath into my cheeks, slumped back against the cushion of the booth.

Finally, Cindy said, "We've been behind you all the way. We're not going to abandon you now."

Jill shook her head. "You want me to let him go, guys, while we reopen the case? If we don't try him, Cleveland will."

"I don't want you to let him go," I said. "I only want to be one hundred percent sure."

"I *am* sure," Jill replied, her eyes ablaze.

I sought out Claire, and even she had a skeptical expression fixed firmly in my direction. "There's an awful lot of physical evidence that makes it pretty clear."

"If this gets out," Jill warned, "you can toss my career out with the cat litter. Bennett wants this guy's blood on the courthouse wall."

"Look at it this way," Cindy said, chuckling, "if Lindsay's right, and you send Jenks up, they'll be studying this case as a 'how *not* to' for twenty years to come."

Numbly, we looked around the table. It was as if we were staring at the pieces of some shattered, irreplaceable vase.

"Okay, so if it's not him," Claire said with a sigh, "then how do we go about proving who it is?"

It was as if we were all the way back at the beginning — all the way back at the first crime. I felt awful.

"What was the thing that nailed our suspicion on Jenks?" I asked.

"The hair," said Claire.

"Not quite. We had to get to him before we knew who it belonged to."

"Merrill Shortley," Jill said. "*Jenks and Merrill?* You think?"

I shook my head. "We still needed one more thing before we could take him in."

Cindy said, "*Always a Bridesmaid. His first wife.*"

I nodded slowly as I left Susie's.

# Chapter 104

Over the next few days, I went back over everything we had on Joanna Wade.

First, I reread the domestic complaint she had filed against Jenks. I looked at pictures of Joanna taken at the station, bruised, puffy faced. I read through the officers' account of what they found at the scene. *Exchanges laced with invectives. Jenks swinging wildly,* clearly enraged. *He had to be subdued, resisted arrest.*

The report was signed by two officers from Northern, Samuel Delgado and Anthony Fazziola.

The following day, I went back out to visit

Greg Marks, Jenks's former agent. He was even more surprised at my visit when I told him I was there on a different aspect of Jenks's past. "Joanna?" he replied with an amused smile. "Bad judge of men, Inspector, but a worse judge of timing."

He explained that their divorce had been finalized only six months before *Crossed Wire* hit the stands. He said the book sold nearly a million copies in hardcover alone. "To have to put up with Nicholas through all the lean years, then come away with barely more than cab fare . . ." He shook his head. "The settlement was a pittance compared to what it would've been if they had filed a year later."

What he told me painted a different picture of the woman I had met in the gym. She seemed to have put it all behind her.

"She felt used, dropped like worn baggage. Joanna had put him through school, supported him when he first started writing. When Nick bagged law school, she even went back to her job."

"And afterward," I asked, "did she continue to hate him?"

"I believe she continued to try and *sue*

him. After they split up, she tried to sue him for a lien against future earnings. Nonperformance, breach of contract. Anything she could find."

I felt sorry for Joanna Wade. But could it drive her to *that* kind of revenge? Could it cause her to kill six people?

The following day, I obtained a copy of the divorce proceedings from County Records. Through the usual boilerplate, I got the sense it was an especially bitter case. She was seeking three million dollars judgment against future earnings. She ended up with five thousand a month, escalating to ten if Jenks's earnings substantially increased.

I couldn't believe the bizarre transformation that was starting to take over my mind.

It had been Joanna who had first mentioned the book. Who felt cheated, spurned, and carried a resentment far deeper than what she had revealed. *Joanna*, the Tae-Bo instructor who was strong enough to take down a man twice her size. Who even had access to the Jenkses' home.

It seemed crazy to be thinking this way.

More than preposterous . . . it was impossible.

*The murders were committed by a male, by Nicholas Jenks.*

# Chapter 105

The next day, as we shared a hot dog and a pretzel in front of City Hall, I told Chris what I had found.

He looked at me in much the same way the girls had a few days before. Shock, confusion. Disbelief. But he didn't get negative.

"She could've set the whole thing up," I said. "She knew about the book. She lobbed it out there for us to find. She knew Jenks's taste — champagne, clothes — his involvement with Sparrow Ridge. She even had access to the house."

"I might buy it," he said, "but these murders were committed by a man. *Jenks,* Lindsay. We even have him on film."

"Or someone made up to look like Jenks. Every sighting of him was inconclusive."

"Lindsay, the DNA was a match."

"I spoke to the officers who went to the house when he beat Joanna," I pressed on. "They said, as enraged as Jenks was, she was dishing it right back to him, just as strong. They had to restrain *her* as they took him away in the car."

"She dropped the charges, Lindsay. She got tired of being abused. She may not have gotten what she deserved, but she filed and started a new life."

"That's just it, Chris. *She* didn't file. It was Jenks who left her. She sacrificed everything for Jenks. Marks described her as a model of codependency."

I could see Chris wanted to believe, but he was unconvinced. I had a man in jail with almost incontrovertible evidence against him. And here I was unraveling everything. What was the matter with me?

Then, out of the blue, something came back to me, something I had filed away long ago. Laurie Birnbaum, the witness from the Brandt wedding. How she had described the man she saw. *Something strange . . . The beard made him seem older, but the rest of him was young.*

Joanna Wade, medium-height, right-handed, the Tae-Bo instructor, was strong enough to handle a man twice her size. And Jenks's nine millimeter. He said he hadn't seen it in years. *At the house in Montana . . .* The records showed he had bought the gun ten years ago. When he was married to Joanna.

"You should *see* her," I said with rising conviction. "She's tough enough to handle any of us. She's the one link who knew about everything: wine, clothes, *Always a Bridesmaid.* She had the means to pull it all together. The photos, the sightings were inconclusive. What if it was her, Chris?"

I was holding his hand — my mind racing with the possibilities — when I felt a sudden, awful tightness in my chest. I thought it was the shock of what I had just proposed, but it hit me with the speed of an oncoming train.

Vertigo, nausea. It swept from my stomach to my head.

"*Lindsay?*" Chris said. I felt his hand bracing my shoulder.

"I feel kind of weird," I muttered. The sweats, a rush, then terrible light-headedness. As if armies were marching and clashing in my chest.

"Lindsay?" he said again, this time with real concern.

I leaned into him. This was the weirdest, scariest sensation. I felt both momentarily robbed of strength and then back in control; lucid, then very woozy again.

I saw Chris, and then I didn't.

I saw who killed the brides and grooms. And then it faded away.

I felt myself falling toward the sidewalk.

# Chapter 106

I found myself coming to on a wooden park bench in Chris's arms. He held me tightly while my strength returned.

Orenthaler had warned me. *It was stage three.* Crunch time in my body.

I didn't know which held more apprehension for me: going on chemo and gearing up for a bone marrow transplant or feeling my strength eaten away from the inside.

*You can't let it win.*

"I'm okay," I told him, my voice getting stronger. "I was told to expect this."

"You're trying to do too much, Lindsay.

Now you're talking about reopening a whole new investigation."

I took a deep breath and nodded. "I just need to be strong enough to see this through."

We sat there for a while. I could feel the color in my face reviving, the strength in my limbs returning. Chris held me, cuddled me tenderly. We must've looked like two lovers trying to find privacy in a very public place.

Finally, he said, "What you were describing, Lindsay, about Joanna, you really think it's true?"

It could still add up to nothing. She hadn't lied about her separation from Jenks. Or about her current relationship with both him and Chessy. Had she concealed a bitter hatred? She had the knowledge, the means.

"I think the killer is still out there," I said.

# Chapter 107

I decided to take a huge risk. If I blew it, it could knock the lid right off my case.

I decided to run what I suspected by Jenks.

I met him in the same visiting room. He was accompanied by his lawyer, Leff. He didn't want to meet, convinced there was no longer a point in talking with the police. And I didn't want to convey my true intent and end up feeding their defense arguments if I was wrong.

Jenks seemed sullen, almost depressed.

His cool and meticulous appearance had deteriorated into an edgy, unshaven mess.

"What do you want now?" he sneered, barely meeting my eyes.

"I want to know if you were able to come up with anyone who would like to see you in here," I said.

"Pounding the lid on my coffin?" he said with a mirthless smile.

"Let's just say, in the interest of doing my duty, I'm giving you one final chance to pry it back open."

Jenks snorted skeptically. "Sherman tells me I'm about to be charged in Napa with two more murders. Isn't that great? If this is an offer of assistance, I think I'll take my chances on proving it myself."

"I didn't come here to trap you, Mr. Jenks. I came to hear you out."

Leff leaned over and whispered in his ear. He seemed to be encouraging Jenks to talk.

The prisoner looked up with a disgusted glare. "Someone's running around, intent to look like me, familiar with my first novel. This person also wants to see me suffer. Is it so hard to figure out?"

"I'm willing to hear any names," I told him.

"Greg Marks."

"Your former agent?"

"He feels like I owe him my fucking career. I've cost him millions. Since I left, he hasn't gotten a worthwhile client. And he's *violent*. Marks belongs to a shooting club."

"How would he have gotten his hands on your clothing? Or been able to get a sample of your hair?"

"You find that out. You're the police."

"Did he know you'd be in Cleveland that night? Did he know about you and Kathy Kogut?"

"Nick is merely proposing," Leff cut in, "that other possibilities do exist for who could be behind these crimes."

I shifted in my seat. "Who else knew about the book?"

Jenks twitched. "It wasn't something I paraded around. Couple of old friends. My first wife, Joanna. . . ."

"Any of them have any reason to want to set you up?"

Jenks sighed uncomfortably. "My divorce, as you may know, was not exactly what they call mutually agreeable. No doubt there was a time Joanna would've been delighted to find me on a deserted road while she was cruising along at sixty. But now that she's back on her feet, with a new life, now that she's even gotten to know Chessy . . . I don't think so. No. It isn't Joanna. Trust me on that."

I ignored the remark and looked firmly into his eyes. "You told me your ex-wife's been to your house."

"Maybe once or twice."

"So, she'd have access to certain things. Maybe the wine? Maybe what was in your closet?"

Jenks seemed to contemplate the possibility for a moment, then his mouth crinkled into a contemptuous smile. "Impossible. No. It isn't Joanna."

"How can you be so sure?"

He looked at me as if he were stating an understood fact. "Joanna loved me. *She still does.* Why do you think she hangs around, covets a relationship with my new wife? Because she misses the view? It's because she cannot replace what I gave her. How I loved her. She is empty without me.

"What do you think?" he snorted. "Joanna's been holding specimens of my hair in a jar ever since we were divorced?" He sat there, stroking his beard, while the resolve on his face softened into a glimmer of possibility. "Someone has it in for me . . . but Joanna . . . she was just a little clerk when I met her. She didn't know Ralph Lauren from JCPenneys. I gave her self-esteem. I devoted myself to her, and she to me. She sacrificed for me, even worked two jobs when I decided to write."

It was hard to think of Jenks as anything other than the ruthless bastard who was responsible for these horrible crimes, but I pressed on. "You said the tuxedo was an old suit. You didn't even recognize it. And the gun, Mr. Jenks, the nine millimeter. You said you hadn't seen it in years. That you thought it was kept somewhere at your house in Montana. Are you so sure this might not have been planned for some time?"

I could see Jenks subtly shifting his expression as he came around to the impossible conclusion.

"You said that when you started writing, Joanna took a second job to help support you. Just what sort of work?"

Jenks stared up toward the ceiling, then he seemed to remember.

"She worked at Saks."

# Chapter 108

Slowly, unavoidably, I was starting to feel as if I were on the wrong airplane, heading to the wrong city.

Against all logic, I was growing surer and surer that Nicholas Jenks might not be the killer. *Oh, brother!*

I had to figure out what to do. Jenks in handcuffs was the lead picture in both *Time* and *Newsweek*. He was being arraigned in Napa for two additional murders the following day. Maybe I should just stay on the wrong plane, get out of town, never show my face in San Francisco again.

I got the girls together. I took them

through the mosaic that was starting to come clear: the acrimonious contest over the divorce, Joanna's sense of being discarded, her direct access to the victims through her contacts at Saks.

"She was an assistant store manager," I told them. "Coincidence?"

"Get me *proof*," Jill said. "Because as of now, I have proof against Nick Jenks. All the proof I need."

I could hear the worry and frustration in her voice. The whole country was watching this case, watching her every move. We had worked so hard to sell Mercer and her boss, Sinclair, on the idea that it was Jenks. And now, after all that — to propose a new theory and suspect.

"Authorize a search," I told Jill. "Joanna Wade's house. Something has to be there. The missing rings, a weapon, details on the victims. It's the only way we'll ever pin it down."

"Authorize a search on what basis? Suspicion of new evidence? I can't do that without blowing this case wide open again. If we show we're not even sure, how can I convince a jury?"

"We could check where she worked,"

proposed Cindy. "See if she had specific access to information on the brides."

"That's circumstantial. It's crap," Jill cried. "One of my neighbors works at Saks. Maybe she's the murderer."

"You can't go through with this," argued Cindy, "if we still have doubt."

"*You* have doubt," said Jill. "What I have is everything in place for a slam-dunk conviction. To you, it's a story, you follow it where it leads. My whole career is on the line."

Cindy looked stunned. "You think I'm here for just the story? You think I sat on every lead, agonized over not being able to go to copy, just so I could wind up with the book rights later on?"

"C'mon girls," said Claire, her arm on Cindy's shoulder. "We have to be together on this."

Slowly, Jill's intense blue eyes softened. She turned to Cindy. "I'm sorry," she said. "It's just that when this gets out, Leff will be able to plant huge doubts in that jury's mind."

"But we can't back down now just because it's bad tactics," said Claire. "There *could* be a murderer out there, a multiple murderer."

I said to Jill, "Authorize a search. C'mon, Jill."

I had never seen Jill look so upset. Everything she had achieved in her career, everything she stood for, was being placed squarely on the line. She shook her head. "Let's try it Cindy's way. We'll start with Saks, check Joanna out there."

"Thank you, Jill," I said. "You're the best."

She exhaled resignedly. "Find out if she's had any contact with anyone who had access to those names. Connect Joanna with those names, and I'll get you what you want. But if you can't, be prepared to fry Jenks."

From across the table, I took her hand. She gripped mine. We exchanged a nervous smile.

Jill finally joked, "Personally, I hope all you come back with is the hot item to be featured in the next Christmas catalog."

Claire laughed loudly. "Now that wouldn't be a total loss, would it?"

# Chapter 109

The following day, the day Nicholas Jenks was set to be arraigned for the murders of Rebecca and Michael DeGeorge, I set out to track down a new killer.

I couldn't let Jenks know we were looking that closely at Joanna. Of course, I didn't want Joanna to know we were focusing suspicion on her, either. And I didn't want to face Mercer's or Roth's reactions.

With all this going on, it was my Medved day, too. After that spell in the park with Chris three days before, I had gone for a blood test. Medved called back himself, told me he wanted me to come in. Being called in again like that scared me. Like that first time with Dr. Roy.

That morning, Medved kept me waiting. When he finally called me in, there was another doctor in his office — older, with white hair and bushy white eyebrows. He introduced himself as Dr. Robert Yatto.

The sight of a new doctor sent a chill through me. He could only be there to talk about the bone marrow procedure.

"Dr. Yatto is head of hematology at Moffett," Medved said. "I asked him to look at your latest sample."

Yatto smiled. "How are you feeling, Lindsay?"

"Sometimes okay, sometimes incredibly weak," I answered. My chest felt tight. *Why did I have to go through this with someone new?*

"Tell me about the other day."

I did my best to recount the reeling spell I'd had in City Hall Park.

"Any emissions of blood?" Yatto asked matter-of-factly.

"No, not lately."

"Vomiting?"

"Not since last week."

Dr. Yatto got up, came across the desk to

me. "Do you mind?" he asked, as he cradled my face in his hands. He expressionlessly pressed my cheeks with his thumb, pulled down my eyes and peered into my pupils, under my lids.

"I know I'm getting worse," I said.

Yatto released my face, nodded toward Medved.

Then, for the first time since I'd started seeing him, Medved actually smiled.

"It's not getting worse, Lindsay. That's why I asked Bob to consult. Your erythrocytic count jumped back up. To twenty-eight hundred."

I gave a double take to make sure I had heard right. That it wasn't some kind of wishful dream I was playing out in my own mind. "But the spells . . . the hot and cold flashes? The other day, I felt like a war was going on in me."

"There is a war," Dr. Yatto said. "You're reproducing cells. The other day, that wasn't Negli's talking. That was you. That's how it feels to heal."

I was stunned. My throat was dry. "Say that again?"

"It's working, Lindsay," Medved said. "Your red blood count has increased for the second time in a row. I didn't want to tell you in case it was an error, but as Dr. Yatto said, you're building new cells."

I didn't know whether to laugh or cry. "This is real? I can trust this?" I asked.

"This is *very* real," Medved said with a nod.

I stood up, my whole body shaking, tingling with disbelief. For a moment, all the joys that I had suppressed — a chance at my career, running on Marina Green, a life with Chris — came tumbling through my brain. For so long, I had been so scared to let them free. Now, they seemed to burst out of me.

Medved leaned forward and warned, "You're not cured, Lindsay. We'll continue the treatments, twice a week. But this is hopeful. More than hopeful, Lindsay. This is good."

"I don't know what to say." My body was totally numb. "I don't know what to do."

"If I were you," Dr. Yatto said, "I'd bring to mind the one thing you might've thought you'd miss most, and go do that today."

I wandered out of the office in a haze. Down the elevator, through the sterile lobby, into a flowered courtyard that overlooked Golden Gate Park.

The sky was bluer than I'd ever seen it, the air off the bay sweeter and cooler and more pure. I stood there, just hearing the beautiful sounds of my own breaths.

Something crept back into my life that had been away, something I never thought I would embrace again.

Hope.

# Chapter 110

"I have something to tell you," I said to Chris on the phone, my voice ringing with urgency. "Can you meet me for lunch?"

"Sure. You bet. Where?" No doubt he thought I had some important news to break on the case.

"Casa Boxer," I said with a smile.

"That urgent, huh?" Chris laughed into the phone. "I must be starting to have a bad effect on you. When should I come?"

"I'm waiting now."

It took him barely fifteen minutes to arrive at the door. I'd stopped on the way at Nestor's bakery and picked up some freshly baked cinnamon buns. Then I popped a bottle of Piper-Heidsieck that I had saved in my fridge.

Never in six years had I bugged out on a case in the middle of the afternoon. Especially one of this magnitude. But I felt no guilt, none at all. I thought of the craziest way I could break the good news.

I met him at the door, wrapped in a bed-sheet. His big blue eyes went wide with sur-prise.

"I'll need to see some ID." I grinned.

"Have you been drinking?" he said.

"No, but we're about to." I pulled him into the bedroom.

At the sight of the champagne, he shook his head. "What is it you want to tell me?"

"Later," I said. I poured him a glass and began to unfasten the buttons of his shirt. "But trust me, it's good."

"It's your birthday?" he said smiling.

I let the bedsheet drop. "I would never do this for just my birthday."

"*My* birthday, then."

"Don't ask. I'll tell you later."

"You broke the case," he exclaimed. "It

was Joanna. You found something that broke the case."

I put my fingers to his lips. "Tell me that you love me."

"I do love you," he said.

"Tell me again, like you did at Heavenly. Tell me that you won't ever leave me."

Maybe he sensed it was Negli's talking, some crazy hysteria, or that I just needed to feel close. He hugged me. "I won't leave you, Lindsay. I'm right here."

I took his shirt off — slowly, very slowly — then his trousers. He must've felt like the delivery boy who had stumbled into a sure thing. He was as hard as a rock.

I brought a glass of champagne to his lips, and we both took a sip from it.

"Okay, I'll just go with this. Shouldn't be too difficult," he said.

I drew him to the bed, and for the next hour we did the one thing I knew I would have missed most in the world.

We were in the middle of things when I felt the first terrifying rumbling.

At first it was so weird, as if the bed had speeded up and was rocking faster than we were; then there was a deep, grinding sound coming from all directions, as if we were in an echo chamber; then the sound of glass breaking — my kitchen, a picture frame falling off the wall — and I knew, we knew.

"It's a goddamn quake," I said.

I had been through many of these — anyone who lived here had — but it was startling and terrifying every time. You never knew if this was the Big One.

It wasn't. The room shook, a few dishes broke. Outside, I heard the bleat of horns and triggered car alarms. The whole thing lasted maybe twenty seconds — two, three, four vibrating tremors.

I ran to the window. The city was still there. There was a rumble, like a massive humpback whale breaching underground.

Then it was still — eerie, insecure, as if the whole town were holding on for balance.

I heard wailing sirens, the sound of voices shouting on the street.

"You think we should go?" I asked.

"Probably . . . we're cops." He touched me again, and suddenly I was tingling all over, and we melted into each other's arms. "What the heck, we're Homicide, anyway."

We kissed, and once again we were locked into a single, intertwined shape. I started to laugh. *The list,* I was thinking. The skybox. Now an earthquake. *This sucker's starting to get pretty long.*

My beeper went off. I cursed, rolled over, glanced at the screen.

It was the office.

"Code one eleven," I told Chris.

Emergency Alert.

"Shit," I muttered, "it's just an earthquake."

I sat up, pulled the sheet over me, called in on the phone next to the bed.

It was Roth buzzing me. Roth *never* buzzed me. *What was going on?* Immediately, I transferred to his line.

"Where are you?" he asked.

"Dusting off some debris," I said, and smiled toward Chris.

"Get in here. Get in here fast," he barked.

"What's going on, Sam? This about the quake?"

"Uh-uh," he replied. "Worse. Nicholas Jenks has escaped."

# Chapter 111

As he sat shackled to the seat of the police van on the way back from Napa, Nicholas Jenks watched the impassive eyes of the patrolman across from him. He plotted, schemed. He wondered how much it would take to buy his freedom.

*One million? Two million? After all, what did the fool take home? Forty grand a year?*

He figured the steely-eyed officer was someone above reproach, whose commitment to his duty was unquestioned. If he were writing it, that's who he would have put in the car with him.

*Five million, then.* He smirked.

If *he* were writing it. That notion possessed a cold, punishing irony for him. He *had* written it.

Jenks shifted in his restraints — wrists cuffed, torso strapped to the seat. Only minutes earlier, he had stood in the redbrick courthouse in Santa Rosa while the prosecutor in her little Liz Claiborne suit pointed her finger at him. Over and over, she accused him of things only a mind as cultivated as his would think up and do.

All he could do was stare coldly while she accused him of being this *monster.* Sometime, he'd like to lock her in the law library and show her what he was really capable of.

Jenks caught a glimpse of the sky and the sun-browned hills through the narrow window in the rear door and tried to get a fix on their bearings. *Novato. Just hitting Marin.*

He pressed his face to the steel restraining wall. *He had to get out.* If he were writing it, there would always be a way out.

He looked at the guard. *So what was the story,* Joe Friday? What happened next?

"You married?" he asked.

The policeman stared through him at first, then he nodded.

"Kids?"

"Two." He nodded again, even breaking a slight smile.

No matter how hard they tried to resist, they were always fascinated to talk with the monster. The guy who killed the honeymooners. They could tell their wives and friends, justify the miserable six hundred a week they brought home. He was a celebrity.

"Wife work?" Jenks probed.

The cop nodded. "Teacher. Business ed. Eighth grade."

*Business ed, huh? Maybe he would understand a business proposition.*

"My wife used to work," Jenks grunted back. "My first wife. In retail. My current wife worked, too, in television. Course, now she only works *out.*"

The remark produced a snicker. The tight-assed bastard was loosening up.

Jenks saw a landmark he recognized. Twenty minutes from the Golden Gate Bridge. There wasn't much time left.

He glanced out the window at the patrol car following them. There was another in front. A bitter resignation took hold. There *was* no way out. No elegant escape. That was in his books. This was life. He was screwed.

Then, out of nowhere, the police van lurched violently. Jenks was hurled forward in his seat, toward the guard across from him. For a second, he wondered what was going on, then the van lurched again. He heard a chilling rumbling sound outside.

*It's a fucking quake.*

Jenks could see the lead police car swerve to avoid the charge of another car. Then it skidded off the road.

One of the cops yelled, "Shit," but the van continued on.

Jenks spun around in panic, trying to hold on to anything that was fixed in the compartment. The van was bucking and jolting.

The police car following them jumped over a sudden hump in the highway and, to his total amazement, flipped. The driver of Jenks's van looked behind him in shock.

Then suddenly the other cop in front screamed for the driver to stop.

An eighteen-wheeler was breached in their way. They were headed right toward it. The van swerved, and when it did, the road buckled again. Then they were out of control — flying.

*I am going to die here,* Nicholas Jenks thought. *Die here, without anyone ever knowing the whole truth.*

The van crashed into the stanchions of a Conoco station. It screeched to a stop, spinning twice on its side. The officer across from him was hurled against the metal wall. He was writhing and moaning as he looked at Jenks.

"Don't move," the officer panted.

*How the hell could he?* He was still shackled to the seat.

Then came this horrid wrenching sound, and they both looked up. The towering steel light above the station toppled like a redwood and crashed down on them. It smashed through the door of the van, striking the officer in back, probably killing him on impact.

Jenks was sure he would be killed — all the smoke, the screams, the twisting of metal.

But he wasn't. He was clear. The streetlight had torn a hole in the side of the car, ripped his restraints right out of the seat. He was able to kick himself free, even with shackled hands and feet, and push himself through the gaping hole.

People were running in the street, screaming in panic. Motorists pulled off the road, some dazed, others jumping out of their vehicles to help.

*This was it!* He knew if he didn't run he would replay this moment for the rest of his life.

Nicholas Jenks crawled out of the van, dazed and disoriented. He spotted no cops. Only frightened passersby streaking past. He limped out and joined the chaotic street scene.

*I'm free!* Jenks exulted.

*And I know who's setting me up. The cops won't get it in a million years.*

# Chapter 112

It took about three minutes for Chris and me to throw on clothes and head back to the Hall. In the rush, I never told him my news.

By disaster standards, the quake was nothing much — unless you had spent the past five weeks tracking down the country's most notorious killer. Most of the damage ended up confined to shattered storefronts and traffic accidents north of the city, but as we pushed our way through the clamoring throng of press in the Hall's lobby, the quake's biggest news crackled with the fierceness of a live wire:

*The bride and groom killer was free.*

Nicholas Jenks had managed to flee after the police van taking him back to jail had flipped over outside Novato, the result of a chain of automobile accidents caused by the tremor. The policeman guarding him had been fatally injured. Two more, in the front seat of the overturned van, were hospitalized.

A huge command center was set up down the hall from Homicide. Roth himself took charge. The place was crawling with brass from downtown and, of course, the press.

An APB was released, Jenks's description and photo distributed to cops on both sides of the bridge. All city exits and highway tolls were being monitored; traffic slowed to a crawl. Airports, hotels, and car-rental ports were put on alert.

Since we had tracked Nicholas Jenks down originally, Raleigh and I found ourselves at the center of the search.

We placed an immediate surveillance on his residence. Cops spread out all over the Sea Cliff area, from the Presidio to Lands End.

In searches like this, the first six hours were critical. The key was to contain Jenks in the grid where he had bolted, not let him contact anyone who could help him. He had no resources, no funds, no one to take him in. Jenks couldn't stay on the loose — unless he was a lot craftier than I thought he was.

The escape left me stunned. The man I had hunted down was free, but I was also left conflicted. *Were we hunting the right man?*

Everyone had a theory about where he might head: the wine country, east into Nevada. I had my own theory. I didn't think he'd head back to the house. He was too smart, and there was nothing to be gained there. I asked Roth if I could borrow Jacobi and Paul Chin, to play out a hunch.

I took Jacobi aside. "I need you to do me a big favor, Warren." I asked him to do surveillance outside Joanna Wade's apartment on Russian Hill. I asked Chin to do the same outside the house of Jenks's former agent, Greg Marks.

If Jenks really believed he was being set up, those were two places he might go.

Jacobi gave me a look as if I were sending him out on another champagne lead. The entire corps of inspectors was following up leads. "What the hell, Lindsay . . . why?"

I needed him to trust me. "Because it struck me as funny, too," I said, begging his support, "why Jenks would leave that damn tuxedo jacket behind. I think he might go after Joanna. Trust me on it."

With Warren and Paul Chin in place, there was nothing I could do except monitor the wires. Six hours into the search, there was still no sign of Nicholas Jenks.

# Chapter 113

Around four, I saw Jill pushing her way through the crowd buzzing outside my office. She looked ready to kill somebody, probably me.

"I'm glad you're here," I said grabbing her. "Trust me, please, Jill."

"Cindy's downstairs," she said. "Let's go talk."

We sneaked out and were able to find Cindy amid a throng of reporters clawing at anyone who came down from the third floor. We called Claire, and in five minutes we were sitting around a table at a coffee shop just down the block. Jenks's escape had thrown all of my speculations into disarray.

"You still believe he's innocent?" Jill pressed the issue immediately.

"That depends on where he turns up next." I informed them that I had stationed a couple of men around the homes of Greg Marks and Joanna Wade.

"Even now?" Jill shook her head and looked close to blowing. "Innocent men don't run from police custody, Lindsay."

"Innocent people might," I said. "If they don't believe the justice system is being just!"

Claire looked around with a nervous swallow. "Ladies, it strikes me we're entering into very sensitive territory here, all right? We've got a manhunt trying to locate Jenks — he could be shot on sight — and at the same time, we're talking about trying to firm up a case against someone else. If this comes out, heads will roll. I'm looking at some of those pretty heads right now."

"If you *really* believe this, Lindsay, you need to take it to someone," Jill lectured me. "Roth. Mercer."

"Mercer's away. And right now, everybody's focused on locating Jenks.

Anyway, who the hell would believe this? As you say, all I have is a bunch of hypotheticals."

"Have you told Raleigh?" asked Claire.

I nodded.

"What does he think?"

"Right now, he can't get past the hair. Jenks's escape didn't help my case."

"I knew there was something I liked about that guy." Jill finally smiled thinly.

I looked at Claire for support.

"It's hard to argue your side of things, Lindsay," she said with a sigh. "That said, your instincts are usually good."

"So then bust in on Joanna, like Lindsay proposed," said Cindy. The more I was around her, the more I loved her.

Things had suddenly gotten very sticky in the way of accountability. I turned to Claire. "Is there anything we might have missed that could implicate Joanna?"

She shook her head. "We've been through all that. All the evidence points the finger *directly* at Nicholas Jenks."

"Claire, I'm talking about something that was there, right in front of us, that we just didn't see."

"I want to be with you on this, Lindsay,"

Claire said, "but we've been through it. Everything."

"There's got to be something. Something that could tell us if the killer is male or female. If Joanna did it, she's no different from any killer I've tracked down. She *left* something. We just haven't seen it. Jenks did — or someone did for him — and we found him."

"And we ought to be out looking for him now," urged Jill, "before we end up with couple number four."

I felt alone, but I just couldn't surrender. It wouldn't be right. "Please," I begged Claire, "go through everything one more time. I think we've got the wrong man."

# Chapter 114

In the light of the makeup mirror, the killer sat transfixed by soft blue eyes that were about to become gray.

The first thing was to smear her hair until all the blond had been dyed away, then brush it back *smooth,* a hundred times, until it had lost its luster and shine.

*"You forced me into this,"* she said to the changing face. *"Forced me to come out one more time. I should have expected as much. You love games, don't you, Nick?"*

With a cotton swab, she applied the base, a clear, sticky balm with a gluelike smell. She dabbed it over her temples, down the curve of her chin, in the soft space between her upper lip and her nose.

Then, with a tweezer, she matted on the hair. Tufts of reddish brown.

The face was almost complete. But the eyes . . . anyone could see they were still hers.

She slipped out a pair of tinted contacts from the case, moistening them, stretching her lids to insert each one.

She blinked, well satisfied with the result.

The familiarity was gone. The change was complete. Her eyes now reflected a steely, lifeless gray.

Nicholas's color.

*She was him.*

# Chapter 115

Claire's call woke me out of a deep sleep.

"Come down here," her voice commanded.

I blinked groggily at the clock. It was ten after five. "Come down *where?*" I moaned.

"I'm at the damn office. In the damn lab. The guard at the front counter will let you in. *Come right now.*"

I heard the urgency in her voice, and it took only seconds for me to come to my senses. "You're at the lab?"

"Since two-thirty, sleepyhead. It's about

Nicholas Jenks. I think I found something, and Lindsay, it is a mind-blower."

At that hour, it didn't take me more than ten minutes to get to the morgue. I parked in the circular area outside the coroner's entrance reserved for official vehicles. I rushed in, my hair uncombed, dressed in a sweatshirt and jeans.

The guard buzzed me in and let me through. He was expecting me. Claire met me at the entrance to the lab.

"Okay," I said, "my expectations are high."

She didn't answer. Only pressed me up against the door of the lab, without a word of greeting or explanation.

"We're back at the Hyatt," she started in. "Murder number one. David Brandt is about to open the door.

"Pretend you're the groom," she said, placing her hand on my shoulder and gently easing me into place, "and I'll be the killer. I surprise you as you open the door, and stab — *right-handed,* not that it makes any difference now."

She thrust her fist into the space under my left breast. "So you fall, and that's where we find you, later, at the scene."

I nodded, letting her know that I was following along so far.

"So what do we find around you?" she asked, wide eyed.

I made a mental picture of the scene. "Champagne bottle, tuxedo jacket."

"True, but that's not where I'm headed."

"Blood . . . a lot of blood."

"Closer. Remember, he died of a cardiac, electromechanical collapse. We simply assumed he was scared to death."

I stood up, gazed down at the floor. Then suddenly I saw it as if I were there with the body.

"Urine."

"Right!" exclaimed Claire. "We find a small residue of urine. On his shoes, on the floor. About six cubic centimeters' worth, that I was able to save. It seemed logical that it belonged to the groom — voiding is a natural response to sudden fear, or death. But I was thinking last night, there were traces of urine in Cleveland, too. And here, back at the Hyatt, I never even had it tested. *Why would I?* I always assumed it was from David Brandt.

"But if you were here, crumpled on the floor, and I was the killer standing above you, and the pee was *here,*" she said, pointing to the floor around me, "who the hell's urine would it be?"

Our eyes locked in one of those shining moments of epiphany. "The killer's," I said.

Claire smiled at her bright student. "The annals of forensic medicine are rich with examples of murderers 'getting off' when they kill, so *peeing* isn't so far-fetched. Your nerves would be on end. And good old compulsive me, obsessive down to the last detail, refrigerates it in a vial, never knowing what for. And the thing that makes this all come together is, *urine can be tested.*"

"Tested? For what?"

"For *sex,* Lindsay. Urine can reveal sex."

"Jesus, Claire." I was stunned.

She took me into the lab to a counter with two microscopes, some chemicals in bottles, and a device I recognized from college chemistry classes as a centrifuge.

"There aren't any flashing gender signs in urine, but there are things to look for. First, I took a sample and spun it down in the centrifuge with this KOH stain, which is something we can use to isolate impurities in blood cultures." She motioned for me to look in the first scope.

"See . . . these tiny, filamentlike branches with little clusters of cells like grapes. *Candida albicans.*"

I looked at her blankly.

"Yeast cells, honey. This urine's laced with high deposits of yeast. Boys don't get them."

I started to smile, but before I could even reply, she dragged me on. "Then I put the other sample under the scope and brought it up three thousand mag. Check this out."

I lowered myself over the scope and squinted in.

"You see those dark, crescent-shaped cells swimming around?" Claire asked.

"Uh-huh."

"Red blood cells. Lots of them."

I lifted my head from the scope and looked at her.

"They wouldn't show up in a man's urine. Not to anywhere near this degree. Not unless they've got a bleeding kidney, which to my knowledge, none of our principals show any signs of."

"Or" — I shook my head slowly — "unless the killer was menstruating."

# Chapter 116

I stared at Claire as the information settled in my mind. All along, Nicholas Jenks *had* been telling the truth.

He hadn't been in the room when David and Melanie Brandt were killed that night. Nor in Napa. Probably not even near the Hall of Fame in Cleveland. I had hated Jenks so much I couldn't see past it. None of us had been able to get past the fact that we wanted him to be guilty.

All the evidence — the hair, the jacket, the champagne — had been an incredible deception. Jenks was a master of the surprise ending, but someone had set the master up.

I put my arms around Claire and hugged her. "You're the best."

"You're damn right I am. I don't know what it proves," she answered, patting my back, "but the person standing over that poor boy at the murder scene was a woman. And I'm just as sure that she stabbed David Brandt to death with her right hand."

My mind was spinning. Jenks was loose, hundreds of cops on the chase — and he was innocent.

"So?" Claire looked at me and smiled.

"It's the second-best news I've heard lately," I said.

*"Second best?"*

I took her hand. I told Claire what Medved had shared with me. We hugged again. We even did a little victory dance. Then both of us got back to work.

# Chapter 117

Upstairs at my desk, I radioed Jacobi. Poor guy, he was still sitting outside Joanna Wade's home at the corner of Filbert and Hyde. "You all right, Warren?"

"Nothing that a shower and a couple of hours of sleep wouldn't improve."

"Tell me what's going on."

*"What's going on?"* Jacobi recited, as if he were resentfully going over his log. "Four-fifteen yesterday afternoon, target comes out, struts down the block to Gold's Gym. Six-ten, target reemerges, proceeds down block to Pasqua Coffee, comes out with plastic bag. I suspect it's Almond

Roast. Goes into the Contempo Casuals boutique, comes out empty. I gotta figure the new fall stuff hasn't arrived yet, Boxer. She makes her way home. Lights go on on the third floor. Is it chicken I smell? I don't know — I'm so fucking hungry I might be dreaming. Lights go out about ten-twenty-five. Since then, she's been doing what I'd like to be doing. Why you got me out here like a rookie, Lindsay?"

"Because Nicholas Jenks is going to try to find his ex-wife. He believes she's setting him up. I think he knows that Joanna is the murderer."

"You trying to cheer me up, Boxer? Bring meaning into my life?"

"Maybe. And how's this . . . *I think she is, too.* I want to know immediately if you spot Jenks."

Chris Raleigh came in about eight, tossing a surprised look at my bleary eyes and disheveled appearance. "You should try a brush in the morning."

"Claire called me at five-ten. I was in the morgue at five-thirty."

He looked at me funny. "What the hell for?"

"It's a little hard to explain. I want you to meet some friends of mine."

"Friends? At eight in the morning?"

"Uh-huh. My girlfriends."

He looked completely confused. "What am I not following here?"

"Chris." I seized his arm. "I think we broke the case."

# Chapter 118

An hour later, I got everyone together on the Jenks case, hopefully for the last time.

There had been a few alleged sightings of Nicholas Jenks — in Tiburon down by the marina, and south of Market, huddled around a gathering of homeless men. Both of them proved false. He had eluded us, and the longer he remained free, the greater the speculation.

We got together in a vacant interrogation room that Sex Crimes sometimes used. Claire smuggled Cindy up from the lobby, then we rang down Jill.

"I see we've loosened the requirements,"

Jill commented, when she came in and saw Chris.

Raleigh looked surprised, too. "Don't mind me — I'm just the token male."

"You remember Claire, and Jill Bernhardt from the district attorney's office," I said. "Cindy you may recall from Napa. The team."

Slowly, Chris looked from one face to another until he settled on me. "You've been working on this independently of the task force?"

"Don't ask," said Jill, plunking herself down in a wooden chair. "Just listen."

In the cramped, narrow room, all eyes turned to me. I looked at Claire. "You want to begin?"

She nodded, scanned the group as if she were presenting at a medical conference. "On Lindsay's urging, I spent all last night going through the three case files; I was looking for anything that would implicate Joanna. At first, nothing. Other than coming to the same conclusion I had before — that from the angle of the first victims' wounds, the killer was right-handed. Jenks is *left-*

*handed.* But it was clear that it wouldn't stick.

"Then something struck me that I had never noticed before. At both the first and third crime scenes there were traces of urine. Individually, I guess neither the medical examiner in Cleveland nor I ever thought much of it. But as I thought through the crimes scenes in my head, the *locations* of these deposits didn't make any sense. Early this morning, very early, I rushed down here and performed some tests."

There was barely a breath in the room.

"The urine we found at the Grand Hyatt demonstrated large deposits of yeast, as well as atypically large counts of red blood cells. Red blood cells in that amount appear in the urine during menstruation. Coupled with the yeast, there's no doubt in my mind that the urine was a woman's. A woman killed David Brandt, and I have no doubt we'll find a woman was in the stall in Cleveland, too."

Jill blinked, dumbfounded. Cindy's bright red lips parted in an incredulous half smile.

Raleigh just shook his head.

"Jenks didn't do it," I said. "Joanna must

have. He abused her, then he dumped her for his new wife, Chessy, just as he was about to strike it rich. Joanna tried to sue him twice, unsuccessfully. Ended up with a settlement many times smaller than she would have gotten a year later. She watched him gain celebrity and wealth, and a new, seemingly happy, life."

Chris looked amazed. "You really believe a woman could physically pull this off? The first victims were stabbed, the second were dragged twenty, thirty yards to where they were dumped."

"You haven't seen her," I replied. "She knew how to set Jenks up. She knew his tastes, his investments, and had access to his possessions. She even worked at Saks."

Cindy chipped in, "She was one of the few people who would've been aware of *Always a Bridesmaid.*"

I nodded toward Jill. "She had the means, the motive, and I'm damned sure she had the desire."

A really heavy silence filled the room.

"So how do you want to play this?" Chris finally said. "Half the force is looking for Jenks."

"I want to inform Mercer, try to get Jenks

brought in without someone killing him. Then I want to go ahead and pierce Joanna's cover. Phone calls, credit cards. If she was in Cleveland, something will tie her there. I think you'd agree now," I said to Jill, "we have enough to authorize a search."

Jill nodded, at first hesitantly, then with more resolve. "It's just impossible to believe that after all this, we now have to defend that bastard."

Suddenly, there was a loud rap on the glass window of the door. John Keresty, an inspector on the task force, broke in on us.

"It's Jenks. . . . He's just been sighted. He's up in Pacific Heights."

# Chapter 119

Raleigh and I leaped up, almost as one, racing back to the command center.

It appeared Jenks had been seen in the lobby of a small hotel called the El Drisco. A bellboy spotted him. Free of his cuffs. Now he was on the streets, somewhere up in Pacific Heights.

*Why there?* My mind ratcheted through the possibilities. Then it became clear.

*Greg Marks lived up there.*

I radioed Paul Chin, who was still sitting surveillance on the agent's brownstone. "Paul, be on the alert," I told him. "Jenks may be headed your way. He was seen in Pacific Heights."

There was a beep on my cell phone. It was Jacobi. Everything was happening at once.

"Boxer, there's an All Available Units on Jenks up in the Heights about a mile from here. I'm headed up there."

"Warren, *don't leave,*" I shouted into the receiver. I still believed Joanna was the murderer. I couldn't leave her unmonitored — especially with Jenks on the loose. "Stay at your post."

"This takes precedence," Jacobi argued. "Besides, nothing's happening here. I'll call a radio car to relieve."

"*Jacobi,*" I shouted, but he had already signed off and was on his way to the Heights. I turned to Chris. "Warren's left Joanna's."

Suddenly, Karen, our civilian clerical, shouted for me. *"Lindsay, call for you on one."*

"We're headed out," I hollered back to her. I had strapped on my gun, grabbed the keys to my car. "Who is it?"

"Says you'd want to talk to him about the Jenks case," Karen said. "Says his name is Phillip Campbell."

# Chapter 120

I froze, fixed on Raleigh, and lunged back toward my desk.

I signaled Karen to put it through. At the same time, I hissed under my breath to Raleigh, "Start a trace."

I waited in a trance; seconds could mean the difference. The breath was tightening in my chest. Then I picked up.

"You know who this is," Nicholas Jenks's arrogant voice declared.

"I know who it is. Where are you?"

"Not a chance, Inspector. I only called to let you know, whatever happens, I didn't kill any of them. I'm not a murderer."

"I know that," I told him.

He seemed surprised. "You know . . . ?"

I couldn't let Jenks know who it was. Not with him on the loose. "I promise, we can prove it wasn't you. Tell me where you are."

"Hey, guess what? I don't believe you," Jenks declared. "Besides, it's too late. I told you I'd take this into my own hands. I'm going to solve these murders for you."

Jenks could hang up any moment and we'd lose him. This was my only chance. "Jenks, I'll meet you. Anywhere you want."

"Why would I want to meet you? I've seen enough of you to last a lifetime."

"Because I know who did it," I told him.

What he said next jolted me.

"So do *I*."

And *then* he hung up.

# Chapter 121

*Sixth . . . Market . . . Taylor . . .* the  streets shot by, the top hat on the roof of Chris Raleigh's car flashing wildly.

*Ellis.*

*Hyde.*

We shot up Larkin, climbing through the lights, then rocked over the bumps as we careened over Nob Hill. In a matter of minutes, we arrived in Russian Hill.

Joanna lived on the top floor of a town house on the corner of Filbert and Hyde. We were no longer waiting to flush her out.

Jenks was loose; he had probably homed

in on her. Now it was a matter of preventing more killing.

We slowed, cut the lights as we wove through the quiet, hilly streets. The house had been unguarded for maybe fifteen minutes. I didn't know if Joanna was up there. Or where the hell Jenks was.

Chris pulled to the curb. We checked our guns and decided how to proceed.

Then I saw a sight that tore the breath from my lungs.

Chris saw it, too. "Christ, he's here."

From a narrow alley two houses away, a man in a beard and baggy sport coat emerged. He looked both ways as he hit the street, then he made his way down the block.

*It was Jenks.*

Raleigh pulled out his gun and reached for the door. I looked closer in disbelief, grabbed onto him. "Wait. Look again, Chris."

We both gaped in amazement. He had the same look: the short reddish-gray hair, the same unmistakable beard.

*But it wasn't Jenks.*

The figure was thinner, fairer; the hair was

slicked back, hiding a longer length, not cut short. I could see that much.

*It was a woman.*

"That's Joanna," I said.

"Where's Jenks?" Chris grunted. "This just keeps getting creepier."

We watched the figure slink down the block as a frenzy of possibilities ran through my mind. This *was* creepy.

"I'll follow her," said Chris. "You go upstairs. Make *sure* it's her, Lindsay. I'll radio for support. Go on, Lindsay. Go."

The next moment, I was out of the car, crossing the street toward Joanna's apartment. Chris eased the Taurus down the block.

I pushed random buttons until a woman's angry voice replied. I identified myself, and a gray-haired woman emerged from the apartment next to the front door. She announced that she was the landlady.

I badged her, got her to locate a key pronto. Then I told her to get back in her apartment.

I had my gun out, took off the safety. A film of hot sweat was building up on my face and neck.

I reached Joanna's apartment on the third

floor. My heart was pounding. *Careful, Lindsay,* a voice inside me said, then came a cautioning chill. *Could Nicholas Jenks be here?*

I had certainly entered enough hostile environments during my police career. None worse than this. I inserted the key, turned, and when the lock caught, pushed the door with my foot.

It swung open . . . revealing the bright, stylishly decorated apartment of Joanna Wade.

"Anyone here?" I shouted.

No one answered.

There was no one in the living room. Same for the dining room, kitchen. A coffee mug in the sink. The *Chronicle* out and folded to the Datebook section.

No sign that I was in the home of a psycho. That bothered me.

I moved on. Magazines — *Food and Wine, San Francisco* — on the coffee table. A few yoga posture books.

In the bedroom, the bed, unmade. The entire place had a relaxed, unforbidding feel.

Joanna Wade lived like any ordinary woman. She read, had coffee in her kitchen, taught exercise, paid her bills. *Killers were preoccupied with their victims.* This didn't make sense.

I turned into the master bath.

"Oh, damn it!" The case had made a last, irrevocable turn.

On the floor, in her workout tights, was Joanna Wade.

She was leaned against the tub looking at me, but not really — actually, she was still looking at her killer. Her eyes were wide and terrified.

He had used a knife. *Jenks? If not him, then who?*

"Oh, Christ," I gasped. My head was spinning and it *hurt.*

I hurried over to her, but there was nothing I could do. Everything had twisted again. I knelt over the dead woman as a final, shuddering thought filled my mind:

*If it wasn't Joanna, who was Chris following?*

# Chapter 122

Within minutes, two blue-and-whites screeched to a stop outside. I directed the patrol officers upstairs to the grisly body of Joanna, but my thoughts had turned to Chris. *And whoever he was following.*

I had been up in the apartment for ten, maybe twelve minutes, without a word from him. I was worried. He was following a murderer, and a murderer who had just killed Joanna Wade.

I ran downstairs to an open patrol car. I called in what had happened to Command Central. A riot of doubts was crashing in my mind.

*Could it somehow have been Jenks after all?* Could Jill have been right? Was he manipulating us, right from the start? Had he set everything up, even the sighting in Pacific Heights?

But if it was him, *why? Why,* after I had told him I believed him? Why would he kill her now? Was Joanna's death something I could have prevented? What in hell was going on? Where was Chris, damn it?

My cell phone finally beeped. To my relief it was Chris.

"Where are you? You had me scared to death. Don't do that to me."

"Down by the marina. The suspect's in a blue Saab."

"Chris, be careful. It's *not* Joanna. Joanna's dead. She was stabbed a bunch of times in her apartment."

*"Dead?"* he repeated. I could feel the frantic question slowly sinking into his mind. "Then who the hell is driving the Saab up ahead of me?"

"Tell me where you are *exactly.*"

"Chestnut and Scott. The suspect just pulled up to the curb. The suspect is getting out of the car."

Somehow, this sounded familiar. *Chest-*

*nut and Scott? What was down there?* In the tumult of blue-and-whites screeching up in front of Joanna's building and reporting in, I raked my mind for a connection.

"He's heading away from the car, Lindsay. He's starting to run."

Then it hit me. The photo I had picked up at Jenks's house. The beautiful and unmistakable moonlit dome. The Palace of Fine Arts.

*It was where he had been married.*

"I think I know where he's going!" I shouted. "The Palace of Fine Arts."

# Chapter 123

I took off in the radio car with the siren blaring all the way to the Presidio.

It took me no more than seven minutes, with traffic wildly shifting out of my way, to speed down Lombard over to Richardson to the south tip of the Presidio. Up ahead, the golden rotunda of the Palace of Fine Arts loomed powerfully above a calm, gleaming pond.

I saw Chris's blue Taurus pulled up diagonally across from the tip of the park and jackknifed the patrol car to a halt next to it. I didn't see a sign of any other cops.

*Why hadn't any backup arrived? What the hell was going on now?*

I clicked my gun off safety and made my way into the park underneath the giant rotunda. No way I was waiting.

I was startled by people running toward me, away from the rotunda grounds.

"Someone's shooting," one of them screamed.

Suddenly, my legs were flying. "Everyone out! I'm San Francisco police!" I screamed as I bumped through the people rushing by.

"Maniac with a gun," one of them yelled.

I ran around the pond alongside a massive marble colonnade. There was no sound up ahead. No more shots.

Leading with my gun, I rounded corners until I was in sight of the main rotunda. Huge Corinthian columns soared above me, capped with ornate heroic carvings.

I could hear voices in the distance: a woman's mocking tone: *"It's just you and me, Nick. Imagine that. Isn't it romantic?"*

And a man's voice, Jenks's: *"Look at you, you're pathetic. As always."*

The voices echoed out of the huge dome of the main rotunda.

*Where was Chris? And where was our backup?*

Cops should have been here by now. I held my breath, straining to hear the first police siren.

Every step I took, I heard my own footsteps echoing to the roof.

*"What do you want?"* I heard Jenks's cry reverberating off the stone. Then the woman shouting back, *"I want you to remember them. All the women you fucked."*

Still no sign of Chris. I was tight with worry.

I decided to go around the side of a row of low arches that ran down to where the voices were coming from. I ducked around the corner of the colonnade.

Then I saw Chris.

He was sitting there, propped against a pillar, watching everything unfold.

My first reaction was to say something like, *Chris, get down, someone will see you.* It was one of those slow-motion perceptions where my eyes were faster than my mind.

Then I was seized with horrible fright, nausea, and sadness.

Chris wasn't watching, and he wasn't hiding.

The front of his shirt was covered with blood.

All my police training nearly gave way. I wanted to scream, to cry out. It took everything I had to hold it in.

Two dark bloodstains were soaking through Chris's shirt. My legs were paralyzed. Somehow I forced myself over to him. I knelt down. My heart was pounding.

Chris's eyes were remote, his face as gray as stone. I checked for a pulse and felt the slightest rhythm of a heartbeat.

"Oh, Chris, no." I stifled a sob.

When I spoke, he looked up, eyes glimmering as he saw my face. His lips parted into a weak smile. His breath wheezed, heavy and labored.

My eyes filled with tears. I applied pressure to the holes in his chest, trying to push back the blood. "Oh, Chris, hang in there. Hang in there. I'll get help."

He reached for my arm. He tried to speak, but it was only a weak, guttural whisper.

"Don't talk. Please."

I raced back to the patrol car and fumbled with the transmitter until I heard Dispatch.

"Officer down, officer down," I shouted. "Four-oh-six. I repeat, four-oh-six!" The statewide call for alarm. "Officer shot, rotunda of the Palace of Fine Arts. Need immediate EMS and SWAT backup. Possible Nicholas Jenks sighting. Second officer on the scene inside. Repeat, four-oh-six, emergency."

As soon as the dispatcher repeated the location back to me with a *"Copy,"* I threw down the transmitter and headed back inside.

When I got to him, Chris was still holding on to small breaths. A bubble of blood popped on his lip. "I love you, Chris," I whispered, squeezing his hand.

Voices rang out ahead in the rotunda. I couldn't make them out, but it was the same man and woman. Then there was a gunshot.

"Go," Chris whispered. "I'm holding on."

Our hands touched.

"I've got rear," he muttered with a smile. Then he pushed me away.

I scurried ahead, my gun drawn, glancing back twice. Chris was watching — *watching my back.*

I ran in a low crouch all the way down the

length of the row of columns closest in, clear up to the side of the main rotunda. The voices echoed, intensified. My eyes were riveted.

They were straight across the basilica. Jenks, in a plain white shirt. He was holding one arm, bleeding. He'd been shot.

And across from him, holding a gun and dressed in a man's clothes, Chessy Jenks.

# Chapter 124

She looked like a bizarre disfigurement of the beautiful woman she was. Her hair was matted and dyed gray and red. Her face still carried the marks of her disguise, a man's sideburns and flecks of a red beard.

She was holding a gun tightly, pointing it directly at him. "I have a present for you, Nick."

"A present?" Jenks said in desperation. "What the hell are you talking about?"

"That's why we're *here.* I want to renew our vows."

Chessy took a small pouch out of her

jacket and tossed it at his feet. "Go ahead. Open it."

Nicholas Jenks knelt stiffly and picked up the pouch. He opened it, the contents spilling into his palm. His eyes bulged in horror.

*The six missing rings.*

"Chessy, Christ," he said. "You're out of your mind. What do you want me to do with *these?*" He held out a ring. "These will put you in the gas chamber."

"No, Nick," Chessy said, shaking her head. "I want you to swallow them. Get rid of the evidence for me."

Jenks's face twitched in apprehension. "You want me to *what?*"

"Swallow them. Each one is someone you've destroyed. Someone whose beauty you've killed. They were innocent. Like *me.* Little girls on our wedding days. You killed us all, Nick — me, Kathy, Joanna. So now give us something back. *With this ring, I do pledge.*"

Jenks glared and shouted at her. "That's enough, Chessy!"

"I'll say when it's enough. You love games, so play the game. Play *my* game this time. *Swallow them!*" She pointed the gun. "No sense pretending I won't shoot, is there, dear?"

Jenks took one of the rings, raised it to his lips. His hand was shaking badly.

"That was Melanie, Nicky. You would've liked her. Athletic . . . a skier . . . a diver. Your type, huh? She fought me to the end. But you don't like us to fight, do you? You like to be in total control."

She cocked the gun and leveled it at Jenks's head.

Jenks put the ring in his mouth. With a sickened expression, he forced it down his throat.

Chessy was losing it. She was sobbing, trembling. I didn't think I could wait any longer.

"Police," I yelled. I stepped forward, two hands on my .38, leveling it at her.

She spun at me, not even showing surprise, then back to Jenks. "*He* has to be punished!"

"It's over," I said, carefully advancing toward her. "Please, Chessy, no more killing."

As if she suddenly realized what she had become, the sickening things she'd done, she looked at me. "I'm sorry . . . I'm sorry for everything that happened — except this!"

She fired, *at Jenks.*

I fired, too, at her.

Chessy's slender body flew backward, hitting the wall hard and crumpling against it. Her beautiful eyes widened, and her mouth sagged open.

I looked and saw that she'd missed Jenks. He was staring at her in disbelief. He didn't think she could do it, didn't think she hated him that much. He still believed he controlled Chessy, and probably that she loved him.

I hurried to her, but it was too late. Her eyes were already glazed, and the blood was streaming from her chest. I held her head and thought that she was so beautiful — like Melanie, Rebecca, Kathy — and now she was dead, too.

Nicholas Jenks turned toward me with a gasp of relief. "I told you . . . I told you I was innocent."

I looked at him in disgust. Eight people were dead. The brides and grooms, Joanna, now his own wife. *I told you I was innocent?* Is that what he thought?

I swung, my fist catching him square in the teeth. I felt something shatter as Jenks dropped to his knees. "So much for innocence, Jenks!"

# Chapter 125

I was running and I realized that I no longer knew exactly what I was doing, where I was. Somehow my instincts brought me back to where Chris had been shot.

He was still up against the pillar in the same position. He looked as if he'd been waiting for me to return.

I rushed up to him, knelt down as close as I could get. I could see police and the EMS medical crew finally arriving. What took them so long?

"What happened?" Chris whispered. I could barely hear him.

"I got her, Chris. Chessy Jenks was the killer."

He managed to nod his head. "That's my girl," he whispered.

Then Chris smiled faintly and he died on me.

I never would have imagined, or dreamed, that Chris would be the first to die. That was the most terrible and dreadful shock. I was the sick one, the one whom death had brushed against.

I put my head down close to his chest. There was no movement, no breath, just a terrifying stillness. Everything seemed so unreal.

Then the medics were working on Chris, doing heroic, useless things, and I just sat there holding his hand.

I felt hollowed out and empty and incredibly sad. I was sobbing, but I had something to say to him; I had to tell Chris one last thing.

"Medved told me, Chris. I'm going to be okay."

# Chapter 126

I couldn't go near my office at the Hall. I was given a one-week leave. I figured I'd take another of my own time on top of that. I sat around, watched some videos of old movies, went for my treatments, took a jog or two down by the marina.

I even cooked and sat out on the terrace overlooking the bay, just as I had with Chris that first night. On one of those nights, I got really drunk and started playing with my gun. It was Sweet Martha who talked me off the ledge. That, and the fact that if I killed myself, I would be betraying Chris's memory. I couldn't do that. Also, the girls would never have forgiven me, right?

I felt a hole tear at my heart, larger and more painful than anything I had ever felt, even with Negli's. I felt a void of connection, of commitment. Claire called me three times a day, but I just couldn't speak for very long, not even to her.

"It wasn't you, Lindsay. There was nothing you could've done," she consoled.

"I kind of know that," I replied. But I just couldn't convince myself it was true.

Mostly, I tried to persuade myself I still felt a sense of purpose. The bride and groom murders were solved. Nicholas Jenks was shamelessly milking his celebrity status on *Dateline* and *20/20.* My Negli's seemed to be in remission. Chris was gone. I tried to think of what I would do next. Nothing very appealing came to mind.

Then I remembered what I had told Claire when my fears of Negli's were the strongest. *Nailing this guy was the one clear thing that gave me the strength to go on.*

It wasn't just about right or wrong. It wasn't about guilt or innocence. It was about what I was good at, and what I loved to do.

Four days after the shooting, I went to Chris's funeral. It was in a Catholic church out in Hayward, where he was from.

I took my place in the ranks with Roth and Jacobi. With Chief Mercer, who was dressed in blues.

But my heart was aching so bad. I wanted to be up near Chris. I wanted to be next to him.

I watched his ex-wife and his two boys struggling to keep it together. I was thinking about how very close I had come to their lives. And they didn't know it.

*Hero cop,* they were eulogizing him.

*He was a marketing guy,* I thought, smiling. And then I started to cry.

Of all people, I felt Jacobi grasp my hand. And of all the improbable things, I found myself holding his back. *Go ahead,* he seemed to be saying. Go ahead and weep.

Afterward, at the graveside, I went up to Chris's ex-wife, Marion. "I wanted to meet you," I said. "I was with him when he died."

She looked at me with the fragile courage only another woman could understand.

"I know who you are," she said with a compassionate smile. "You *are* pretty. Chris told me you were pretty. And smart."

I smiled and took her hand. We both squeezed hard.

"He also said you were very brave."

I felt my eyes well up. Then she took my arm and said the one thing I wanted most to hear.

"Why don't you stand with us, Lindsay."

The department gave Chris a hero's burial. Sad, mournful bagpipers opened the ceremony. Row after row of cops in dress blues. A twenty-one-gun salute.

When it was over, I found myself walking back to the car, wondering what in God's name I was going to do next.

At the cemetery gates I spotted Cindy and Jill and Claire. They were waiting there for me.

I didn't move. I stood there, my legs trembling badly. They could see that if they didn't make the first move, I could break down.

"Why don't you ride back with us?" Claire said.

My voice cracked. I could barely utter the words. "It was supposed to be me, not him," I said to them. Then one by one they all hugged me.

I put my arms around all of them and

melted into their embrace as deeply as I could. All four of us were crying. "Don't ever leave me, guys."

*"Leave?"* Jill said with wide eyes.

"None of us," promised Cindy. "We're a team, remember? We will *always* be together."

Claire took hold of my arm.

"We love you, sweetie," she whispered.

The four of us walked arm in arm out of the cemetery. A cooling breeze was blowing in our faces, drying our tears.

At six o'clock that night, I was back inside the halls of the Hall of Justice.

There was something important I had to do.

In the lobby, almost the first thing you see, there's a large marble plaque. On it are ninety-three names, the names and dates of ninety-one men and two women who wore the uniform of the SFPD and died in the line of duty. A mason is working on the plaque.

It's an unwritten rule on the force, you never count them. But tonight, I did. Ninety-three, starting with James S. Coonts on October 5, 1878, when the SFPD was first formed.

Tomorrow there will be one more:

Christopher John Raleigh. The mayor will be there; Mercer, too. The reporters who cover the city beat. Marion and the boys. They will memorialize him as a hero cop. I will be there, too.

But tonight, I don't want speeches or ceremonies. Tonight, I want it to be just him and me.

The mason finishes up the engraving of his name. I wait while he sands the marble, vacuums away the last particle of dust. Then I walk up and run my hand over the smooth marble. Over his name.

*Christopher John Raleigh.*

The mason looks at me. He can see the pain welling in my eyes. "You knew him, huh?"

I nod, and from somewhere deep in my heart, a smile comes forth. *I knew him.*

"Partner," I say.

## Epilogue

# COUP DE GRÂCE

I have come to learn that murder investigations always have loose ends and questions that cry out to be answered. Always.

But not this time.

I was home one night about a month after we buried Chris. I had finished dinner for one, fed and walked Her Sweetness, when there was a knock on the door, a single, authoritative rap.

I hadn't buzzed anyone up from downstairs, so I went and looked through the peephole before I opened up. I couldn't believe my eyes. It was Nicholas Jenks.

He had on a blue blazer over a white shirt

and dark gray slacks. He looked as arrogant and obnoxious as ever.

"Aren't you going to let me in?" he asked, then smiled as if to say, *Of course you are. You can't resist, can you?*

"No, actually I'm not," I told him. I walked away from the door. "Get lost, asshole."

Jenks knocked again, and I stopped walking. "We have nothing to talk about," I called loudly enough for him to hear.

"Oh, but we do," Jenks called back. "You *blew* it, Inspector. I'm here to tell you how."

I froze. I could feel my eyes blazing, heat burning the back of my neck. I walked back to the door, paused, then opened it, my heart beating fast. *You blew it.*

He was smiling, or maybe laughing at me. "I'm celebrating," he said. "I'm a happy fella! Guess how come?"

"Don't tell me, because you're a bachelor again."

"Well, there's that. But I also just sold North American rights to my latest book. Eight million dollars. Then the movies paid four. This one's nonfiction, Lindsay. Guess the subject. Go ahead, take a stab."

I wanted desperately to punch Jenks out again. "And I'm the one you have to share your news with? How goddamn sad for you."

Jenks continued to grin. "Actually, I came here to share something else. You *are* the only one I want to share this with. Do I have your attention yet, Lindsay? You blew it big-time, babe."

He was so creepy and inappropriate that he was scaring me. I didn't want him to see it. What did he mean, I *blew* it?

"I'd offer you a drink, but I hate your guts." I smirked.

He threw up his hands, imitated my smirk. "You know, I feel exactly the same thing toward you. That's why I wanted to tell you this, Lindsay, *only you.*" He lowered his voice to a whisper. "*Chessy did what I told her to do,* right up until the very end. The murders? We were playing a terrible, wonderful game. Tragic husband and wife kill happy, innocent husbands and wives. We were *living out* the plot of a novel. My novel. You blew it, Lindsay. I got away clean. I'm free. I'm *so* free. And now I'm richer than ever."

He stared at me, then he started to laugh.

It was probably the most sickening sound I'd heard in my life.

"It's true. Chessy would do anything I wanted her to do. All of them would — that's why I picked them. I used to play a game where they barked like dogs. They loved it. Want to play, Lindsay? Ruff, ruff?"

I glared at him. "Don't you feel kind of inadequate — playing your father's old games? Joanna told me."

"I took things way past anything my father ever imagined. I've done it all, Inspector, *and I got away with it.* I planned every murder. Doesn't that make your fucking skin crawl? Doesn't it make you feel inadequate?"

Suddenly, Jenks was putting on plastic gloves he took out of his jacket pockets. *What the hell?*

"This is perfect, too," he said. "I'm *not here,* Lindsay. I'm with this sweet little liar of a bitch in Tahoe. I have an alibi bought and paid for. Perfect crimes, Lindsay. My specialty."

As I turned to run, Jenks took out a knife. "I want to feel this going inside you, Lindsay. Deep. The coup de grâce."

"Help!" I screamed, but then he hit me

hard. I was shocked at how fast he moved and how powerful he was.

I slammed into a living room wall and almost went out. Martha instinctively went after him. I'd never seen her bare her teeth before. He lashed out and cut her shoulder. Martha fell over, whining horribly.

*"Stay away, Martha!"* I screamed at her.

Jenks picked me up and threw me into my bedroom. He shut the door.

"There was supposed to be another bride and groom murder while I was in jail. New evidence was going to slowly reveal itself. It would become clear that I was innocent — framed. Then I'd write the book! But Chessy turned around and double-crossed me. I never respected her more, Lindsay. I almost loved her for it. She showed some goddamn guts for once!"

I crawled away from Jenks, but he could see there was nowhere for me to go in the bedroom. I thought I might have a broken rib.

"You'll have to kill me first," I told him in a hoarse whisper.

"Okay." He grinned. "Glad to oblige. My pleasure."

I crawled hand over hand toward my bed,

the side facing a window on the bay. It was hard to breathe.

Jenks came after me.

"Stop, Jenks!" I yelled at the top of my voice. "Stop right there, Jenks!"

He didn't stop. Why should he? He slashed back and forth with the knife. Christ, he was enjoying this. He was laughing. Another perfect murder.

I reached under the bed to where I'd fastened a holster and revolver, my home security system.

I didn't have time to aim, but I didn't have to. Nicholas Jenks was stunned, the knife poised over his left shoulder.

I fired three times. Jenks screamed, his gray eyes bulged in disbelief, then he collapsed dead on top of me. "Burn in hell," I whispered.

I called Claire first — the medical examiner; then Cindy — the best crime reporter in San Francisco; then Jill — my lawyer.

The girls came running.